Six Poppies

LISA CARTER

PENGUIN

MICHAEL M J JOSEPH

Est. 1936

PENGUIN MICHAEL JOSEPH

UK | USA | Canada | Ireland | Australia
India | New Zealand | South Africa

Penguin Michael Joseph is part of the Penguin Random House group of companies
whose addresses can be found at global.penguinrandomhouse.com

Penguin Michael Joseph, Penguin Random House UK,
One Embassy Gardens, 8 Viaduct Gardens, London SW11 7BW

penguin.co.uk

| Penguin
Random House
UK

First published 2024

001

Set in 12.5/14.75pt Garamond MT Std
Typeset by Jouve (UK), Milton Keynes
Printed and bound in Great Britain by Clays Ltd, Elcograf S.p.A.

The authorized representative in the EEA is Penguin Random House Ireland,
Morrison Chambers, 32 Nassau Street, Dublin D02 YH68

A CIP catalogue record for this book is available from the British Library

PAPERBACK ISBN: 978-1-405-97541-4

MIX
Paper | Supporting
responsible forestry
FSC® C018179

For Andrew, Jack, Alfie and Ted

When you go home, tell them of us and say
For your tomorrow, we gave our today.

John Maxwell Edmonds

Prologue

Dust had settled in the mesh fabric of my training shoes. The rubber sole, the collar of the heel, my white running socks. Nothing stayed its original colour out here for long. Loose sand – or 'moon dust', as we called it. The powdery, flour-like substance that covered everything in southern Afghanistan. And I mean everything. You could shower twice a day but it never really went away. Sometimes great threatening clouds of the stuff would scud across the sky, making visibility so bad all military aircraft had to be grounded and the roads in and out of camp closed.

But today the sky was a clear blue and the sun on my back already felt warm even though it was early still, just gone six. Half an hour until the start of the camp run. Stretching my arm behind my back, I stared into the distance, looking beyond the perimeter fence and its crown of coiled barbed wire, to the fields of poppies, their vivid red flowers waving in the wind.

It all looked so serene – no sign of violence or war. No sign of life at all. I could sense him though, out there somewhere. The enemy. Watching. Waiting. Ready to catch me unawares.

1

A Land Rover screeched to a halt beside me, kicking up a cloud of dust in its wake. Lieutenant Christopher Harris jumped out.

'Morning,' he said cheerfully. 'Just been putting out the direction signs.' Taking in the fifty or so fellow runners already gathered at the starting line, he let out an appreciative whistle. 'Looks like the most people we've ever had.'

He loitered awkwardly for a moment, watching me stretch. 'Right, well, better go and warm up myself. See you at the starting line.'

'Have a good one, sir,' I called after him as he walked away.

'Sucking up to top brass as usual, I see.' Fridge slapped me on the back so hard I lost my balance and stumbled forward.

I shoved him back. 'You bloody idiot.'

We both laughed. It had always been this way between us, an affectionate, needling banter of jokes and teasing, ever since we were eight-year-old schoolboys sitting side by side in class. We could make each other laugh until tears rolled down our cheeks.

He brandished a blurry black and white photograph in front of my face. 'It's a little girl!' He stared at the scan in wonder. 'A little girl,' he said again, but more quietly this time, as if taking in the news for the first time.

I thought of four-year-old Billy – Fridge's dinosaur-obsessed son at home, strong-jawed and blond like his dad – and pictured a sweet little girl with his wife Angela's flame-coloured curls and serious blue eyes.

'Congratulations!' I told him.

'Congratulations on what?' Squadron asked as he walked towards us, still rubbing sleep from his eyes.

He was wearing mismatched socks and a T-shirt that was much too small for his hulking six-foot-three frame.

'Good morning, my gentlemen friends,' Assami, our interpreter, called out from behind him. 'And what a very beautiful morning it is.'

'How can you be so cheerful at this time of the morning?' Squadron groaned, tugging at his T-shirt.

'I'm cheerful because I am not the one doing the running.' Assami laughed his great booming laugh. 'And why is your T-shirt so small?'

The others turned up in dribs and drabs. First Jobbo and Caroline, holding hands and deep in conversation. Her long, dark hair immaculate, as always, braided and pinned neatly on top of her head like a maid in a Bavarian bierkeller.

Then Cherub with Jenni, the nurse he had just started dating. She laughed at something he said and reached up to kiss him, leaving the bright red imprint of her lips on his cheek.

Finally Danny appeared, throwing a rugby ball back and forth with Sarge, while Sarah, lost in thought, followed closely behind. I noticed she was the only one of us dressed in proper running kit. Expensive-looking training shoes too.

She brushed aside a stray strand of hair that had escaped from her ponytail and tucked it behind her ear.

In the three weeks she'd been out with us I'd watched her do it a handful of times. I couldn't help but find it sexy, even though I knew I shouldn't. Sarah and Danny were childhood sweethearts. There was no going there. Her eyes flickered towards mine. I looked away.

'Right, you lot,' Sarge shouted. 'I need a photo for the camp newsletter, so get your sorry arses together and line yourselves up in two rows.'

We obediently shuffled into position. Squadron, Jobbo, Cherub and Fridge made up the back line with me, while in front of us Assami, Caroline, Jenni, Sarah and Danny took their places.

'I'll count down from three and then I want you all to shout "Bastion!"' Sarge grinned.

On the count of one we all yelled *Bastion!* at the same time.

My eyes stayed trained on the camera throughout. It was only when I looked at the photo much later that I noticed Sarah's face turned towards mine, her eyes locked on me.

Poppy #1

They say that when you get a tattoo done you need to be able to 'trust your artist'. That they should be someone who 'speaks to you'. I have no idea what that means — only that I need to say something, and the words won't come. This is the only way I can think of saying it, so here goes.

I push open the heavy glass door and an old-fashioned bell rings above my head. The same sound as the school bell — the distant clattering chime that told me I was already in trouble. I was always late.

Inside, the tattoo parlour isn't what I was expecting. I imagined a doctor's waiting room — a bit tired, with plastic chairs, dusty plants and a stack of out-of-date magazines. But it's not like that at all. It's more like one of those trendy hotels, all slate-grey walls and matching skirting boards, with a dark, shiny concrete floor. There's a big, squishy velvet sofa that my bad knee is crying out for me to sink into and behind

5

that, on the wall, an electric sign that simply says 'Tattoo' in blue neon.

A skinny young girl with a shaved blonde head is already sitting on the sofa. She smiles at me briefly before reaching into a bag at her feet and pulling out a magazine with a picture of Kate Middleton in her wedding dress on the cover.

While she flicks through the pages I stare at the huge tattoo on her upper arm – a long black scythe with an angry red blade and the words 'Vampire Slayer' snaked around it on a scroll. Crikey.

A door opens in the back and Barry, the tattoo artist, emerges.

'You must be Carl,' he says, warmly clasping my hand in his. It's a firm, cool grip. Reassuringly so. This isn't the sort of thing you want done by someone with trembling fingers and sweaty palms.

Barry looks at me steadily. His eyes are dark, but not troubled; not haunted by images he'd do anything to unsee, not ringed black and blue with fatigue. They're nothing like the eyes I see when I look in the mirror.

He's young and wiry, with a mass of dense curly hair pulled up into a knot on top of his head. He has substantial holes in his ear lobes plugged by copper rings – the sort you'd find in a plumber's toolbox.

The lobes are so stretched the hole is definitely over a centimetre wide. How is that even possible? I realize I'm staring and quickly shift my attention back to his face.

He smiles, unphased, and holds up the sketch – or 'flash', as he calls it – of my tattoo. 'Just checking you're happy with the final drawing?'

I stare at it and feel my stomach tense. Am I really doing this?

6

Deliberately inflicting a new wound on my already battle-scarred body? I take a deep breath and nod.

'Let's get started, then,' he says.

He apologizes to the girl for keeping her waiting and says his colleague will be out in a minute, then he leads me to a small room at the back of the shop, its red walls plastered with flashes of Barry's other tattoo designs.

Skulls clearly do brisk business. One is particularly disturbing: snakes spilling out of the top of it like brains, black crosses where pupils should be. It stares at me with eerie, emerald-green eyes. I wouldn't want to bump into whoever had that tattoo done on a dark night.

But there are other, exquisitely beautiful designs too. Elaborate Chinese drawings I find bewitching and unfathomable. I stare at the symbols, fascinated, and wonder what they mean.

Barry clears his throat.

'I'll give you a few minutes to get settled,' he says. Then he's gone.

I take my lucky T-shirt off, the one I bought in Blackpool on Fridge's stag do. We all bought T-shirts that day – me, Fridge, Cherub and Squadron. It was our last lads' trip before being deployed, and we were all on such a high. Young enough and stupid enough to think we were untouchable.

Hanging it carefully on the silver metal hook behind the door, I brush the tips of my fingers over the letters emblazoned on the front: JOHNSON MOTORS MOTORCYCLES, 36 COLORADO BLVD, PASADENA CA.

It's so worn now, there are holes under the armpits and on the seam of the neck, but I can't bring myself to get rid of it. It's one of the last links left that connects me to my old life – the life I led

7

before the war changed everything – and I cling to it like a child with a comfort blanket.

Turning back to face the bed, I see it's covered in a layer of cling film. It looks like a scene off the telly where the murderer has carefully laid out plastic sheets, preparing to bash his victim's head in.

A shiver runs down my back – the sort of shiver I used to feel before we went out on patrol. I steel myself, as I learned to do when I was on ops back then, and pick up the dark blue towel Barry has left folded neatly on the end of the bed. I lay it out in front of me, then gingerly ease myself down on top of it.

Barry comes back into the room whistling. 'Ready?'

I nod, watching as he busies himself with his equipment.

'Remember, we're going to be at this for a while, so I hope you've had a good lunch,' he says.

When Barry explained to me on the phone that the first session would take five hours, I was shocked. But it's not as if I have anywhere else to be. This is the first date I've had in the diary for months.

'All set,' I say, remembering the dry cheese sandwich I'd forced myself to eat before leaving the house.

'In that case, I just have one more question,' Barry says. 'Music?'

I smile, remembering.

' "Boys Don't Cry". The Cure.' Then I bury my face in the pillow.

I hear the snapping sound of rubber being stretched, like someone pulling on a balloon before they blow it up. It must be Barry putting on nitrile gloves, but I don't look round. I don't want to watch.

8

Robert Smith starts to sing. He sings about trying to hide his tears, about trying to laugh it off because boys don't cry, and for a moment I'm back on Fridge's stag do – singing this as we walk along the sea front in the pouring rain on our way back to the B&B. Six weeks before our first deployment.

I feel a sharp scorch of pain on my shoulder blade, followed by an intense vibration. Barry tells me to relax and to breathe slowly. His voice is warm and soothing.

There is a shocking realization of a needle being dragged across the skin on my back. When my brain catches up with the pain, it registers a stinging and burning and scratching sensation – like a dentist scraping away at the same tooth for too long – and I want to scream at him to stop.

Barry wipes something across my back. I recognize the distinctive sharp, musty odour of surgical spirit. It's the smell of the medical room where we all went to have our shots for Afghanistan.

Cholera, diphtheria, hepatitis B, rabies. We had to have the lot. I flinched when the nurse jabbed the needle in, but at least it was over in seconds. And we were all together, like we always were, messing around. Everything was a joke back then.

But this – the pain of this doesn't stop. Every time the needle pierces my skin it feels like it's vibrating right through to my bone. It hurts so much it takes my breath away. My body starts shaking.

Barry stops.

He turns off the electric fan heater and, with an energetic shove, opens the window. The blast of cold air steadies me and I force myself to focus on the items on the metal medical trolley by the bed.

I study them as if trying to memorize them for one of those kids' party games. A clear glass bottle of surgical spirit, some swabs and pads of cotton wool, a door key, a packet of spearmint Extra chewing gum and a mobile phone.

A couple of minutes later I'm ready for him to start again. And then, after another ten minutes, something happens. The adrenaline kicks in, like Barry said it would, and my breathing goes back to normal.

I zone out, like I used to do when I was out on patrol on the streets of Kandahar. When every fibre would be strained, anticipating the next attack. Alert for the moment when the villagers and their kids would suddenly disappear.

That was our cue. Silence but for the pounding of your heart, knowing it was about to kick off.

All at once I'm back there. The searing humidity. The parched, dry mouth. And the smell. The smell of heat, dust and sweat, that oh-so-familiar soup of fear. I can taste it.

The pain I feel in my back is almost soothing now. As if I'm finally getting my due . . .

And then it stops.

Barry – as if communicating from another dimension, I'm so spaced out – asks me if I'm okay.

It takes me a second to remember where I am, and then it hits me. The tattoo parlour.

'Congratulations,' he says. 'The first one's done.' Smiling, he holds out a mirror. 'Ready to take a look?'

Slowly, I raise myself up on the bed to face him, then peer over my shoulder to look in the mirror.

I stare at this new image of myself. At the violent red and the powerful black and the bright green that weaves in between.

It has been drawn beautifully, much better than I'd dared to hope.

'What do you think?' Barry says after a moment.

'It's great,' I say. 'Really great.'

Because it is. It's everything I need it to be.

Big.

Significant.

Permanent.

And shocking.

'Thank you,' I tell him, although a simple thank you doesn't cover it, this vision of mine that Barry has somehow managed to bring to life.

He bows his head in acknowledgement, tells me to take it easy for a day or so, and warns me that the tattoo will start to dry out and peel, like sunburn. It may even scab over. Also, that it will itch like hell. Then he leaves me to get dressed.

I slip my lucky T-shirt over my head and follow Barry out to the front of the shop, where I pay up and arrange to see him again in a couple of weeks.

Outside, I check my watch. It's early still. But I feel exhausted and a bit shaky, so I decide to head over the road to the pub. A whiskey will straighten me out.

Inside, I'm relieved to see there's only one other bloke in there. I used to love a rowdy pub, being packed in with the lads, music blaring in the background. But these days my nerves are shot, and loud places make me feel on edge.

I'm constantly on the lookout for aggressive behaviour, but I don't think the old boy nursing his pint of bitter or the young lad serving are going to give me any trouble.

I can't sit with my back to a door – or window either – but as the place is nearly empty I settle myself on a stool where I can scope any movement behind me in the mirror above the bar.

I order a Jack Daniels.

In the background, Adele is belting her heart out. I listen as she sings about how they almost had it all.

The barman pushes my drink in front of me. I wait for him to move away and then I raise the glass in a toast, looking at myself in the mirror. As I lift my arm, I can feel the newly tattooed skin on my back prickling beneath my T-shirt. The pain gives me a burn of satisfaction.

I take a long gulp. The grainy taste takes me straight back to toasts made long ago.

'To you,' I say silently. 'To all of you.'

Afghanistan

2007

1. Carl

August

Every morning felt like a particularly unforgiving version of Groundhog Day. Waking up early in a tent to face the stench of boots that had been worn too long. The solar bag filled with water to hang overhead as an improvised shower. The long queue for breakfast in the cookhouse.

But not this particular morning.

Standing in front of me with an empty tray in her hands, she looked lost – as if she wasn't quite sure how she happened to have ended up here. Her uniform hung loose on her slight frame. It looked like it belonged to someone else.

She was alarmingly pretty, with flawless skin, sculpted cheekbones and yellow-blonde hair that was somehow all the colours of summer. As she took in her surroundings she absent-mindedly twirled the end of her ponytail between her fingers.

Just then a bunch of boisterous lads jostled past her, looking for somewhere to sit, and she stumbled sideways into the counter.

'Don't mind them,' I said, bending down to pick up the tray they had accidentally knocked out of her hands.

15

She slowly straightened herself up from the counter and stared at me.

'I'm Carl,' I said, holding out my hand.

Her fingers, enclosed in mine, felt small and delicate and soft. I could still feel their touch even after she pulled them away.

She told me her name, but I didn't hear it. Her quiet voice was lost amid the clash of trays on tables, the clatter of knives and forks battling it out like gunfire on plates all around us.

'I think he's talking to you,' she said, nodding towards the chef.

'Ketchup?' he repeated wearily.

I nodded. When I looked back at her she was yawning.

'Something I said?'

'Sorry,' she laughed. 'Last night was my first in camp and I didn't get much sleep. Is it always this –'

Right on cue a tray smashed to the floor behind us, scattering food in all directions. A loud cheer echoed around the tent.

'Noisy?' she said, and we both laughed.

'Yes,' I shouted above the din. 'You get used to it though.'

I thought back to my own first sleepless night here, lying in my bunk listening to the sound of aircraft flying overhead, the rumble of trucks moving in and out of camp, and the constant whir of generators.

It was true, you did get used to it. The noise, the chaos. I'd been told this morning that a suicide bomber

16

had rammed his motorcycle into an armoured column just outside the camp perimeter during the night. I'd slept right through it.

I decided not to tell her about that.

She reached forward to help herself to a carton of juice.

I noticed the red cross, mounted on a white square of fabric, stitched neatly on the arm of her camouflage jacket. 'Medic?' I asked.

'Nurse,' she said, nodding. 'I wanted to do my bit. Look after the soldiers who are doing theirs. I worked in Intensive Care back home, thought it would give me a good grounding for the work out here.'

As she spoke, her hand reached up to touch the badge on her arm, as if to reassure herself. 'I wanted to be part of something bigger, part of a team,' she said.

I recognized that need to belong. It was what had driven me to sign up too. The pull to believe in something, to be able to tell myself that somehow, somewhere, I might be doing something good.

'Sorry, I'm rambling,' she apologized.

She smiled then, a gorgeous wide smile, and pushed the stray strand of blonde hair that danced across her face behind her ears. We held each other's gaze. For a split second I thought I saw a spark of interest in her eyes.

I mentally rehearsed the list of reasons why this was a bad idea. I couldn't afford to be distracted. My usual MO of one night stands might be awkward – I was bound to bump into her again around camp.

But then . . . there was something arresting about this girl. More than the fact she was distractingly pretty. She was clearly smart and brave, or she wouldn't be out here.

There was something I couldn't pin down. In the slight huskiness of her voice, in the way her hands flew through the air as she spoke, in the way she absent-mindedly pushed her hair away from her face. I wanted to talk to her, find out more about her.

'I see you've met Sarah,' a voice said from behind me.

Danny stepped past me, reaching an arm around her and stooping down to kiss the top of her head. 'Sorry to keep you waiting, babe.'

Sarah.

Danny had been talking about his girlfriend from home, who was due out here soon. I didn't realize it was this week. Besides, I'd assumed she would have a Welsh accent, like him. Crestfallen, I looked away.

I was relieved to see Fridge and Squadron walking towards us in the queue.

'Here,' Fridge said, holding out a carefully folded piece of newspaper. 'Dad said to give this to you when I'd read it. It's a piece on the new Leeds squad. He reckons the gaffer's on his way out – I hope so, he's been –'

Danny interrupted him. 'This is Fridge,' he said to Sarah. 'Don't ask me why he's called Fridge, because I honestly couldn't tell you.'

'Fridge . . .' she repeated, looking completely baffled.

'And this is Squadron,' Danny continued. 'He seems

mild enough, but believe me, you don't want to be near him if they run out of Black Forest gateau. It gets ugly.'

She shook Squadron's hand, then darted a glance back at me.

'And Carl I think you've met?' Danny said.

She opened her mouth to say something, but then another gang of rowdy soldiers bowled past her. This time Danny nudged her out of the way, pulling her protectively towards himself.

'I can't believe you're actually here,' he said, holding her in a tight embrace. She stepped back to say something and then he drew her close again, pressing her face into his chest. 'You're actually here,' he repeated, breathing her in.

Danny seemed different with Sarah at his side. While she spoke he listened carefully, nodded his head and smiled. His hand kept drifting towards her – her arm, her elbow, her thigh.

It was as if, standing next to her, touching her, seeing himself reflected in her calm green eyes, he had found something he'd been looking for. He was more relaxed, more confident.

I felt pleased for him. Truly.

That was the thing about being at Bastion that I'd never expected – how quickly strangers could feel like brothers. And Danny, unlike the others, felt like a younger brother to me.

Maybe it was the sense of family I'd never known when I was growing up – a feeling of belonging. Who knows? I just knew I cared about the lads I was with. All of them. I had their backs, like they had mine.

So, even if a part of me did feel jealous, it was good to know Danny had someone who could make him feel like that. Someone whose physical presence made him light up.

'Bacon roll,' the chef yelled, slamming the plate down on the counter in front of me.

I picked it up, smiled at Sarah one more time – she was twirling her ponytail again – then slowly walked away.

It was for the best. This was the last place in the world where I could afford for things to get messy.

2. Sarah

Walking from the canteen to the hospital that first morning, I was struck by the lack of colour. Row after row of canvas tents, bomb-proof barriers, and storage yards paved with endless slabs of concrete. As far as the eye could see across this vast rubble-strewn camp, everything was beige. Even the sand I walked on.

It had been the same in the cookhouse – a sea of camouflage, the bodies all blending into one as the soldiers queued for food or hunkered down over tables to eat.

Maybe that was what had made the blueness of his eyes so striking. Steel blue.

'Sarah, are you okay? You're miles away.'

Danny had stopped walking and was staring straight at me.

'Sarah?' he asked again.

'Sorry, I'm just tired.' I smiled at him.

It was true. I'd been too nervous to sleep on the flight out from Brize Norton. And I'd been feeling on edge ever since the pilot announced that our approach into Camp Bastion would be in total darkness and we should put our body armour on.

I listened now to the rotor blades of helicopters thumping away in the sky above us. To the message being broadcast on the camp tannoy, calling all emergency medical teams to the hospital.

'It just all feels a bit of a shock, being here . . . the reality of it.'

He smiled and put his arms around me. 'I remember that feeling, but you'll be surprised how quickly you acclimatize.'

It was so good to see Danny, to know he was safe, to breathe him in after being apart for so long. He smelled of soap and mints, as always. But something was missing. The smell of the Welsh countryside that was usually on him from the hours he spent outdoors, playing, practising or watching his beloved rugby.

As I stood back to look at him I noticed the signs of strain – the lines etched around his eyes that hadn't been there when he'd left. In the canteen earlier he had seemed agitated when he introduced me to everyone. I realized now he'd been talking non-stop, with a febrile, nervous energy, all the time we'd been walking.

'What about you?' I asked. 'Are you okay?'

'I am, now you're here,' he said, kissing me. 'I hated not being with you, I've missed you so much.' He drew in a deep breath. 'I've missed all of you, I miss home. This place . . .' He trailed off.

Danny had always been so sure about wanting to join the army. His dad had trained as a mechanic with the RAF, and Danny worshipped him – or the memory of him. His dad died during a routine operation when Danny was just six years old.

He was so desperate to be like his dad, to feel his dad

would have been proud of him, I don't think he ever questioned whether being in the army was actually what he wanted. It never even occurred to him.

He enlisted during our last month at school and begged me to do the same, so we could stay together. But I was set on a career as a nurse. It was only after I'd started my training, when one of the other student nurses mentioned being a member of the Territorial Army, that I considered joining up.

She talked about combat operations and peacekeeping missions and highly charged training weekends, and it all sounded so vital and exciting. Besides, I missed Danny. Being in the TA felt like a way of being closer to him.

I'm not sure I ever actually expected to see action, but then I found myself loving my part-time army life. I learned about leadership and management and, as I grew to be more direct, becoming firm in my decision-making, so I grew in confidence too.

Until then, I had always thought I was so lucky to have met Danny when I was young. While my friends were desperately searching for 'the one', love had already found me. All that angst they went through – worrying about whether they would meet someone, and if they did, whether that person would like them in return – it passed me by.

But I started to see that, wonderful as Danny was, being with him had held me back too. I'd been co-dependent for so long, I hadn't learned how to be me. To have faith and confidence in who I was.

By the time the opportunity came along for me to deploy to Afghanistan, it was no longer about Danny, about wanting to be out here with him, although people assumed that it was.

No, going to Afghanistan was about my career. It was about sixteen-hour days, seven days a week. Becoming the best nurse I could possibly be.

'I thought I'd love it out here,' Danny said, pulling me into a tight embrace. 'And I do – well, parts of it. I just didn't expect to miss home so much. The little things, the boring routine you take for granted: the pub on a Friday, rugby with the lads, Sunday lunch at Mam' s –' He broke off and we both fell silent.

A heaviness crept over me. I realized then that I didn't miss that old world. Rather, I couldn't wait for my new life to begin.

'And you,' Danny whispered into my ear. 'I missed you the most.'

How could I possibly tell him that now, when we were finally together again, I craved independence, the chance to prove myself on my own terms.

'Come on, you,' I said, gently peeling his arms away from me. 'You're meant to be showing me the quickest way to the hospital. I don't want to be late on my first day.'

Danny resumed his nervous chatter as we carried on walking across the camp, but for the first time in our five years together the sound of his voice, the familiar gesture of him reaching for my hand, no longer made me feel anchored.

We were walking side by side, but with every pace it felt as if the distance between us was getting wider.

If we'd known then what we were walking towards, would we have walked a little more slowly?

Turned back, even?

3. Carl

24 December, Christmas Eve

We ended up leaving camp two and a half hours later than planned, delayed by a monster sandstorm. We holed up in the canteen, not that any of us had any appetite.

Sarah, Jenni and Caroline joined us, Caroline clambering over my lap and Fridge's outstretched legs to squeeze in next to Jobbo, Jenni trying to make us all laugh with a pair of light-up reindeer antlers.

Sarah smiled, but the smile didn't quite reach her eyes. Something seemed wrong; she looked preoccupied, worried. Or maybe it was just that the innocence which had marked her out as new to camp, back when I first met her in August, had gone.

Waiting to go out on patrol was never fun. The anticipation. The fear. The tightness in the pit of my stomach. The endless clock-watching because I just wanted the waiting to end so I could get on with whatever I was going to have to deal with out there.

Caroline slipped her hand into Jobbo's, and he gave it a reassuring squeeze. 'You okay?' she whispered, and he nodded, pulled her closer towards him.

Sarge, cigar in mouth as always, could sense the mood and was doing his best to keep our nerves at bay by distracting us with stories about his missus. 'I love that woman with all my heart,' he was saying. 'She's a great wife and a wonderful mother. But my God, she's a shocking cook. Gravy so thick it needs spreading, and don't even get me started on her turkey. I'd rather eat my own biceps.'

Everyone laughed. Sarge could always be relied upon to rally everyone's spirits. He was a great ox of a man who loved life, the army and cigars. He was fiercely loyal, considered no sentence complete without at least one swear word in it, and was a force to be reckoned with in the bar.

But despite Sarge's best efforts, it's fair to say we were all more on edge than usual by the time the storm finally passed and we were given the all-clear to get going.

'Come on, then, lads,' Sarge rallied as his walkie-talkie crackled into life. He stood up, tucked what was left of his cigar behind his ear, then reached for his helmet. 'Let's get to work.' The delay in starting the patrol meant the sun had almost set. It was that eerie sort of orange light that presaged day becoming night, and cold, like the biting Yorkshire winds back home.

As we settled into the back of the truck I looked at Fridge, his eyes just visible beneath the lip of his helmet. He was staring straight at his rifle, his jaw clenched. I wanted to talk to him but he had his game face on, and I knew better than to bother him.

I'd seen that look so many times. I saw it that first

day I met him, aged eight, sitting next to him in class, watching as he painstakingly wrote his name in his new exercise book.

As the years passed I witnessed that very same look before every football game, every exam, every military training exercise. The mask that came down over his features. The mask that told the world he was ready. He was on a mission.

I knew that kid better than I knew myself. I knew his favourite song was 'Life Is A Rollercoaster' by Ronan Keating, even though he pretended it was 'Going Underground' by The Jam.

I knew he lived for Leeds United, could quote every line from the first two Rocky movies, that his favourite meal was spaghetti Bolognese, and that the small scar above his upper lip wasn't a battle scar. It was from the morning when, aged five, he'd decided to use his dad's razor to give himself a shave.

And I knew there was something wrong now.

I'd heard him on the phone to Angela earlier that day, back in the mess. He'd been laughing, telling her she must look like a Christmas pudding, and she must have been laughing too, and then suddenly she can't have been laughing any more – because he was pleading with her to stop crying.

'Please, Ange. Please, babe,' he'd begged. 'I can't stand it when you cry. I promise I'll be safe, I promise I'll come home.'

I'd flinched as he said it. None of us ever promised that.

We were driving past what had once been the town's grand mosque, now just a giant hole in the ground. Only the pole with the loudspeaker that announced the daily calls to prayer stood defiantly intact.

It was the route we always took when we headed out into insurgent country, but tonight I had a funny feeling as I looked at that mosque-shaped hole and the rubble that surrounded it.

Suddenly we lurched wildly to the left and Danny fell sideways into me. I caught sight of the expression on his face as I reached out to help him back into his seat. It was a look of sheer terror.

'You're all right, lad,' I told him. 'It's just a pothole.'

He sat back in his seat and started to hum quietly. He always hummed to himself when he was nervous.

Listening to him then, I felt overcome with a sense of protectiveness. A need to see him home safe. To see everyone home safe. I ran my hand over my grenades and ammunition for reassurance.

Hyper-aware now, I scanned the countryside for signs of an ambush, even though I knew I wouldn't see any. The insurgents were too sophisticated to let themselves be seen. They had become expert at rigging up invisible tripwires, then waiting for a military vehicle to pass by before detonating the bomb using radio or mobile phone signals.

Danny hummed the first verse of 'God Rest Ye Merry Gentlemen' and then he started to sing. Quietly at first, but then Sarge joined in, and a moment later Cherub.

After that, we all did, belting out the words from somewhere deep within us. By the time we got to the second round of 'Oh tidings of comfort and joy', Danny no longer looked scared, and the shadow that had clouded Fridge's face earlier had completely disappeared.

Fridge had always been a sucker for Christmas. I thought back to when we were little boys, dressed up as shepherds in the school Nativity play, wearing old dressing gowns. Fridge had got into trouble for wearing a Leeds United shirt underneath.

Our eyes locked and he grinned at me – a big, contagious grin that illuminated his whole face.

Nothing ever felt as frightening when Fridge was with me. Best mates since we were nippers, bound together by the highs and lows of our lives – the good, the bad, and everything in between. I was so glad to have him out here with me.

I smiled back.

'Happy days,' he said.

Then:

BOOM!

4. Sarah

'Incoming in five!'

It was Jenni, the head nurse.

'We're on, pet,' she said, yanking a plastic apron over her head and tying the strings expertly behind her back.

A look passed between us as we listened to Colonel Blackstone, the chief surgeon, relay the news.

'It seems that one of the patrol vehicles drove over an IED,' he announced solemnly.

A shudder travelled through me. Danny's patrol had left the compound an hour earlier. Cherub – 'Jenni's Cherub', as I thought of him now – was with him in the same vehicle. So were Sarge, Squadron, Jobbo, Fridge and Carl.

The radio rasped again. A second vehicle had also come under attack. Three more severely wounded casualties were on their way.

Dear God, don't let Danny's patrol be one of the ones that was hit.

Doctors rushed past me, their blue surgical gowns hastily pulled on over their camouflage uniforms. Two headed straight for theatre, while another gave orders to the X-ray team.

'Bloods,' yelled Jenni.

'On it,' I said, making my way to the fridge door. Outside, I heard the sound of a helicopter.

Less than a minute later, the wounded were being wheeled in. A crazy, electric energy took over, as it always did when traumas were arriving. Soldiers were triaged in seconds, clothes and boots cut away and dropped unceremoniously into plastic bags to be incinerated later.

Someone's boots. Someone's uniform. Someone's life.

'He's gone,' I heard the chief surgeon say, pulling a sheet over the blond-haired patient on the first trolley.

'Blood pressure a hundred and forty over forty-six,' Jenni called out, frantically working on the second patient.

Steeling myself not to think about the sheet-covered corpse, I joined the colonel at the side of the third casualty. Before he even had time to ask, I reached for the dose of adrenaline and handed it to him.

I watched as he pushed it into the patient, the magic fluid that would keep the soldier's heart pumping. I scanned the lad's heart rate, his blood pressure and blood oxygen level. It wasn't until I moved to check his temperature that I realized he was awake. His eyes scanned my face urgently. Another desperate stranger, just a boy, a long way from home, searching for reassurance. My heart contracted.

'Hey,' I said, pressing my gloved palm gently on his forehead. 'It's okay. You're in the hospital. You're safe.'

'I need you to get a message to my wife,' he said shakily. 'I need you to tell her how much I love her.'

It was the universal request of almost all the injured soldiers brought into the hospital. With each new request my heart hardened a little bit more towards this war they were fighting. I always contacted the families of the ones who didn't make it, their frightened faces etched into my mind forever.

'I will.' I nodded. 'I promise.'

The colonel laid a hand on the lad's chest and tilted his head down so he could look him in the eye. 'You're going to be all right, soldier. You're in good hands. We're going to take you into surgery now.'

The soldier reached for my arm as we wheeled him into the operating theatre. 'You won't forget, will you?' he said, his voice weak. 'Her name is Ellie. Tell her she's the love of my life.'

'I won't forget,' I told him as I inserted the cannula into the vein on his forearm. I looked back at him and smiled my brightest nurse's smile. 'But you'll be able to tell her yourself soon enough.'

A single tear rolled down his cheek, leaving a strip of clean flesh on his otherwise bloody, soot-blackened face.

The anaesthetist placed the oxygen mask over the soldier's face and told him to count backwards from ten. He made it to six before his hand released its fierce grip on my arm.

I thought of his wife back at home, unaware of what had happened. I thought of Danny, still out there some-where, imagined him hurt and asking one of the lads to tell me how much he loved me, and my breath caught in my throat.

Poor Danny. He'd been so clingy these last few weeks, anxious and jumpy in a way he never was back home.

Even when we were alone, he was never really able to fully disconnect from what was going on outside the camp.

I'd seen how afraid he was sometimes; told myself, and him, that it was his fear that would keep him alive. That being afraid would make him alert, keep him safe. How useless those words seemed now. Being afraid, being brave, they wouldn't stop him from being blown up by a roadside bomb. From being hit by a bullet, or from accidentally stepping on an IED.

And what did I know of what it felt like to be overcome by a fear like that? To head out on another patrol, wondering if this would be the day you didn't make it back.

Around camp the lads were always full of bravado, but in the hospital tent I got to see how scared they really were. Sometimes patients woke screaming from nightmares so vivid they looked around them as if expecting to see bullets whooshing by their beds. Even when I told them where they were, that they were safe, they were still too afraid to go back to sleep. Suspicious of the hospital's silence, they forced themselves to stay awake, alert to the invisible enemy that stalked them.

The same deadly enemy that lay in wait for Danny and the others.

A sudden terror descended on me.

I listened to my patients' cries, I held their hands, but I couldn't help them. What if Danny's patrol had come under attack by that same enemy and I couldn't help him either?

5. Carl

It's hard to say what hit my senses first after the blast. The heat, the dust, the noise, the pressure. The wave literally rushed through me. I didn't see the light. My life didn't flash before me.

Everything just went very quiet.

Time stood still for a couple of seconds, then the adrenaline started pumping its way through my body at speed and I was back. Back in the moment, knowing that if I didn't move fast I risked being shot at.

Instinctively I patted myself down. The uniform on my right arm and my stomach felt sticky to the touch. I couldn't feel a thing, but I realized I must be wounded because when I pulled away my fingers they were covered in blood.

Jobbo's voice as he shouted a damage report into the radio sounded strange and echoey through the buzzing sound that was ringing in my ears.

I hauled myself up to face Danny. He had gaping chunks of flesh missing on his right arm and hand, and he was bleeding from deep shrapnel wounds to his face which was blank with shock.

He was staring past me. I turned my head to see that his gaze was focused on Sarge, lying on the ground next to us, his leg blown clean off below the knee. His teeth were clenched together and he was moaning in pain.

I was still stunned and half deafened by the explosion, but Sarge needed me and I was going to do everything I could for him. My brain fizzed into action.

'Sarge,' I heard myself say. I didn't recognize my own voice, it sounded so distorted. 'You're going to be fine,' I told him. 'It's just a scratch.'

He laughed, and turned to look at me. Then he stopped laughing, and tears started to roll down his face. The sight of Sarge crying was far worse than the sight of his bloodied, brutally truncated leg.

He tried to sit up but I held him down. 'Stay still. We need to get a tourniquet on you.' I knew from my first-aid training back home that I needed to apply pressure to what was left of the limb.

I dug into my sleeve pocket for a bandage. Grimly, I pulled back the scorched remnants of Sarge's trousers and, doing my best to ignore the horror of the blackened fabric, drenched with his warm, pumping blood, I eased the bandage under his thigh and pulled it tight.

'All set,' I said. I forced myself to smile at him, despite the fact that my insides were cramping, my whole body shaking with the fear that he might not make it. That I might not be able to save him.

'How you doing back there?' Jobbo yelled.

'All good,' I lied, looking across at Danny's ashen face.

All this time Danny had been sitting next to me and Sarge, not uttering a sound.

'Danny? Danny, mate, are you okay?' I asked.

He didn't respond.

'Hang in there,' Jobbo yelled. 'Backup's on its way.'

'You hear that, Danny?' I said. 'We'll be out of here in no time.'

Sarge was swearing under his breath. I turned back to him and saw that he had started to shiver. I shrugged my jacket off and felt a sharp stab of pain in my stomach.

'Are you okay?' Sarge asked as I winced.

'I'm fine,' I told him, laying my jacket across his chest. 'Don't worry about the rest of us. We're all fine.'

That was the moment I realized I couldn't see Fridge.

I called his name but there was no answer. 'Jobbo,' I called out desperately. 'Can you see Fridge?'

Before he could respond I saw a military vehicle screech to a halt beside us. The quick reaction force.

'You see, Danny,' I said, 'I told you everything's going to be okay.'

He blinked then and let out a long sigh, as if for all this time he hadn't dared to breathe.

I patted him on the shoulder. 'You're all right.'

He nodded and I hauled myself out of the way so that the lads with the stretcher could set it down next to Sarge. I watched as they pumped a shot of morphine into him and scribbled a large M plus the time on his forehead, so the doctors who treated him later would know what he'd been given and when.

The time they wrote on his forehead was 5.23. I'll never, ever forget that time.

Because as they lifted Sarge up on to the stretcher,

that's when I saw the body lying in the mangled wreckage of the Warrior. It was maybe a hundred yards ahead of me, the arm at a weird angle to the rest of the body, and covered in blood.

I knew straight away it was Fridge.

I could tell by his hair and his body and his tattoo – a tattoo I knew so well, it might as well have been my own. It was his wife's face, drawn next to an outline of a tiny baby's foot.

Billy's foot.

I had drawn that outline while Fridge gently pressed his son's foot on a piece of paper the day Billy was born.

'Fridge!' I screamed. Then again, *'Fridge!'*

Desperate to reach him, I tried to haul myself up but a strong hand on my shoulder forced me back down.

'Not so fast,' the medic said. 'We need to get a dressing on your stomach.'

I craned my head to look at Fridge.

'Fridge,' I called out.

I felt the medic push a needle into my arm.

'Fridge,' I called again, my voice now barely a whisper.

Fridge.

6. Sarah

My heart plunged as I heard the news that Danny's patrol had been hit. One dead, two seriously injured. They were bringing them into the hospital now.

Danny was the first in. My eyes skittered over him. He had blood-soaked dressings on his arm and hand and extensive shrapnel wounds to his face which was caked in blood and soot. His eyes were closed.

'Danny!' I cried, rushing over to him.

'He's going to be fine,' the medic wheeling him in told me. 'We had to sedate him.'

Sedate him? I wanted to ask more, but there wasn't time. Other trollies were being wheeled in behind him.

'Sarah!' It was Colonel Blackstone.

'Go,' the medic smiled. 'I've got this.'

I rushed to the second trolley and saw that it was Carl. His eyes registered my presence for just a second. They were the same striking blue as the day I'd first met him in the canteen, but his focus drifted off now.

'Carl, Carl, can you hear me?'

He closed his eyes.

'Carl,' I pleaded. 'Carl!' I reached for his hand.

'He's going into shock,' the colonel said. 'Let's get him into surgery.'

Carl's breathing was shallow and rapid, his hand cold

and clammy. I had an awful feeling that he didn't want to wake up. I gripped his hand as we wheeled him into theatre.

'Carl, it's Sarah.' I tried to sound calm, even though my heart was racing. 'We're taking you into surgery now. You're hurt but you're going to be okay. You hear me? You're going to be okay. So hang in there. Will you do that, Carl? Will you do that for me?'

I stepped back to let the anaesthetist place the mask over his face. I thought of the young soldier I'd watched him put the very same mask on, less than an hour ago. He hadn't made it.

'You okay?' Jenni asked as I came out of theatre. 'You look shattered. Why don't you go and sit with Danny.'

I shook my head. I felt guilty about not going to him, but I knew Danny would be sleeping. My emotions were with Carl, I couldn't leave him. How could I explain that to Jenni? I could barely explain it to myself. Something about him just seemed so achingly vulnerable, lying on that hospital trolley. And so alone.

I looked over my shoulder, peeked through the glass panel into the operating theatre, and scanned the monitors by Carl's side. His vitals were steady. Thank God.

I turned back to Jenni. 'Who . . . ?' I asked her. 'Who . . .' I couldn't bring myself to finish the sentence.

'Sarge is injured but he's going to be okay,' Jenni said. 'Fridge . . .' She looked stricken.

Oh God. Fridge. His poor family.

I wondered if Carl knew. The loss of his friend

would hit him hard. All the lads were good mates but none more so than those two. Best friends since way before they joined the army, they were like brothers. They ordered the same food, laughed at the same jokes, finished each other's sentences.

Carl had spent time in care as a kid – like Caroline, Jobbo's girlfriend – and from what I could gather Fridge and his parents had, to all intents and purposes, been his family. And now Fridge was gone.

How was it possible that just a few short hours ago we had all been sitting in the canteen together joking?

'Go on,' Jenni insisted. 'Go check on Danny. I've got this.'

After one more glance into the operating theatre, to reassure myself that Carl was going to be all right, I went to check on Danny. He was fast asleep, his wounds cleaned and dressed.

I kissed him on the forehead. 'Sleep well, sweetheart,' I whispered. Then, knowing that he was peaceful – for now, at least – I busied myself in recovery. I checked patients' pulse rates and blood pressures. I assessed surgical sites and monitored IV fluids. I went over levels of sensation. Then I checked pulse rates and blood pressures and IV fluids again.

My mind flicked back to the training base I'd been sent to before I came out here. The endless drills we rehearsed, over and over again, on dummies and volunteer patients, doing precisely this.

It felt strange to think of the person I was then. I had thought I knew it all. I had thought I was ready for anything. But nothing could have prepared me for the real thing. How could it?

For the sheer overwhelming, relentless sadness of war.

For the sight of Danny's bloodied, soot-blackened face.

For Fridge.

For Ellie, the wife I would write to at the end of my shift, to tell her that her husband's last words had been how much he loved her.

The doors swung open and Jenni and another nurse pushed Carl's trolley into the room.

'He's going to be fine,' she said. 'How's Danny doing?'

'Fast asleep,' I told her. 'But . . .'

Jenni looked at me.

'I'm worried. About them having to sedate him. Apparently, he was in shock.'

She nodded. 'I wouldn't worry too much,' she said kindly. 'Plenty of the lads who come through here suffer from the accumulated effects of stress. Coming under attack, facing IEDs every day, they're bound to. I'd say it's to be expected, after what Danny's been through today.' She looked down at Carl. 'What they've all been through.'

Jenni started to run through his post-operative checks.

I reached my hand out for the chart she was holding. 'Why don't you grab a coffee?'

She looked at me gratefully. 'You sure?'

I prised the chart out of her hands in response.

'I'll bring one back for you,' she said, disappearing out of the room.

When the door opened again, half an hour later, I assumed it was Jenni.

But then I heard Caroline's voice.

'Hey,' she said quietly. 'I hope it's okay to be here. I just wanted to check on you all.' Ashen-faced, she stared at Carl. 'How is he doing?'

'He's going to be fine.'

'Thank God.' She sighed heavily. 'Does he know?' she whispered. 'About Fridge?'

'I'm not sure. He didn't say anything when they brought him in.'

'Carl will be lost without him.'

I nodded.

'I still can't believe he's gone,' Caroline said. 'It doesn't seem real.'

We both stared at the tubes running in and out of Carl's body.

When I looked up, I saw that Caroline was staring at me. I didn't realize I was crying until she put her arms around me.

Home

2011

7. Carl

Yorkshire

Stepping out of the shower on a sunny September morning, I catch sight of the vivid red scar that criss-crosses my stomach. The ugly souvenir I brought home from Afghanistan that reminds me every day of all I've lost.

Normally I pull a T-shirt over it as quickly as possible, but today I have to put a fresh dressing on the tattoo, so I wrap a towel across my midriff to cover it instead. Then, twisting my head over my shoulder, I stare in the mirror at the new image on my back and smile. My tribute to Fridge.

Awkwardly I reach over my shoulder and think of Sarah changing my dressing that Christmas morning. In my mind's eye I see her face so clearly, her brow furrowed in concentration, her cool fingers as they moved quickly and efficiently over my skin. She was so gentle, so kind.

I'm ashamed to say I don't think I was a very gracious patient. I was too angry, in too much pain. I didn't want to be nursed back to health. I wanted to be with Fridge. For the longest time that's all I wanted.

Suddenly, there's an almighty crash downstairs and

Elsa leaps up from the bed, barking. Her paws skid and clatter on the bare wooden floorboards as she bolts through the bedroom and hurtles downstairs.

Maggie must be here.

I smile as I listen to Maggie greet Elsa.

'Did you miss me? Did you? Did you? Yes, you did. Of course you did. What's not to miss? I'm wonderful. Yes, I am. Yes, I am.'

Maggie is the object of Elsa's undying adoration and my assistant in a flourishing dog walking and dog sitting business. She is skinny as a whippet, with a pale, spectral face, dyed black hair cut brutally short, and big grey-blue eyes that are always ringed in heavy black eyeliner.

Her clothes are black – skinny jeans held up by a black belt studded with silver bullets, and T-shirts with pictures of bands on the front I've never heard of. Even the nails on her silver-skull-beringed hands are black.

It's funny – she's the most frightening-looking person I've ever known, and yet the least threatening. She is gentle and big-hearted and lovely and, much as I hate to admit it, I couldn't run my business without her. The last three months have been crazily busy, with a bunch of new dogs to walk and look after. I'd never manage it on my own.

The business itself is down to Fridge's dad, Michael. I can't remember a time when that man hasn't been there for me. If anything, he's been even more of a rock since Fridge died.

He lent me the money to buy the van I needed to get the business going. He took me to the dealership, negotiated a discount. They were happy to do him a favour; he's one of those men everyone wants to do a favour for. Fridge was the same.

Michael had bought vans off the local dealer for decades, for his carpentry business. Vans with seats that were always covered in a smattering of sawdust, and crumbs from opened packets of shortbread.

Vans in which Michael drove me and Fridge to our endless football games, dropping me back home at the end of the day. He always insisted I wait in the van while he knocked on the door. I realize now he was checking to see how drunk Mum was. Nine times out of ten he'd climb back into the passenger seat and drive me to their house again.

'Your mum's not feeling too good,' he'd say, offering me a packet of shortbread.

Back at Fridge's home, his mum, Kathleen, would hand me a pair of pyjamas that smelled just like their sheets did – of summer. Laundry definitely didn't smell like that in our house. Everything in our house smelled of ashtrays or the stale odour of minced beef and onion pancakes.

Not being at home was a relief, because it meant I didn't have to think about the dishes stacked up in the sink. About the empty bottles by the bin. About the empty bedroom Scott and Adam had shared before they were taken into care. And I didn't have to worry about looking after Mum.

On those nights I spent at Fridge's house I got to be a kid. We would lie awake in bunk beds that Michael had made himself, talking about everything – football, music, girls – until his dad opened the bedroom door and told us both to belt up.

'Or at least keep it down a bit,' he'd say, with a wink.

After Fridge died, when I was well enough to go back to camp, I would lie awake in my bunk and curse myself for not protecting him like he and his dad had always protected me.

Nothing assuaged the loneliness, and nothing purged the guilt. Nothing. I thought his mum and dad would blame me too, but they never did. I often thought it would have been easier if they had.

All the time I was still in Afghanistan, and Fridge wasn't, they carried on sending me letters. Cuttings from *The Yorkshire Post* about Leeds United, pictures of Billy and his new baby sister, Lottie, and updates on all our mates back home.

Kathleen talked about her vegetable patch and the weather, and Michael talked about his building projects and the footie. They talked about Fridge and how proud they were of him. And they told me how proud they were of me.

For months, I couldn't bring myself to answer those letters. Their kindness was too much to bear.

Before heading downstairs now, I glance at the picture I keep in a frame by my bed – the one Sarge took of us all on the morning of the camp run, just a couple of weeks after Sarah arrived at camp. For a brief moment I imagine myself back there. Before Fridge died, and everything changed.

It's the same every morning. That one fleeting second where I take in Fridge's reassuring presence by my side, Sarah's smile, Squadron's ridiculous too-tight T shirt, Assami's unfailing grin, Danny's anxious frown, and the two loved-up couples. Cherub and Jenni. Jobbo and Caroline.

And then I remember. All of it.

My eyes wander back to Squadron.

I should get a move on. I can't be late. Not for him.

Downstairs Maggie is filling the house with noise. She tops up the kettle, flicks on the radio and triggers another round of jubilant barking from Elsa as she opens the cupboard to take out her food.

I smile as I pull on my clothes.

Noise.

Noise is good.

It drowns out the sound of my loneliness.

8. Sarah

At work in the Intensive Care Unit, when awful things are happening around me, it's reassuring to listen to the voices on the radio burbling away in the background. To know that out there — in the rest of the world — the safe, mundane banalities of everyday life rumble on as usual.

Here, too, in Danny's mum's house, where these days it feels dark no matter what time of day it is or how many lights are switched on, the radio is reliably cheerful. Annie keeps it on all the time, as if its noise alone will make the house, and her son, happy again.

Through the open living-room door I can just make out Danny's face as he stares, unseeing, at the TV. He has that faraway look in his eyes. The thousand-yard stare. Or, to give it its medical definition: 'The unfocused gaze of a traumatized soldier who has become emotionally detached.'

His hair is so long now, it falls below his shoulders. Matted and greasy and black, it mirrors the wild, unkempt beard that obscures the bottom half of his face.

Danny used to take such pride in his appearance.

When we were younger, the other lads in his rugby team used to tease him about how long he spent on fixing his hair. Not any more.

'Is it possible,' the DJ asks over the airwaves, 'to cook an egg in the bath? Or even,' he pauses, a smile in his voice, 'in a dishwasher?'

He must be a stand-in, because I don't recognize the voice, and yet there is something familiar in his northern accent and easy charm. A memory pulls at the edges of my mind.

'There you go, lass,' he says, handing the show over to his co-host.

And suddenly I am transported fully back there, to a crowded military canteen. Deep blue eyes, warm skin pressed against mine for the briefest of moments as he shakes my hand.

Whenever I think of him, it is always his face on that first morning that I recall, before he knew I was Danny's girlfriend. Before the shutters came down and locked me out.

The kettle boils, spewing out angry steam. I pour the bubbling-hot liquid into two mugs and fish out the teabags quickly – he doesn't like it too strong – and toss them in the bin. Then I take a deep breath, paste on a smile, and carry the mugs of tea through to the living room.

Gently, I sit down on the sofa.

'Sweetheart, I made you some tea.'

Carefully, I hold it out for him, but his hands remain rigid, steadfastly gripping the edge of his armchair.

Hands I would know anywhere.

The purple thread of veins that twist and pop below the thin, shrapnel-scarred skin. The slightly crooked middle finger, broken in a schoolboy rugby tackle. How they used to turn bright red like a pair of gloves in the cold – even getting something out of the freezer would make them change colour. He would fold his hands in mine to warm them up again.

He doesn't reach for my hands any more. In fact, he barely acknowledges me at all.

'Danny?' I try again.

They say that every war has its after-war. This is Danny's. His mind separated from his body, forever stuck in some desert battlefield. A place where none of us can visit him.

He may not have been a direct victim of a bomb or a missile, but Danny is another casualty all the same. The deep psychological injuries have never healed. The old Danny – the sweet, gentle, uncomplicated Danny with the happy, dancing eyes – the boy I fell in love with when I was seventeen years old, is gone.

Back then, he didn't have a care in the world. Life came easily to him. School, sport, friendship, girls.

The first time I ever saw him, he was onstage rehearsing for the school musical. A bunch of girls were whispering and giggling as they watched him through the doors of the school hall. I went to see what all the fuss was about.

The fuss was Danny.

After that, I'd notice him around school, always

surrounded by a gaggle of cool friends. So I couldn't believe it when, a couple of weeks after first setting eyes on him in rehearsal, he waved at me as I crossed the playground at the end of the day.

We had been back in Mum's Welsh hometown barely a month by then. I was still feeling lost and lonely, without any of my old friends, without my dad who had stayed in London, now living with his new girlfriend. I felt invisible. At the very least, not worth noticing.

So when Danny lifted his hand in my direction, I turned around, expecting to see the popular kids he normally hung out with. But there was nobody else there. Only me.

'Hey, London girl,' he said, casually throwing a rugby ball up in the air. 'Can I walk you home?' He caught the ball and casually raked a hand through his ink-black hair, pushing it out of his eyes which were the same pale grey as the Welsh sky above us.

He smiled, and I saw that one front tooth ever so slightly overlapped the other. It was the only thing that wasn't absolutely perfect about him.

'Sure,' I said, trying to sound casual.

When I closed the front door of the hated new house behind me that afternoon, it felt for the first time like it could become a home for us after all.

Mum peered at me from behind one of the removal company's enormous cardboard boxes, still stacked in the kitchen.

'You look different,' she said.

Mum was right. Being with Danny changed everything

for me. Until then, I had missed London. Missed my friends. Missed my running club. And I was angry with Mum for taking me away from them. Almost as angry as I was with Dad for leaving us.

Danny made up for all of that. He was sweet and funny, and he made me feel good about myself at a time when Dad, because he had chosen to leave us, had made me feel like I wasn't good enough.

Danny introduced me to his friends, invited me to watch him play rugby, rehearse with his school band. He listened patiently as I told him about Dad's new wife, new baby on the way. He came running with me, laughing and joking as he chased me across fields and valleys and mountains that had been carved in the Ice Age. Their peaks and slopes felt epic after the flat expanses of south London.

Our teenage romance felt epic too.

Mum got a job as an estate agent. Her face was no longer permanently red and swollen from crying. She dyed her hair blonde, bought herself some high-heeled boots. And then one day, towards the end of my first term, I noticed that she'd started to laugh again. We both had.

That Christmas, our first without Dad, Danny's mum invited us to spend the day with them. Annie and Mum got tipsy and burned the turkey while Danny and I kissed under the mistletoe he'd picked himself that morning.

'*Nadolig Llawen*,' he said, as he held it above me and smiled. 'Or as you English like to say, Happy Christmas.'

'*Nadolig Llawen*,' I replied happily, pulling him down next to me to kiss him.

We were sitting on this same, worn blue sofa.

The same spot where we played charades later that day.

Where, weeks later, Danny told me for the first time that he loved me.

Where we drunkenly fell asleep in each other's arms on Saturday nights.

Where we opened the envelopes that held our exam results.

Where Danny told me he'd signed up.

'I want to see the world before it's too late like it was for Dad,' he said. 'There wasn't enough time for him. But there is for you and me. We should make the most of it.'

I breathe out a long sigh. That time stretches ahead of us like a curse now. Minutes and hours and days and months, while we all anxiously wait to see if Danny will get better – or worse. Whether he will hurt me any more than he already has.

'Fifty per cent of veterans with post-traumatic stress disorder commit wife-battering and domestic violence,' the doctor on duty told me matter-of-factly the first time it happened. 'It's not Danny, not the Danny you knew, who did this, it's his illness.'

Now that's what I focus on. I tell myself it wasn't me he saw the first time he wrapped his hands so tightly around my neck that I thought I was going to die. Or when, a year after we came home, he smashed a vodka bottle against my arm.

'Please forgive me, Sarah,' he begged, full of remorse when he came back to himself. '*Please.*'

But there is never anything to forgive.

Because how can I be angry with him for doing something he has no idea he is doing? That's what makes all of this so hard. I can't speak out about it, or complain about it, or escape from it.

Because none of this is his fault.

And because the women whose husbands and partners never came back to them have it so much worse. Like Ellie, the young bride I wrote to, whose husband's last words were about her. And all the other widows too.

Danny's arm jerks involuntarily.

I reach out and carefully lay my hand on top to steady it, as if by touching him I can absorb some of his pain. Bring him back from wherever it is he has disappeared to.

But there is no bringing him back.

Poppy #2

In the kitchen I gulp down the tea Maggie has made for me, then grab the keys to the van and head out. I glance at my watch and am relieved to see there is plenty of time. Squadron always was a stickler for punctuality.

Squadron was born to be a soldier, just like his dad before him and his dad before that. He was given his nickname by a mate in school because all he ever talked about was joining the army. He loved everything about it – the marksmanship, the fitness, the discipline. It really mattered to him.

He made it matter to me too.

'See,' I tell him silently as I push open the door to the tattoo parlour with time to spare. If only he were still here for me to impress.

Barry is waiting for me. 'Ready for poppy number two?'

I nod and follow him into his room.

'So, what music choice will it be today?' Barry asks as he snaps on his gloves.

' "Oliver's Army" by Elvis Costello,' I tell him, before taking a deep breath and lowering my face down on to the pillow.

Squadron's favourite song. It was his dad's too – killed on the streets of Northern Ireland before he ever got a chance to meet his son. Another generation cursed by war. Wasn't it meant to be different for us?

Behind me, above my ear, I hear the needle start to vibrate, then I feel the familiar sharp sting of its tip biting into my skin. I focus on the song and, like the lyrics say, my mind sleep-walks. Back to the day we first met, the very first day of basic training. A bunch of us were waiting outside the train station – you could spot the new recruits from the frightened looks on our faces. When a bus finally pulled up to collect us, the man who was to be our sergeant jumped out. He was terrifying. All angry, writhing muscle, like a pit bull.

'I don't give a rat's arse who you are,' he screamed into the ear of one unfortunate lad who had stepped forward, reached out his hand and politely introduced himself as Michael.

'Well, what are you waiting for? Put your bags in the back and get on the bloody coach.'

While we all immediately reached down to pick up our luggage, the traumatized kid froze. Without saying a word, Squadron picked up his bag for him and hoisted it across his shoulder. He nudged him in the direction of the bus.

'Don't let him get to you,' I heard him whisper into the lad's ear.

That lad was Cherub – so named because of his mass of blond curls. Ironic, given the brutally efficient soldier he turned into. One of the best. Not the best though. That was always going to be Squadron.

He was one of those men built like mountains, with ridiculously long limbs and massive feet and hands. He had deep-set brown eyes and long, thick black lashes that he hated, because everyone always commented on them. He told me once that when he was a little boy he was so sick of his teacher going on about them that he cut them off with his mum's nail scissors. But he couldn't prevent them growing back again.

He was a beast of an athlete – strong and fast. During those first weeks of training he demolished me relentlessly in all the physical challenges. The runs, the bag lifts, the jerrycan tests. Squadron made them look easy – powering ahead of us all with his two cans full of water dangling easily at his sides. He never spilled a drop.

After leaving school, Fridge had gone to work for his dad for a bit – he didn't join up until the Afghan war started. By then, I had come to rely on Squadron in the way I had previously relied on Fridge. We ate together, trained together, practised our change steps and front salutes together.

He taught me how to dismantle and assemble a rifle. Doing it blindfolded was his party piece.

I taught him how to read a map, something that came easily to me after orienteering training. I can see him now, a comically puzzled look on his face as those great big hands of his endlessly rotated the map, trying to make sense of it.

God, those weeks of training were tough. But whenever I complained about Sarge being an unhinged psychopath who had it in for me, Squadron would talk me down.

'It may not feel like it now, but it's how they make us a unit. It's us against them. Every time he has a go at you, at any of us, we all bond together and become that much stronger. You need to think about the bigger picture.'

As training progressed, the possibility of seeing action abroad loomed closer. Some of our boys were already in Afghanistan, and it was a strong possibility that we would be sent out there too.

There was talk of helping the Afghan people against a resurgent Taliban. About winning over the hearts and minds of the population, helping them build schools and hospitals and roads.

I started to understand what Squadron was saying about the bigger picture and began to feel a pride in what I was doing and what I might be able to do for others.

I stopped caring about Sarge shouting at me, about sleeping in barracks that were freezing cold, about sharing my space and a bathroom with thirty other men.

Squadron taught me to keep my rage in check too. He put a stop to a pointless bar fight I got into on a night's leave towards the end of our training. I don't even remember what the guy in the pub had done to annoy me, but I know I was about to land him one when suddenly Squadron was standing between us.

'Don't,' was all he said. His physical presence was enough.

The next morning, his mum left early for work and Squadron cooked me breakfast. As he fried the bacon, without turning to look at me, he said, 'What were you thinking? Someone with your training having a go at him? And what if they kicked you out of the army? Would it have been worth it?'

I realized then that it wasn't. That none of the fights I'd endlessly provoked at school had been worth it either.

I'd always told myself that I was better than my dad, who'd done time for a drunken brawl, but what had I become? I didn't want to be a man like my father. I wanted to be a man like Squadron.

He never stopped offering me bits of wisdom and advice. That

62

very first tour, as the Hercules began its steep descent towards Camp Bastion, I glanced at the helmets stowed around the plane, as if seeing them for the first time, and suddenly it hit me, really hit me.

Squadron must have noticed my anxiety. He tapped me reassuringly on my leg. 'Get your body armour on. It's time to do some good.'

He said that every single time we went out on patrol. Like a prayer that would protect us. It didn't protect him in the end – and neither did I.

But then none of us saw it coming.

We'd just made it back from a patrol. I clocked Squadron's face and he was grinning with relief, grateful to have survived another mission. We all felt the same – every patrol since Fridge's death had been freighted with an extra level of tension.

I watched as he took off his helmet. It was the first thing we all did when we came back through the camp gates. Telling ourselves we could start to relax.

Then he put down his weapon.

And that's how the sniper got him. He waited until we'd all put down our weapons and taken off our helmets, and then the Afghan 'policeman' on the roof of the checkpoint opened fire.

Squadron was killed instantly, six weeks after we lost Fridge.

And somehow, his death was even more shocking to me than Fridge's. Not just the manner of his death, at the hands of someone we thought we could trust, but because I just never envisaged him going before me. He was too good a soldier.

Even now, I struggle to accept the injustice of it. The fact that he was never given a chance to defend himself. That this most honest of men wasn't given an honest death.

63

Sometimes when I can't sleep, I remember how soundly Squadron always slept. 'Contented exhaustion,' he used to call it. 'The exhaustion that means we know we've done a tiny bit of good.'

And I ask myself, did we? Did we do good? It's hard to know in a world where a man you think is on your side waits for you to lay down your weapons and then opens fire . . .

'All done,' Barry says.

I can't believe he's finished already – I had completely disappeared into my head.

Barry holds up the mirror, and I study the fresh art on my back. I feel tears welling up and, embarrassed at my emotion, look away.

'People often react like this,' Barry says kindly. 'It's the endorphins. Your body is flooded with them while you're having the tattoo done, which can lead to a bit of a crash after. Or it could just be that the tattoo really means something to you.'

He smiles and says no more, busying himself pasting ointment over my back and putting on a dressing.

As he works I think about what he said. I hadn't expected to feel so overwhelmed, but already this tattoo means a great deal to me. It's as if my body, which has felt redundant for so long, has a new purpose.

A memorial to my friends.

For you, Squadron. The most unselfish, decent man I ever knew. You were such a big character in my life, the hole you've left will be impossible to fill. But this tattoo, well, maybe it can fill a tiny part of it.

9. Sarah

'We're getting married in December! We're finally going to do it!'

Jenni was screaming so loudly down the phone that I had to hold it away from my ear.

'I don't want to wait until next summer and, in any case, I think December is more romantic, don't you? We can fill the church with flickering candles and fairy lights. It'll be all roaring fires and hot toddies. Also, crucially, there won't be any humidity, so my hair won't frizz . . . Sarah? Sarah, are you crying? You *are*, you're crying! Cherub, Sarah's crying!' Then a pause. 'Oh God, I'm so sorry, I'm such an idiot. Has something happened with Danny again?'

'I am not crying,' I lie. 'Well, maybe a little bit, but only because I'm so happy for you. You deserve it.'

'I do, don't I?' she laughs. Then, without pausing for breath, starts giddily rattling off more details in that gorgeous Geordie accent of hers. 'So, we've booked this amazing hotel that we got a great deal on because Cherub went to school with the manager, can you believe that? And Sarah, it was so romantic, he went down on one knee and . . .'

I settle the phone on my shoulder and lean back against my hospital locker, listening as Jenni merrily talks non-stop about bouquets and dresses and morning suits and wedding lists.

Fleetingly, I find myself thinking of Caroline – of how all she wanted was a simple white slip dress and flowers in her hair – and it makes me smile to think of my two vastly different but equally wonderful friends. Friendships forged in the blazing chaos of our six months in Afghanistan.

Caroline worked in the kennels, looking after the dogs used on patrols for sniffing out drugs and explosives, while Jenni and I spent practically every waking minute together in the hospital. We were working so closely together that by the time I left, our relationship was almost telepathic.

Listening to her now, I can tell just by the tone of her voice how happy she is. And knowing she has got the happy ending she deserves makes me feel happy too.

And she really does deserve it. Not only is she the most loyal, toughest, funniest and most generous person I know, she is also the best nurse I have ever had the privilege of working with. I don't just mean her medical skills, but her sheer will to keep patients alive.

The first time we met, she told me that she had always wanted to be a nurse, that, as a little girl, she had turned her bedroom into a ward for dolls. I used to watch her with injured and frightened soldiers, back when we were working in the camp hospital together – comforting them, making them laugh when there was nothing to laugh about – and I'd catch a glimpse of the little girl who had spent her whole life preparing for this.

She took care of the nurses too. Even when we were pushed to breaking point, mentally and physically exhausted, Jenni would keep us all going. I never once heard her complain. Everyone adored her – even the lads in camp. She'd play Xbox and pool with them – she was wickedly good at both. I remember staring wide-eyed the first time she picked up a cue.

'Four older brothers,' she said by way of explanation as she held her hand out for her winnings – a family-size bar of Dairy Milk chocolate – which she immediately shared with everyone else.

I'm so glad that my wonderful friend is happy, that they both are. That somehow they've managed to escape the curse that has so mercilessly assailed the rest of us. They've been talking about getting married ever since coming home from Afghanistan. But then she got pregnant with the twins, and life just got in the way.

They live in an old farm cottage on the outskirts of Newcastle, with Noah and Toby, who are two now, and an overweight Boxer dog called Mr Brown.

I never knew it was possible for a house to be so full of noise and chaos, discarded toy cars and action figures. It's scruffy, but in a way that makes you feel comfortable and warm, so warm, with an ancient woodburning stove in the kitchen and clothes permanently drying in front of it. Cherub teases Jenni and tells her off for lighting it even in the summer.

In front of the fireplace are two scruffy armchairs

that used to belong to Cherub's grandparents. I picture Jenni bustling around the kitchen as she talks to me now – the woman never, ever sits still – and wish that I was there with her, sitting in one of those old armchairs.

'. . . and afterwards it's going to be the best party. My nephew Maddock is DJ'ing and –' She suddenly interrupts herself. 'That's enough of me rattling on. I haven't even asked how things are with you. How are you, pet? How is Danny? Are the tablets helping?'

I think about the battles I've had with Danny, trying to get him to take the antidepressants he's been prescribed for his PTSD. About him snatching the foil packet out of my hand as I tried to persuade him to take them last weekend, and him ramming its jagged edge into my forehead.

'I think so,' I say. 'I'm fine.'

I can't bear to puncture the happy mood with the truth. Plus, sometimes talking about it is just too hard. It's much easier to pretend everything is all right.

'We're both fine,' I repeat.

'That's great,' Jenni says.

There is a knock on the door. 'Sarah, are you in there? Are you okay?' It's Vihann, one of the ICU nurses.

'I'm fine,' I call out. 'Just changing my scrubs.' I end the conversation with Jenni. 'I've got to go, I'm still at work,' I tell her. 'I love you and I'm so happy for you.'

'I love you too,' she says.

I change out of my scrubs, pull on jeans and a jumper,

68

and head back to the ward. At the nurse's station Vihann holds out a chocolate chip muffin from the canteen. My favourite.

'Oh my God,' I say, immediately taking an enormous bite. 'You're too good to me,' I add, my mouth full of cake.

'I know,' he says, picking up the clipboard in front of him and glancing through the notes.

I watch as he reads, mentally preparing himself for the night shift ahead.

I've worked with Vihann for years. When I told him I was going to Afghanistan, he burst into tears. He was so scared something awful would happen to me. He burst into tears again when I made it home in one piece and came back to my old job.

I was so glad to slip back into my old routine, grateful that at least here nothing had changed, when everything else in my life had. There was comfort, too, in how insignificant I felt, swallowed up by the vast corridors of the Cardiff hospital and its eight-thousand-strong workforce.

And now, each shift I am grateful to disappear into my work, to bury my own feelings beneath the needs of my patients and whatever it is they and their families are going through.

Here, I still feel like I'm helping people. And I don't have to be afraid of Danny's moods.

Vihann finally looks up from his notes. 'You look tired,' he says kindly.

He knows better than to suggest I go home, even

though my shift ended fifteen minutes ago. He is one of the few people who know the truth about how bad Danny is, because he was on duty the night I had to have stitches in A&E. He knows work is my refuge these days.

'I'm just going to check in on my patient,' I tell him, polishing off the last mouthful of muffin and wiping the crumbs from my mouth. 'One quick look, then I'm out of here, I promise.'

He nods, and I pad down the peaceful corridor of the Intensive Care Unit. It's different working here to the rest of the hospital. The ratio of patients to nurses is one to one. That's a good thing, obviously, but it also means that, no matter how short a time you look after someone, you form a bond. Because it's just you and them.

You are the wall that stands between them and their mortality, and the connection that comes with that is like no other. Especially when the patient's condition deteriorates, improves, then deteriorates again. It feels as if I'm battling to survive with them.

I'm relieved to see that the car crash victim I've been looking after all day is still stable. Her husband is sitting by the side of her bed, clinging to her hand, while their little girl is curled up on the chair behind him, fast asleep.

When he looks up at me, tears pool on the tips of his eyelashes – just like they did on Carl's, the morning after Fridge died. All this talk about the wedding . . . Carl will almost certainly be there; he is one of Cherub's closest friends.

At the thought of seeing him again a shiver runs down my spine. Unexpectedly, I'm back in Camp Bastion, the night his patrol was hit, looking down at him in the hospital tent.

Until then, I had enjoyed his company as a friend. He was attractive and funny, but there was no more to it than that. But that Christmas Eve, seeing him unconscious, realizing he might not make it, I couldn't bear it.

When he came to, he was angry. He thought he should have died instead of Fridge. 'It should have been me,' he kept repeating. 'It should have been me.'

He insisted that no one would have missed him if he'd been the one who was killed. But I would have missed him.

10. Carl

I turn the heavy card over in my hand, then brush my fingers over the embossed words in their fancy, looping black italics.

Jenni Jane Richardson and Michael Dermot Cooke
Request the honour of your presence at their wedding

On the fifth of December at two o'clock in the afternoon
At St Edward King and Confessor Catholic Church, Clifford

Dinner and dancing to follow at The White Hart Lodge Hotel

Dress code: Black tie

There's a handwritten note from Cherub inside saying he can't wait to catch up. That Sarah is going to be Jenni's bridesmaid. And how great will it be to have the gang together again?

Sarah.

Just the mention of her name makes my heart beat in a way I thought I had taught it to forget.

'What's up with you?' Maggie says, straining forward to peer at the invitation. Her brow furrows. 'Who are Jenni and Michael? You've never mentioned them.'

She's right. I haven't. It was just so much easier not to, to try and forget about that other life. Coming back home to Yorkshire after Afghanistan, after everything that happened, well, it wasn't the best of times.

It was hard living with Mum and her new fella. They kept telling me how lucky I was to be back, how blessed I was to have made it home in one piece. I would smile while my insides twisted with rage at the notion that I was somehow fortunate.

When they moved up to Scotland for his job it was a relief. It wasn't their fault. I know they tried their best to be there for me. But how could they possibly understand? How could they think I was lucky when all the people I cared about had gone?

I told myself I was better off alone. I closed the door of my run-down, mouldy council flat the Veterans Welfare Service had found for me on the outskirts of Leeds, and locked myself away from the world. I never imagined I'd live anywhere else.

My heart hurt all the time, it still does, but I've got used to that. I've learned to live with all the loss. And that's okay. I'm not the only one – so many people lost someone over there. All those young lads with their lives ahead of them. All those families they didn't return to. So much conflict. So much death.

A familiar wave of sadness washes over me.

'I better get going,' I tell Maggie, ignoring her

73

questions and heading for the door. I whistle for the dogs, who eagerly follow me, and before she can say anything I am outside.

I pull my jacket on, easing it over my shoulders, feel the satisfying burn of the new tattoo smarting beneath it, and set off across the blustery moors. Blood is still pulsing in my ears, like it always does when I think back to the war now. But I know that if I just keep putting one foot in front of the other I can walk myself back to being okay. Or if not okay, at least calm. This is the one place that can force the noisy chatter in my brain to keep quiet.

The Chevin towers above me, the wide ancient ridge of rock that soars over the town of Otley, guarding us like a soldier in a watchtower. Fridge and I were brought up here once on a school trip. I remember the teacher telling us that stone quarried from the Chevin was used to help build the Houses of Parliament, and that Oliver Cromwell's army had gathered beneath its protective shadow in the market square on the eve of the Battle of Marston Moor. We all cheered when the teacher told us that they'd drunk the pubs dry before trouncing the enemy the next day.

It makes me wince to think of that now. We were naive schoolboys who thought war was cool. Who grew up to fight in one, still thinking it was cool. Look where that got us.

I take a deep breath. One foot in front of the other. Just keep going. One foot in front of the other.

It was Michael who brought me back up here – after

Mum had moved to Scotland. Those are the words he said to me the first time he came to the flat and knocked on the door. He suggested we go for a walk but I refused, mumbled some excuse about not feeling great.

'Come on,' he said. 'The fresh air will do you good.' Then he smiled. 'I know it's hard, but one foot in front of the other, lad. One foot in front of the other.'

And so we walked. We didn't talk about anything. He didn't ask me about Fridge. He didn't ask me about the war. He didn't ask me about my plans for the future. We just walked.

He kept coming back. He kept not taking no for an answer. And slowly I found myself looking forward to his knock on the door. To our walks across the moors. To the cup of tea from Michael's flask, sitting in his car at the end.

On the days he said he was coming I started to wait for him outside the door, with my coat and trainers on already – just like I used to do when I was a kid, when he and Fridge would come to pick me up in the van.

Sometimes, after one of our walks, I would go back with him for tea. One of Kathleen's delicious home-made chicken pies or lasagne. Michael and I would talk about the state of Leeds United, and Kathleen would talk to me about her vegetable patch while we did the dishes afterwards.

Then one day Michael turned up at the flat and said, 'It's time.'

'What for?' I asked, puzzled.

'To get you some proper help. I've found a charity

that helps ex-servicemen get back on their feet. You've got an appointment this afternoon.'

No bit of me wanted to go with him. But how could I say no to this man I loved like a father who had done so much for me?

It was over an hour's drive from Otley to the small town of Beverley, but Michael talked all the way, so I didn't have time to think about where we were going and what we were doing.

He chatted about his sister, Jean, who ran an animal rescue centre in Leeds, and about some Labrador puppies that had been brought in. He thought we should go and visit.

I told myself I was doing it for Michael, right up until the moment he knocked on the scruffy front door. I didn't see how some well-meaning counsellor could possibly help me or understand what I had been through.

But then the door swung open and an enormous, jug-eared bald man appeared wearing a red T-shirt that said 'I went to Afghanistan and all I got was this crappy false leg'.

And I realized straight away that of course he understood. I could see it in his eyes. He led me into a small, chaotic office filled with piles of paperwork, unwashed coffee mugs, an antique computer and a precarious tower of Poppy Appeal collection boxes.

Brian fussed around making us coffee, then he sat down in front of me.

He studied me for a while as he sipped from his mug,

then finally he said, 'I see lads like you all the time. You think that if you'd done your job better your friends would still be alive. You've seen things, terrible things, that no man should ever see, and you can never unsee them. And you come back home and you're not sure what to expect, but it isn't this. It isn't mood swings and nightmares and flashbacks and rage. But you don't want to ask for help because you're so wedded to your rough, tough soldier image, you don't know who you'd be without it, and you think because you haven't lost a leg you don't deserve any sympathy.' He paused. 'Sound about right so far?'

I nodded.

'You can tell me you're fine if you want, and I'll let you go on your way. Or you can accept you're not fine and consider the possibility that I might be able to help you.'

Neither of us spoke for a while. I stared at the floor.

Then Brian started to talk again, but his tone was softer this time. 'It's like living behind glass, isn't it? Feeling like you don't connect with people?'

That's exactly how it did feel, and when I looked at him it wasn't pity I saw written on his face, it was understanding. The relief and shock of somebody not just getting it but saying it out loud made me cry.

Brian leaned forward. 'Let's see if we can't do something to help you, eh?'

I must have looked startled, because then he said, 'It's all right, lad, I'm not going to hold your hand and sing "Kumbaya", I'm just going to sign you up for a couple of workshops.'

The first workshop was a business experience course, and that's where I met Roz – Maggie's mum. Roz was the accountancy teacher, and on the last day of the course she arrived for class with an enormously fat dog in tow.

'She was my dad's dog,' she said. 'I know it sounds stupid but I honestly think she's been depressed since he died –'

She broke off, looking at me as if making her mind up about something. I waited for her to continue.

'He'd have liked you, my dad. He was a soldier himself once upon a time. He was devoted to Hatty. They used to go on long treks over the moors. He knew those moors like the back of his hand. But then he got Alzheimer's and started to lose his way. He'd turn up all over the place – pubs, hotels, strangers' houses, a caravan park once – generally wet and covered in mud, hungry and confused. Hatty would always be there with him – she never left his side. Then, last summer, Dad died very suddenly. My poor brother found him dead in his armchair, Hatty lying at his feet.' She paused at the memory. 'I'm so sorry,' she said, wiping away a tear. 'I don't know what made me tell you all this.'

'You don't have to say sorry,' I smiled. 'I know what it's like to lose people.'

The dog sighed and relaxed her head on my leg. I realized she was mirroring me; just stroking her made me feel better. I felt calm. The panic I had been feeling all morning about not having a ready-to-launch business idea had disappeared.

I imagined Hatty on her walks over the moors with Roz's dad. I thought of her never leaving his side all those times he got lost and then at the end, still guarding him, reaching up to nuzzle his wizened old hands as they relaxed their grip on the edge of his armchair.

I thought of my walks with Michael, how much I'd grown to love them, and suddenly something the careers guidance officer had said sprang into my mind. He'd said that not all jobs have to be behind a desk, that I might be more suited to something active and outdoors.

'What if I walked her for you?' I said to Roz.

'Really? Would you? I'd pay you.'

So that was that. My ready-to-launch business idea. Although it's never once felt like work. I loved Hatty from the get-go, and I felt honoured to be taking care of this dog for Roz's dad, the gnarly old soldier of my imagination.

Then Elsa made two. I took up Michael's offer to go and visit the Labrador puppies at the animal shelter where his sister worked. Elsa was the runt. She needed me as much as I needed her.

A couple of months after that, I was walking them both in the park when someone I'd bumped into a few times walking her Border terrier asked if I'd look after him for a couple of weeks while she was on holiday.

Someone else did the same when they saw me with the Border terrier, and before I knew it I had so many dogs to look after that Roz, who was helping me sort out a business grant, suggested her daughter Maggie – who had just left school – might give me a hand.

As the months passed, I spent my days literally walking away my grief. Exhausted from the fresh air, I started to sleep for longer stretches at night. I'd found a new purpose for getting up in the morning.

I still have my bad days, and long stretches of the night when, tormented by flashbacks and grief, I lie awake for hours on end, desperately trying to calm my fractious brain.

But right now, striding across my beloved moors with my crazy pack of dogs, well, it's enough. More of a life than I could ever have hoped for. Maybe more than I deserve. That's what the tattooing is about. An acknowledgement that I might be moving on but I will never forget my friends who can't.

I'd been thinking about it for a while. Robert, a lad who used to work with Caroline in the kennels at the camp, had a tattoo of his dog's paw on his arm. The dog, Rixo, was a beautiful, dark brown cocker spaniel with flapping ears and boundless energy. She was killed when his squadron came under fire – shot while Robert was trying to pull her to safety in a ditch. She died in his arms.

Caroline burst into tears when he showed us the tattoo. 'It's so beautiful,' she said.

'It's to remember her,' Robert explained. 'She saved so many lives, her life should mean something too.'

I wanted to do something similar, I just wasn't sure what. And then, last Remembrance Day, I thought of the poppies. It was one of those light bulb moments when something just feels right. I looked at the sea of poppies being worn by people on the telly standing in front of the Cenotaph, and I knew that was the tattoo I was going to have. The symbol that represents all those who have lost their lives on active service.

But remembering lost friends is one thing. Having to face the living is very different. I just don't think I'm strong enough. I'll ring Cherub. Tell him I can't face the thought of being with all those people, that it would be too hard.

I won't be lying. Without Fridge or Squadron by my side, the thought of going to a big social occasion like Cherub and Jenni's wedding is flat-out terrifying. For so long, I've managed not to feel too much. Why go reminding myself of everything I've tried so hard to forget?

Afghanistan

2008

11. Sarah

February

'Doing your *dhobi*?' Carl asked as he walked into the camp launderette.

Quickly, I shoved my washing into the giant machine. But in my haste a pair of knickers escaped and fell to the floor in all their hammock-sized, sexless navy glory. I snatched them up and threw them in with the rest of the load, my cheeks burning. Carl was the last person on that camp I wanted to see my comfy old work knickers.

He looked at me and raised his eyebrows. My God, those eyebrows had a life of their own.

'Hey,' he said, throwing his arms up in the air. 'No judgement here. I've never been a fan of barely there, frilly, lacey, skimpy underwear. Nothing says sexy to me like a pair of pants big enough to sail home in.'

I felt almost guilty laughing. It was only six weeks since Fridge's death, and emotions were still raw. All of us were on edge, bracing ourselves for the next loss. We didn't know it that day, but the next loss would be Squadron – just a few days later.

'Package from home?' Carl nodded at the parcel sitting in my now empty laundry basket.

I nodded. 'From my mum.'

The parcel had arrived that morning, and I'd been saving it to open later. Now we both stared at it. Something told me Carl didn't get many care packages.

I picked it up and started to open it, smoothing out the paper, then carefully turning it over and unpeeling the sticky flap at the back and . . .

'Oh my God, just open it!' He laughed.

I obediently ripped it open. Inside were a bunch of women's magazines – *Marie Claire*, *Woman*, *Woman's Own* – six bars of my favourite salted caramel Lindt chocolate, some marmalade and a box of cigars.

'So, you're a cigar smoker?' Carl asked. He whistled admiringly.

As puzzled by the sight of the cigars as he was, I read Mum's note out loud. 'Some Cuban cigars the Americans might like.'

'She does know this isn't the Second World War, right?' he asked.

There went the eyebrows again. Eyebrows that alone were capable of breaking your heart.

There was an old CD player on the floor by one of the washing machines. It suddenly caught his eye. He looked at me. 'Don't go anywhere. I'll be right back.' And he sprinted out of the door.

I watched another soldier shake a bag of washing into one of the machines. I checked on mine, which was spinning happily, and couldn't resist a peek at Carl's load. A tangle of black Calvin Klein boxer briefs. Of course.

Danny's underpants were Autograph from Marks & Spencer. Lovely Danny. He didn't tease me about my big pants.

I opened my copy of *Marie Claire*.

'Are you reading the problem page?'

Carl was back, holding a Bruce Springsteen CD. He waved it in the air. 'Assami's always banging on about him. I thought I'd see what all the fuss is about. You opening that chocolate any time soon?'

Smiling, I held out a bar to him. He unwrapped it and snapped off a chunk. Then he opened the magazine.

'"Twenty signs he's in love with you,"' he read from the page at which it fell open, his mouth full of chocolate.

He stopped for a moment to swallow his chocolate, then carried on reading. '"He brings you flowers for no reason."'

He peered at me from behind the magazine. '"He wants you to hang out with his friends."'

Another glance, this time with a mild raise of his eyebrows. '"He begrudgingly gets into some of your girly habits."'

Feigning incredulity now. '"He makes you dinner after a bad day."'

He looked up again. 'No wonder I've never been in a long-term relationship.'

As darkness closed in, we listened to Bruce Springsteen, ate chocolate and laughed at the articles we took it in turn to read aloud from the magazines.

A stranger watching us would never have guessed that, just a few weeks ago, he'd been lying seriously injured in a hospital bed, with me standing over him while I changed his dressing, praying that he would make it.

Suddenly the room fell silent as the rhythmic thud of clothes going round and round in the tumble dryer ground to a halt. For a moment neither of us said anything.

'How are you?' I asked.

'Fine,' he said. 'I'm fine.'

I wanted him to see me as someone he could talk to, properly talk to. Wanted him to know that, although he had lost Fridge, I was still there. And I wanted to be there for him. This sweet man with his haunted, deep blue eyes.

'The last few weeks can't have been easy,' I said.

He ran his hand backwards and forwards over his shaved head.

'No, well, I don't think it's been a great time for any of us.'

I thought about Danny. There had been an increasing nerviness to him since the day of the explosion. He talked endlessly of our lives back home. How I'd go back to work at the hospital while he'd join his uncles in the garage they had set up with his dad.

He even talked about the house he'd build for us and the children we'd have – a boy he'd teach to play rugby, and a little girl who might want him to teach her too.

Once upon a time I'd wanted all those things as well. The trouble was, I didn't want them any more. Too many things had changed. But how could I possibly tell Danny?

I turned to face Carl, and our knees brushed together. We were so close to each other, I could feel his breath on my face. I longed to reach out, to place my palm on his cheek.

'You and Danny,' he said, clearing his throat.

'It's complicated –'

'I should get going,' he said suddenly, standing up and walking to the tumble dryer.

He rammed his clothes into a duffel bag, threw it across his shoulder and headed for the door. Just before he disappeared, he turned to look back at me one more time. He looked as if he was going to say something but then thought better of it and opened the door.

I wanted to call him back, I wanted to tell him how I really felt, but already the swirling dust outside was obscuring his face. I willed him not to walk away, willed him to turn around and look at me.

But if he did, I didn't see. The wind kicked up a thick cloud of dust, swallowing up his shadowy bulk in seconds.

12. Carl

The storm that had rolled in was so bad I couldn't see anything in front of me, but I had to get away from the launderette. In my haste to escape, I walked straight into Assami. Dust ricocheted off us both.

'Whoa there,' he chuckled. 'Who are you in such a rush to get to? Or is it get away from?'

He was right. I was running away from Sarah. From how much I'd just realized I felt for her. Sitting next to her, I'd so wanted to reach forward and kiss her. But how could I even think of doing that, knowing that she was with Danny? What sort of man was I?

I'd wanted to talk to her about Fridge, too, about how much I missed him. My grief and guilt at not being able to save him were eating me up inside, but I didn't know how to express it, where to start.

Mine wasn't the sort of family that encouraged us to discuss our feelings. 'Don't let's go opening up a whole new can of worms,' Mum used to say whenever I tried to talk to her about something that was upsetting either of us.

I wanted to tell her how much I missed my brothers. I needed her to tell me it wasn't my fault they'd been taken away.

'Best not to think about it,' she would add, closing the conversation down.

It was why she drank. So she didn't have to think about her life – specifically about being abandoned by her husband and having two of her three sons, my two kid brothers, taken into care.

'Carl?' Assami pressed me. 'Are you okay?'

When I didn't respond, he put his arm around my shoulder. 'Let's get out of this dust.'

He led me to the canteen – which was mercifully quiet – and sat patiently while I went to get us a couple of coffees.

'Peace be upon you,' he said, placing his right hand over his heart, when I came back to join him. 'Now talk to me, Carl. Tell me what is troubling you.'

I shook my head. 'I'm fine.'

'You are my brother,' he continued. 'You can tell me anything.'

I looked up from my coffee, took in his wild, thick black hair and grizzled beard. His lined face. His dark, sympathetic eyes.

He reached forward and put his hand on my shoulder. Something in the way he did it was so reassuring, like the way Michael used to comfort me when I was a kid. I can't explain it, but I found myself opening up to him.

'I miss Fridge,' I told him.

He nodded. 'He was like a brother to you.'

'He was. He and his mum and dad were like my family.'

Assami looked at me quizzically. 'But what about your own family?'

'I never really knew my dad. It's always been just Mum and me – and my two younger brothers, Adam and Scott.'

'So your brothers, you can talk to them?' Assami asked.

I shook my head. 'I lost touch with them a long time ago. They were taken into care. My mum drank, so the authorities took them away from her. Me, too, in the beginning. Adam and Scott were placed with a foster family, good people, who adopted them. I was too much of a handful.'

At this Assami smiled.

'Nobody wanted me, so when Mum got her act together, I was allowed to leave my foster family and go home. She was still drinking, but I learned to look after myself. Looked after her as best I could.

'And then I met Fridge. His mum and dad were amazing, they became everything to me. Let me stay at theirs when Mum was too drunk to pick me up. Took me to footie training. Fed me. Washed my clothes. All the things parents should do.'

My whole life I'd avoided telling people the truth about my mother, my time in care. I felt ashamed. I didn't want people judging her, judging me. Fridge and Squadron knew, but I never once felt judged by them, and I didn't feel judged by Assami now.

'It must have been hard for you. For your mother too,' he said kindly.

'It was tough on Mum,' I agreed. 'She never forgave herself for losing Scott and Adam. She has a new boyfriend now, but she still drinks too much. They both do.'

Assami made a sympathetic noise and rubbed his hand up and down his beard, the way he always did when he was considering something. 'I understand now why you miss Fridge so much,' he said.

The pain of losing him hit me like a wave all over again. Being in Afghanistan without him, going on patrol, constantly looking over my shoulder, only to remember he wasn't there.

It felt good talking to Assami. Talking about Fridge made him come alive again, if only briefly.

Sharing the truth about who I was felt strange, but liberating. I didn't tell him the truth about everything though.

'And is there a woman in your life?' Assami asked finally.

How could I tell him? Tell him that the only woman in my life I'd ever been seriously interested in was Danny's girlfriend.

Sarah.

Even thinking about her made me burn with guilt.

Home

2011

13. Sarah

'Cherub's going to ask Carl to be his best man,' Jenni
tells me from behind the changing-room curtain. 'He
was going to ask his brother, but they've never really
got on. He told me last night that he wants it to be one
of his real brothers – the ones who risked their lives for
him – so he's going to ask Carl. Isn't that lovely?'

'It is,' I say, picturing Carl's blue eyes. 'Very lovely.'

'I wonder if he's seeing anyone,' Jenni says. 'According
to Cherub, he used to be a real ladies' man. Apparently,
Fridge told him once that Carl had a ton of girlfriends
back home, but no one he was ever seriously interested in.'

I feel a sharp twinge of jealousy – a ridiculous rivalry
with these unknown, unattached girls – a feeling I've
never had before and have no right to claim now.

'What do you think?' Jenni emerges triumphantly
from the changing room.

For a moment I think she is asking me for my opinion about whether or not Carl is seeing someone.

'Well?' Jenni asks again, this time doing an elaborate
curtsey.

I realize she is talking about the dress.

Enough, I tell myself sternly. *Enough. This weekend is
about Jenni.*

I clear my throat and look her up and down, assessing her as I would a patient brought in to triage.

The dress is perfectly nice. I just don't recognize my lovely, quirky Jenni in it. Her impressive cleavage, normally so liberally on display, is respectfully constrained behind a shell-shaped bustier.

Her waist, like her breasts, is forcefully cinched in by a corset that runs from her bust to her mid-thigh, where layers of fabric suddenly flare out, giving the dress the curious shape of an upside-down trumpet.

Beneath the hem I catch a glimpse of Jenni's unloved, scaly winter feet, which seem to cower in shame beneath all this glamour. The flash of chipped, fluorescent blue nail varnish on her toes is the only detail that feels authentically, gloriously Jenni.

A strict jeans and T-shirt girl myself, or a silk blouse if I'm feeling really bold, I've always been in equal measure appalled and impressed by Jenni's crazed, scattergun approach to dressing.

Maybe because of where we met, ours has never felt like a normal female friendship. Too much was at stake to talk about things like what outfit to wear on a Saturday night – and in any case, we only ever had scrubs or combats to hand. Although I do remember Caroline warning me about Jenni's 'bold sense of style'.

I thought of her when I saw Jenni outside the wedding dress shop this morning, dressed in denim hot pants, black opaque tights, lilac leather Doc Martens and a faux leopard-print coat. Her flame-red hair – which is now loose, with its long, messy curls swept back over one shoulder – was hidden under a blue silk scarf.

Caroline was right. Jenni does indeed have a 'bold sense of style'. How I wish Caroline could be with us today.

'Go on, then,' Jenni nudges me. 'Tell me what you think.'

'Well,' I say, not quite sure what else to say.

'So elegant . . .' The sales assistant rescues the moment, appearing silently at our side with two flutes of champagne.

Jenni looks crestfallen.

'Yes. But is it sexy?' she asks, leaning forward towards the mirror and jiggling her boobs suggestively.

The sales assistant, paper thin, with an immaculate, shiny black bob and sharp cheekbones, manages to swallow down a look of horror. She smooths the sleeves of the wedding dress, which are long and fitted, and made of fine, transparent gossamer material, staring at Jenni all the while in the mirror.

Then she steps back and confidently declares, 'It's perfect. The silhouette hugs your curves in all the right places, creating an almost magical slimming effect.'

Jenni straightens herself up and downs the glass of champagne in one. 'No, I don't think this is the dress for me,' she says.

Then she hands the glass back to the sales assistant, yanks up her train and waddles awkwardly back into the changing room.

'Slimming effect!' she huffs from behind the curtain. 'Bloody cheek.'

I smile sweetly at the sales assistant and sip my champagne.

'Anyway,' Jenni says, audibly struggling with the effort of getting the dress off. 'Since you're staying for the weekend, we were thinking of having an impromptu engagement dinner for the four of us tomorrow night, if Carl says yes. It's only an hour and a half on the train from Leeds to Newcastle, so he could get to us in no time at all. What do you think?'

I imagine the four of us together, talking, laughing, Carl's eyebrows raised in amusement. All of us happy . . . I can't remember the last time I felt happy, had fun, got drunk with friends. I hear myself sigh.

Jenni's voice floats through the curtain again. 'It's such a shame Danny has flu.'

Jenni knows that Danny has PTSD but she doesn't know how bad it is. I've never told her that Danny is violent. Or that he hurts me. Or that I'm scared of him.

I hate her not knowing the truth, but there's never been a good time to tell her. She was pregnant with the twins when things started getting really bad. She was exhausted, and suffering from terrible morning sickness. I didn't want to burden her with my problems too.

I did think about telling her today, but I can't bear to ruin this special time for her. Or me – it feels so good to have a day when my life isn't overshadowed by Danny. When I can still have some fun. Pretend things are okay.

Jenni yanks back the curtain and raises her arms in the air. 'For the love of God, will you get this thing off me!'

I inch the garment slowly over her head, grateful that her face is hidden from mine by thick layers of satin. If it wasn't, she would see how flushed I am – and not from the champagne.

Carl.

I'm going to see him again tomorrow night.

Poppy #3

'Everything all right?' Barry asks, pouring me a glass of water.

I nod, although the sight of him pulling on his nitrile gloves is enough to make me feel I'm in pain. But today I'm glad of it, because the pain will be a distraction from the fact that, somehow, I've found myself agreeing not only to be Cherub's best man but to go to an engagement dinner tomorrow.

With Sarah, of all people.

I'd called him, fully planning to explain that I couldn't make the wedding. But something about how easy it was to talk to him – to laugh with him – made me hesitate. And then when he asked me to be his best man, I could hardly say no.

'Right, then,' Barry says, interrupting my thoughts. 'Ready for poppy number three? Music?'

He grins when I ask for 'Psycho Killer' by Talking Heads.

Someone was playing this – Danny, I think – on one of our

first nights in Camp Bastion. Background music while we were getting ready for lights out.

I never normally pay attention to the lyrics – but listening to the words of this song now, they could have been written for me. Starting a conversation without being able to finish it. Talking, but not really saying anything.

Like me and Cherub this morning. Stick to banter, that's the rule.

Never mention the flashbacks, the nightmares, the grief I carry for those I feel I let down, the things I saw that were so awful I've buried them in a box in my mind and hope I never have to dig it up and open it.

Being here now, having this tattoo done, talking earlier to Jenni and Cherub, thinking about Sarah, the lid has been prised open again, forcing me to remember all the stories before I can put them away again. First Fridge, then Squadron. Now Tom.

I never knew Tom like I knew those two, but he shared a tent with us. And today, this tattoo, well, it's for him. Because I was the only one with him when he died.

Another one I couldn't save.

Tom and I got separated from the rest of the troop while trying to take cover. 'Living the dream, eh?' he said cheerfully as rounds cooked off all around us.

I grinned back at him. It felt like the heavens were falling in, but since Fridge and Squadron's deaths I'd managed to close my mind off to the fear I used to feel when we first went out on patrols. I guess dying didn't feel as terrifying as it once had.

Tom edged ahead of me, just far enough to take the full force of the landmine alone when he stepped on it. His body was tossed into the air, then crashed back down, falling with a grotesque thud on its side.

A moment later, I saw the blood. A sea of red seeping into the ground below him.

'Tom?' I called. And then again, and again. Even though I knew there would be no response.

I looked away. I couldn't stand to stare at so much loss in the face again.

I told myself he loved his job, that it was an honourable mission, and that his death served some great purpose. But that logic was getting harder and harder to rehearse with each decent man I saw fall. Each wife I knew wouldn't grow old with her husband, each kid growing up without their dad.

There was a heartbreaking picture of her in the newspaper. Tom's little girl. Dressed in a smart red coat, holding her sobbing mum's hand. She was looking up at the camera, her little face a mix of confusion and alarm.

'Why me?' I raged at Assami that night. 'Why is it me who survives when so many better men, men with people who love them and need them, don't make it? Men whose deaths leave huge holes in their families and destroy the people they loved.'

'My brother, your life is every bit as valuable as Tom's,' Assami said calmly.

'It really isn't,' I snorted.

Assami looked at me thoughtfully. 'You must trust that there is another plan for you. Accept that this is the order of things.'

It felt like a mightily messed up order to me.

I'm so sorry, Tom. I'm so sorry that I couldn't save you. And I know this tattoo doesn't make up for that, for a lost lifetime of being a husband, a dad. A lost lifetime of birthdays and sports days and weddings and graduations, and all the precious little details that make up a life in between.

'You okay, mate?' Barry asks, putting his hand on my arm. 'You're shaking.'

'Sorry,' I say, twisting my head around to look up at him.

He smiles. 'No problem. Let's take a minute.'

I turn and sit upright, and he hands me my glass of water. I gratefully take a gulp, then watch Barry studying the tattoo gun in his hand. Splotches of red spit out of the ink cap, and he springs up from his stool to grab a cloth.

He carefully wipes it clean, then he brings it up close to his face. I realize he's inspecting it for damage or flaws. Just as I used to check over my own gun. It's not the same of course but, even so, it makes me feel like there is a connection between us. Like Barry would understand.

'This,' I say hesitantly. 'This tattoo, having it done, it's bringing back memories.'

Barry looks at me and nods.

'Stuff I've worked hard to block out, because it's the only way I know how to protect myself. Things that happened in Afghanistan. Awful things.'

Barry nods again. 'That can happen.' He pauses before he says, 'But it doesn't have to be a bad thing. It can be a way of healing. A way of processing what you need to process.'

I realize that Barry is right. That's exactly what this is. A way of processing the bad memories, so I can live with the good ones in peace.

'Ready to go again?' Barry asks.

The needle comes down on my skin and, for the first time since he died, I think of Tom not as the mangled and bloody heap of my nightmares, but the way he was before.

His freckled skin and the gap between his two front teeth. I'd forgotten how much he used to smile. Lying on his bunk, reading letters from his missus, looking at the pictures his kid had drawn for him, laughing at our lame jokes.

Or whenever he played Xbox. He was an ace player, not as good as Jenni – no one was – but better than the rest of us. I can see him now, punching the air as he scored another imaginary goal.

But the thing I remember so clearly is how generous he was. With his stuff – he never minded anyone borrowing anything. Shampoo, soap, we were welcome to help ourselves. Things sent from home, too, chocolates or biscuits, he always handed them around.

All of a sudden Barry tells me it's done.

'Poppy number three,' he says, holding up a mirror. 'Magic, isn't it?'

The poppies glint in the mirror.

'Magic,' I agree.

Because they are. Not just the way they look but the way they are making me feel. Not happy exactly, but closer to it than I've been for years. The jitters that coursed through me when I arrived have gone.

The idea of seeing Cherub and Jenni – Sarah, even – no longer feels so daunting. I never thought I'd get here – the day everyone told me would come, when I would start to feel better.

But here that day is.

14. Sarah

Cherub is standing in front of their stove, wearing a novelty apron featuring a man with a well-defined hairy six-pack. He's brandishing a can of lager in one hand, a wooden spoon in the other.

He's just told me that Carl is due here any minute.

'How is he?' I ask as nonchalantly as possible.

'All right, I think,' Cherub says. 'But then, you know Carl . . .' He pauses to take a swig of beer. 'He's not one to talk about his feelings.'

I think back to Camp Bastion, to Carl's signature silence, his outward show of supposed invulnerability and toughness. But I paid attention to the details when he was around others, saw the way he showed his love through his actions.

The way he'd shut down sometimes, when the lads' teasing went too far, rather than be cruel, or get drawn into a fight. How he cleared up after them. In the canteen I watched him picking up their forgotten plates, discarded forks, empty cartons. Towels in the gym.

Saw how protective he was of Danny.

How kind he was to Assami, how much he trusted him. How kind he was to Caroline.

Suddenly I feel agitated, nervous at the thought of

seeing him. What if he doesn't care that I'm here? Or doesn't want to see me?

'You look hot,' Jenni says, walking into the kitchen clutching Toby's hand. She settles him in his booster chair at the table with a book.

I'm sitting next to the fire, opposite a slightly terrifying stuffed effigy of a man with his head hanging alarmingly to one side.

'For Bonfire Night,' Jenni says, seeing me staring at it. 'It's meant to be for the kids, but Cherub spent hours making that guy. Honestly, it's his favourite night of the year, any excuse to set fire to something and let off some rockets.' She suddenly swings her head back to look at it again. 'For pity's sake! They're my good pyjamas! Cherub, why is the guy wearing my good pyjamas?'

Sheepishly, he turns to look at her. 'You've still got the ones I bought you for Christmas.'

Jenni snorts. 'Firstly, they are *not* pyjamas,' she says scornfully. 'Secondly, those not-pyjamas are at least three sizes too small. I'm not an Ann Summers model. Disappointing, I know, but something you should probably make your peace with before we get married. And thirdly, I would die of hypothermia if I wore that ridiculous wisp of lace in this cottage. Now take my pyjamas off Worzel Gummidge over here before I cancel the wedding.'

'Yes, ma'am,' he says, saluting her.

I watch as he dutifully undresses the guy.

He still looks exactly like he did the night Jenni and I met him in the camp bar – as if he has stepped straight out of the pages of a 1930s *Boy's Own* annual. Smooth skinned and ruddy cheeked, with a permanent expression of innocence on his face.

The only difference now is his blond hair – which is longer than the army's regulation length, hanging below his shirt collar.

Jenni opens the door of the tumble dryer and pulls out a bundle of laundry. She dumps the knotted spaghetti of socks, vests, pyjamas and multicoloured, teeny-tiny pairs of pants covered in cartoon characters into a basket, and heads towards the table.

'Here, let me,' I say, standing up to take the basket of clothes off her.

I plant myself in a chair in front of the table. Not that any inch of the table's surface is visible beneath the clutter that spills across it.

Wedding magazines, old newspapers, a Hulk figurine with a missing arm, a game of Operation abandoned mid-appendectomy, a Batman lunchbox filled with stale Hula Hoops and orange peel, a hairbrush, a toothbrush, and an enormous box of Pedigree Daily Oral Care Dentastix.

I sit the basket on my lap and start smoothing out the clothes before folding them up.

'Bless you,' says Jenni as she appears by my side with a bottle of wine and three glasses.

She clears a space on the table by sweeping a pile of detritus unceremoniously on to the floor. Then she plants the wine and the glasses in front of us and collapses into the chair next to me.

She sighs. 'I spend my life picking up laundry or loading it into the washing machine. Or drying it, folding it, or putting it away,' she says. 'Or cutting up carrots or wiping bottoms.'

'She loves it.' Cherub appears behind her.

He kisses the top of her head and pours a glass of wine. He takes a large gulp and walks back to the oven, the dog following behind.

'The kids' pasta is ready,' he says, then yells, '*Dinner!*'

'Could you grate some cheese, love?'

'Sheese, sheese, sheese,' chants Toby, kicking his legs out excitedly.

Noah toddles into the kitchen clutching an enormous stripy tiger.

'Nice dress!' I tell him.

Noah gives me a radiant smile. He is dressed as Princess Jasmine from *Aladdin*.

Jenni looks at him indulgently, ruffling the hair on top of his head.

He beams at her, then holds the toy tiger out to show me. 'Rajah,' he says seriously.

My eyes meet Jenni's. He's adorable.

'Not so fast!' Cherub says, scooping him up and sitting him on a chair. 'Dinner first, and then you can show her Rajah. Okay?'

'Kay,' says Noah, helping himself to a carrot stick.

Cherub brushes his son's blond, unevenly cut fringe out of his eyes and hands him a bowl.

He and Jenni move from child to child, sprinkling cheese on top of the pasta, and spooning mouthfuls of food into them. Jenni collects plastic beakers from the drying rack, and as she does so Cherub takes a jug from the cupboard and fills it with water. They glide in and out of each other's way as if performing a well-choreographed dance. I watch Cherub laugh at something Toby does and then wink at Jenni. See him touch her waist as she walks past him to pour water into Noah's cup. He starts to say something and she finishes his sentence for him.

I think of Danny staring at the mute TV, oblivious to my presence, and I long to be enfolded in the cosy cloak of love and domestic chaos that so effortlessly shields these two. The secret world that only they inhabit.

The dog starts to bark, and a moment later the doorbell rings. Noah shuffles down from the table and runs into the hall, with the dog and Cherub hot on his heels.

I hear Carl's voice, and then there he is, standing in the kitchen doorway, holding Noah in his arms. Jenni leaps up to greet him. Toby starts crying at the interruption in being fed his yoghurt.

The dog is still barking, and Cherub is talking to Carl, and the TV is blasting from the living room. And then Toby's crying gets even louder.

But my world is silent – as if Carl and I were the only two people in it.

15. Carl

Coming into the kitchen, I am jolted by the sight of her. I had hoped it would be straightforward. A cheerful get-together with Cherub and Jenni, a brief catch-up with Sarah, then home to my safe, steady life.

But then I, more than anyone, should know how hard it is to get out of these things unscathed.

She is more beautiful than I remember, and as she reaches up to kiss my cheek I feel something shift in my chest. A lurch of longing that I had not expected. That I thought I had locked away.

'Hi, Carl,' she says. 'Good to see you.'

That voice, with its note of huskiness. The smell of her perfume. The way she pushes her hair behind her ear. The way her eyes crinkle at the corner when she smiles.

'Well, get the poor man a drink,' Jenni says to Cherub, pulling me out of my trance.

Cherub hands me a can of John Smith's Extra Smooth bitter, and I smile. 'You remembered,' I say, lifting the tab on top of the can and taking a grateful swig.

'Of course I remembered,' Cherub says. 'Although I still can't believe you and Fridge drank this filth.'

A look passes between us, but it isn't one of sadness. It's the opposite, in fact, it's a happy memory, and I'm taken aback, because it's the first time I've thought of Fridge in a long while without feeling that familiar pull of grief and guilt and regret.

I think of my tattoo and feel reassured. It's as if Fridge is with me now, literally sitting on my shoulder, and I feel braver, more confident, because of it. I know exactly what he would say too.

'What can I tell you? You can take the man out of Yorkshire but you can't take the Yorkshire out of the man.'

Cherub laughs. 'I hope you're hungry,' he says. 'I've made chicken curry.'

Like the beer, he's remembered that this was my favourite meal when we were back in camp, and I suddenly feel such affection for him, for Jenni and Sarah too.

They get it.

We have all lived through something so extraordinary together, experienced so much pain and loss, and I see now that the bond between us is unshakeable.

I grin. 'I'm starving.'

'Right, then,' says Jenni. 'Let's get this show on the road. Carl, do you mind feeding this little perisher while I put some rice on?' She hands me a half-eaten pot of yoghurt.

I pull up a seat next to Toby in the booster chair and survey the rosy-cheeked scrap sitting in front of me. He flashes me an enormous grin when he sees the yoghurt, and opens his mouth wide.

I feed him just like I used to feed Adam and Scott, carefully scooping up the bits of yoghurt that ooze down his chin with the side of the spoon. Sarah is sitting next to me reading a picture book to Noah, who is curled up on her lap.

The sound of her voice is soothing, just like it was when I was in the hospital, and I tell myself that this feeling of friendship and acceptance from her is enough. It doesn't have to be anything more than that. So long as she is happy. So long as they all are.

'How's Danny?' I ask, suddenly feeling bad for dropping off the radar after Afghanistan. For turning my back on everyone. But it was just too hard. I had to walk away to survive.

Now I realize how much I want to be a part of their world again.

'He's okay,' she says. Then adds, 'Well, not really.' She rubs her hand over an angry red scar on the side of her forearm. 'He's been diagnosed with PTSD so, you know, he has his fair share of bad days.'

She pulls her jumper down over her scar, but if she's trying to protect him it's too late. I know those wounds – defensive scars from where the victim has raised their arm to protect their head and face.

My mum has an identical one from some scumbag boyfriend who lunged at her with a broken bottle one time in a pub.

But Danny hurting Sarah? It doesn't make sense. He adored her.

I think back to those last few weeks in Camp Bastion together. How shaky he'd become, how much he relied on her. He couldn't possibly. Could he?

'Dinner is served!' Jenni announces.

Cherub heaps generous portions of chicken curry on to plates and Jenni pours even more generous portions of wine into four glasses.

'To the happy couple,' Sarah says, raising her glass in front of her.

'To the happy couple,' I repeat, my eyes holding hers.

She looks smaller than I remember, and fragile. She seems less sure of herself than she used to. There is something about her that reminds me of the way Mum used to look when she was dating that scumbag.

Suddenly I am overcome by the most intense desire to protect her. To keep her safe. The thought of someone, even Danny – although I still can't get my head around it being Danny – hurting her . . . I can't let that happen.

What if he does it again? What if, and my mind shuts down at this thought, it gets worse? I've heard terrible things about what ex-soldiers with PTSD can be driven to.

My guts twist with the same rage I used to feel when we were under attack, when I couldn't account for all the members of the patrol, when I thought one of them was in danger and I wasn't there to see them right.

Cherub is telling a story about the secondary school where he teaches PE. When we got back from Afghanistan, he signed up for a Troops to Teachers training scheme. Just like that. While I locked myself away, feeling sorry for myself, Cherub was busy getting on with life.

He's always been good at compartmentalizing his

feelings. Training. Fighting. Grief. Jenni. Becoming a teacher. Becoming a dad. And good on him, because look at him. Two kids, a woman he adores and is about to marry, and now he's saying he's just been made head of year.

I bet he's a really good teacher, decent and fair. I bet the kids love him. He's talking about a PE lesson where he told one of the lads to hold on to his balls, meaning the net full of basketballs, but the kid was a cheeky sod and literally dropped his shorts and did just that.

I'm listening and laughing, but all the while I'm watching Sarah. The stray piece of pale gold hair that falls across her face, which I know in a moment she will push behind her ear.

The scar on the side of her arm.

16. Sarah

'Right then, yoos two,' Jenni says to the twins when we finish our dinner. 'Bath time!'

She picks up Toby and carries him upstairs while Cherub, roaring, chases Noah out of the living room and up behind them.

When the sound of Noah's giggles finally disappears, Carl leans forward in his chair.

'Sarah,' he says gently. 'Sarah?'

I'm so used to not talking about Danny, to covering up the sadness that I always carry with me, never articulating what has happened to him, it's only now I see how incredibly lonely I've been. Tears spring into my eyes.

Carl reaches across the table to take my hand. 'Talk to me,' he says.

Carl cared about Danny deeply, I know that, and suddenly it feels selfish, not telling Danny's friends the truth. They, surely, would understand. Maybe even help.

Carl's eyes soften. 'Talk to me,' he says again, but even more tenderly this time.

I swipe at my tears with the back of my hand and let out a shuddering breath.

'Things haven't been right since we got back home,' I begin. 'Little things would set him off at first – like a car's hazard warning lights, or the sound of a car alarm. He said they reminded him of the trucks that were loaded with explosives in Afghanistan.'

Carl nods, as if he understands, and I go on.

'His eyes would glaze over, and his face would take on a strange expression. Like he wasn't seeing what I was seeing, not hearing what I was hearing. Physically he was there, but mentally he would just up and leave, paralysed by whatever it was he was remembering, unable to speak. As the weeks went by, he disappeared inside himself more and more, and he became more and more on edge. Until . . .'

Carl gently squeezes my hand. 'Until . . .' he repeats.

And it all comes tumbling out.

Danny trying to strangle me.

Me reaching for the vodka bottle, the bottle smashing on the floor, me holding my arm above my face to protect myself.

The doctor in A&E telling me Danny had PTSD.

How I've been frightened to be alone with him ever since.

And how I'm even more frightened that he won't get better.

The minute I finish, I feel guilty for betraying Danny. Carl is his friend. There was a time when he would have hated for Carl to think badly of him.

'He didn't mean it,' I say quickly. 'He was devastated when he realized what he'd done. I know somewhere deep inside him the old Danny is still there.' I start to cry again, because I don't know if I believe that any more.

Suddenly Carl is kneeling at my side, gently brushing away my tears with the tips of his thumbs. Then he pulls me towards him and holds me tight.

I breathe him in, let my head rest against his body which feels strong and solid and safe.

The room is quiet but for the sound of the dog snoring in front of the fire.

'Sometimes I think it's my fault,' I say, pulling back. 'And I feel like I've failed him because I don't know how to take away his pain. That maybe if I loved him more . . .'

At this Carl shakes his head. 'Sarah, this is absolutely not your fault,' he says, his voice firm. He puts his hands on my shoulders. 'You do know that, don't you? This has got absolutely nothing to do with you. You mustn't blame yourself.'

I nod, and Carl swings back on his ankles. He goes back to sit in his chair.

'Poor Danny,' he says. 'And poor you.'

For a moment neither of us says anything. Upstairs there is a shriek of laughter, and we both smile.

'Do Jenni and Cherub know?' he asks.

I shake my head. 'They know he has PTSD but not how bad it is. It's easier to pretend everything is fine. A relief, actually. When I'm with them I get to forget about it, at least for a little while.'

'But you shouldn't have to cope with it all on your own. Is Danny getting any help? Are you?'

'He's supposed to be on medication, but he won't take it. He's supposed to be going for therapy, but he refuses. The only medication he's interested in is alcohol.'

We hear Jenni's footsteps on the stairs.

I rub fiercely under my eyes, to wipe away any tell-tale black streaks of mascara.

'Everything okay?' Jenni asks.

'Just feeling a bit tired,' I tell her. 'I've been on early shifts all this week.'

'I know what will wake you up,' she says, grinning. 'Shots!'

She reaches into the cupboard above the fridge and pulls out a bottle of tequila. She twists the red plastic sombrero hat off the top of the bottle, fills it with tequila, and promptly downs it in one.

'Oh God,' Cherub says, walking into the kitchen. 'The tequila's out. This never ends well.'

Jenni holds out the bottle to him.

Cherub looks at Carl.

Carl looks at me.

'Go on, then,' I say, laughing. 'Time for a proper celebration.'

Cherub swallows a shot and then hands the bottle to me. With a sharp tilt of my neck, I slug back the capful of fiery liquid.

And immediately regret it.

I've drunk so much wine on top of the tequila – we all have – that an hour or so later, when Jenni suggests the four of us learn a special dance to do at the wedding, I find myself saying yes.

'Absolutely not,' Carl says. 'Not under any circumstances.'

'What he said,' says Cherub.

Jenni claps her hands in excitement.

'So that's a yes,' she says, reaching out to turn the music up. 'Dad's girlfriend is a dancer, or used to be, on cruise ships. She can teach us.'

Cherub dives across her, deftly moving her hand away from the volume button. 'You'll wake the kids,' he says, putting his arms around her. 'Come on, Tequila Lady. Let's get you upstairs. Good night, all,' he says over his shoulder as he leads Jenni, giggling, out of the room.

'Goodnight, yoos two,' she calls out. 'Make yourselves at home.'

Carl crosses to the CD player. His broad back flexes as he takes a disc out of its box, loads it into the machine and hits play.

He turns, and for a long moment we just stare at each other.

Then he holds out his arms. 'I don't know about you, but if Jenni wants us to do a dance at the wedding, I could seriously use the practice.'

He smiles at me. I smile and walk towards him.

He places one hand on the small of my back, the other on my shoulder. Then I lean in and bury my head in his chest and, slowly, we start to sway in time to the music.

After a few minutes, he pulls his body back so we are looking at each other again.

He cups his hands around my cheeks. 'I can't stand the thought of anyone hurting you,' he says quietly.

Without thinking, I reach up.

But then, just as I'm about to kiss him, I pull away.

17. Carl

For a moment, our lips were about to touch – then she twisted away from me, said something about not being able to do this, and rushed out of the kitchen.

I should never have got that close to her. I don't know what I was thinking. Sarah is still with Danny, no matter how complicated things have become between them.

How could I be so selfish?

As if Danny hasn't been through enough. As if Sarah hasn't. She shouldn't have to be the one to put a stop to it. I should have the decency to do that myself.

After she disappeared upstairs, I lay awake on the sofa. Then I got up early this morning, before Sarah was awake. I didn't want to see that agonized look of regret on her face again.

Jenni begged me to stay for breakfast but I made up an excuse about having to get back for the dogs.

Cherub could tell there was something wrong.

He reached for my arm as I was about to get into the taxi. 'Everything all right?' he asked.

His concern only made me feel even more ashamed.

I thought I'd feel relieved to be out of there, to be on the train on my way home. But as Newcastle city centre shrinks behind me, replaced by open countryside and spiky, leafless trees, the shame grows.

I took advantage of her. Plain and simple. And I took advantage of Danny too. An image flashes before me. His face, rigid with shock, staring at Sarge in the aftermath of the explosion that killed Fridge.

Is that when it started? At the time, I thought he'd been one of the lucky ones. Flesh wounds to his arm and hand, and some deep shrapnel cuts on his face. They patched him up and sent him straight back out there.

Now I wonder. Did a door open in Danny's mind then, letting the horror of what he saw flood in, and then slam shut. Does that awful scene play forever on a loop inside his head?

Poor bloke. I know of other guys it's happened to. Post-traumatic stress disorder – PTSD. Brian talked about them a lot. The poor souls who disconnect from the world for good, because they can't forget the terrible things they witnessed in battle.

Brian talked about it because he saw it in me. And he's right. There are times when I can feel myself slipping down that road. Like when I get into the van and turn the key in the ignition. The radio crackles for a moment with static before the music kicks in. In that moment I'm frozen with fear, back in one of the army trucks, waiting to be driven out on patrol.

Other times it's a smell, a news story, a bad dream. But then it passes, and I wrench myself back to the present. To Maggie and Elsa and the steady rhythm of my new life. I realize now just how lucky I am to have been given another chance. To have been allowed to move on when lads like Danny can't.

The rain outside slams against the train window, making me jump. I turn to watch it lashing furiously against the glass and am taken aback to see my own haunted reflection staring back at me.

I clamp my eyes shut, but it is Danny's face I see then. Danny as he was when he first arrived in camp, not the man Sarah described last night.

I think of him clutching a rugby ball, rolling it across the flat of his hand and then back down again, without letting go of the ball.

Singing. Always singing. He loved the limelight. Being up onstage. But I think what he really liked was making people happy. And no one more than Sarah. He lived to hear her laugh. I try to imagine a world where Danny would hurt Sarah, and find that I can't. Danny adored her. That's the truth.

Before she even got to Bastion he couldn't go a day without talking about her. And then, when she arrived, it was as if something inside him lit up. He would grin from ear to ear whenever Sarah walked into a room, reach for her hand, listen rapt to whatever it was she had to say.

He was dead proud of her, too, for what she was doing out there. He used to tell me how brave she was, how clever she was. How he couldn't believe his luck that she was his.

No. There was never any doubting how much Danny loved Sarah.

It's why I closed down any feelings I might have had for her. Why I walked out of the launderette that afternoon, even though every cell and fibre of me wanted to stay.

'It's complicated,' she'd said when I asked her about him. I know she was trying to tell me something, but I cut her off.

I had to. I didn't trust myself. The flimsiest suggestion that all was not well between them, and I wouldn't have been able to resist her.

And I was right, because look at what happened last night – I told myself that Sarah had feelings for me, and that getting close to her was okay because Danny didn't deserve her.

He had hurt her.

My mind flinches at the memory of the scar on her arm. At the thought of him causing her pain.

It may have been the PTSD, but he still hurt her.

And now I have too.

18. Sarah

I was going to talk to him this morning with a clear head, explain that I have to get things straight with Danny first. Or as straight as they can be with a man who has had his world cruelly pulled down around him.

Danny has already suffered so much. He might not understand what I have to say. He might not even care. But at least I will have tried, and that's the least he deserves.

And if I don't do it this way, I'm no better than my dad. I've always promised myself that I would never play with people's hearts in the glib way that he did. In fact, I'm worse than Dad. At least Mum wasn't sick when Dad cheated on her.

Anyway, it seems I won't get a chance to explain any of this to Carl, because before I get downstairs he's already left.

'You've just missed him,' Jenni says, holding out a fresh cup of coffee.

My heart sinks.

I think of his desolate expression as I pulled away from him last night. What if he believes I still have feelings for Danny? Or thinks that he is the one coming between us.

The truth is, things weren't right between us, even

before Danny got ill. I tried to explain it to Carl once, a long time ago – that afternoon in the camp launderette – how my feelings for Danny had changed, how we'd grown apart. But I didn't get a chance to tell him then either.

'Toast?' Jenni asks.

I shake my head.

'Is everything all right, pet?'

Cherub sits down on the sofa, balancing a bowl of cereal. He pauses between mouthfuls. 'Carl seemed out of sorts too. Dashed off like the house was on fire.'

I think of Carl kneeling next to me last night. Wiping away my tears, holding me in his arms. It felt so good to talk to him – to someone who really understands.

Last night I saw a different side to him. A willingness to open up. Back in camp, apart from in the immediate aftermath of Fridge's death, he always shied away from any sort of serious conversation. Stuck to the safe banter the soldiers all adopted to keep their private terrors at bay.

But yesterday, for the first time, he let me in. A secret thrill runs through me as I remember him cradling my face in his hands. But then the image dissolves and I see him now, alone on the train, not knowing what he did wrong, and I feel a sort of wrenching pain in my chest.

'Hey,' Jenni says, reaching for a pile of papers on the kitchen dresser. 'I meant to show you these yesterday. I found them when I was looking up addresses for the wedding invitations.'

She hands me the bundle. On top is a photograph,

the one that was taken on the day we all did the camp's 5K Park Run.

'See how young we all look,' she says. 'I can't believe it was only four years ago. It feels like a lifetime.'

She looks at Cherub fondly. 'I only signed up for that race because you told me you loved running. We'd just met, so I was still pretending to like the same things. Honest to God, I think if you suggested I went for a jog with you now, I'd punch you.'

Cherub laughs. 'If it makes you feel any better, I only signed up because I wanted you to think I was sporty and dynamic.'

He wipes away a dribble of cereal on his chin with the back of his hand, and we all laugh.

'I better get going,' Cherub says, getting to his feet.

Jenni hands him a sandwich wrapped in tin foil. She's made it for his lunch, and I think how nice it must be to have someone love you enough to fill in the small details like that for you. Someone on the sidelines, always looking out for you.

Cherub kisses us both on the top of the head, and Jenni follows him out into the hall to say goodbye. Noah, Toby and the dog trail after her.

'Help yourself to more coffee,' she calls out as the front door closes behind Cherub. 'I'm going to get these two nippers dressed.'

The kitchen is suddenly silent. I pour myself another coffee, sit back down at the kitchen table and stare at the photograph. I smile at the sight of Squadron in that tiny T-shirt, at Jenni and Cherub, and Assami with his huge smile. At Danny, Fridge, Carl and Jobbo. At Caroline, with her long, glossy, poker-straight hair braided and pinned in two neat, dark brown plaits on top of her head.

Danny looks so handsome, it makes my heart ache to look at him. His black hair is glinting in the sunshine, his shoulders are squared, his earnest face staring straight ahead at the camera.

Finally, I look at me. At the way my face is turned towards Carl. I remember how badly I wanted to impress him on the day. How all I thought about during the race was catching up with him. I didn't give Danny a backwards glance.

Suddenly my skin prickles with guilt.

It's not just that I nearly betrayed Danny last night. It's that I've wanted to betray him for so long.

19. Carl

When I get back to the cottage I see Maggie through the window, bending down to scoop up Mr Jones, the three-legged Jack Russell we've just taken in as a rescue.

I watch as she nuzzles his neck and then carefully plants him on her shoulder, where he sits like a parrot comically surveying the room around him.

Maggie is wearing my Leeds United bobble hat and faded old green parka – the one Kathleen gave me when I started walking the dogs. It used to belong to Michael. I remember him wearing it to take me and Fridge to footie practice when we were kids. A huge man in his huge coat, cheering us on with his huge heart.

That coat is big on me and its enormous scale completely drowns Maggie. She looks like a little girl playing dress-up.

Roz, who has been standing in front of the oven, turns and says something to Maggie. It's almost certainly a complaint about the Rayburn – which she regards as her personal nemesis – and in spite of myself, in spite of last night, I can't help but smile. I'm so relieved to be home. I feel just like I used to feel when I made it back to camp after a patrol. No longer in hostile territory.

When I open the front door I am met by a crazy

kerfuffle of boisterous, noisy dogs. Maggie shouts at them all to calm down, while Roz fights her way through the melee to give me a hug.

'You look done in,' Maggie says.

'Thanks!' I laugh.

'Leave the poor man alone,' Roz chides. Then, looking at me, 'Can I make you a cup of tea, love? Not that this hopeless Rayburn of yours looks like it'll be boiling the kettle any time soon.'

Simultaneously, I say yes to the tea, dump my bag on the floor, nudge the kettle to the hot end of the Rayburn and scratch Elsa's ears. For the first time since I left Jenni and Cherub's this morning, I feel the knot in my chest begin to loosen.

I stare at Roz clucking about the kitchen, at Maggie in her muddy boots leaving muddy footprints everywhere, and suddenly I'm overcome with gratitude for being a part of their world.

These are my new comrades, I realize. Because of them I have a purpose in life, a business with clients who rely on me, a daily routine. They're the reason I get up in the morning.

'What?' Maggie says, seeing me watching her. 'Is it my muddy boots? Sorry, I was just about to take them off.'

'No, no, it's fine,' I say, walking across the kitchen and hugging her.

Maggie pushes me away. 'What is wrong with you?' she asks, her eyes wide with alarm. 'Oh God, are you about to fire me? You are, aren't you?'

I cling on to her even harder, until eventually Roz

gently pats me on the shoulder. 'Come and sit,' she says. 'I'll make you a sandwich.'

'She's made chocolate cake too,' Maggie adds, sitting at the kitchen table and helping herself to a giant wedge.

Roz guides me to the table and nudges me into a chair. I watch as she rounds up plates and mugs, spoons, a knife. She pours milk first and then tea into three mugs, and clouds of synchronized steam rise comfortingly above them.

Roz bustles around and then hands me a sandwich, while Maggie takes a second slice of cake.

'Go on, love,' Roz says to me. 'You'll feel better after having something to eat.'

I eat my sandwich, drink my tea, help myself to a piece of cake. Afterwards, I don't feel better as such, but my mind does feel clearer. I think of something Caroline said to me once. Something about a shield she and I put between us and the world.

'Look,' I'd said, waving my arms in front of me. 'No shield.'

She'd pulled a face. 'You know what I mean.'

I think about it now. Like me, Caroline had spent time in care as a kid. She had a stepdad who hit her, a mum who didn't care. When the bruises got so bad that her PE teacher noticed them, she was placed with a foster family.

Maybe Caroline had a point. I was cautious about who I let into my world, wary of making new friends. But as far as I was concerned, I was right to be and I remember telling her as much.

'I used to be like that too,' she told me, shaking her head. 'Expecting people to let me down because, in the past, everyone had. But the trouble is, you end up living a half-life. Always on the outside.'

Suddenly I understand what Caroline meant. A full life for me would be a life lived with Sarah – but that's not on the cards. And that's okay. I'm used to living on the outside.

What's not okay is finally realizing just how much Caroline lost. She lost a lifetime of living a full life with Jobbo. Caroline, the most deserving, warm, generous person I ever knew.

It was exactly this time of year, and what with everything that's happened in the last twenty-four hours, suddenly the memories are too raw, too real. My mind slams back into its dark place. I can't do this here, not in front of Maggie and Roz. I have to get outside, walk it off, wait for the wall of pain to fall away.

'Carl? Carl, are you all right?' Roz is staring at me, a concerned look on her face.

'I didn't get much sleep,' I tell her, scraping my chair back behind me and reaching for my coat. 'I'm just going to get some fresh air. I won't be long.'

Outside, with Elsa at my side, I retrace my usual route, but the familiar sight of the moors does not restore my calm. The light is beginning to fail and the jagged path I normally feel pulled towards now looks dismal and dangerous, making me feel even more on edge.

How quickly everything shifts, I think.

How quickly it shifted for Caroline.

She and Jobbo would be married by now. Have a home, like Jenni and Cherub, full of noise and clutter and children.

I whistle to Elsa and she comes running. It's the same whistle Caroline used to summon the dogs on camp. It's down to her that I thought of setting up the business.

If it wasn't for Caroline, I wouldn't have everything that I have now.

Afghanistan

2008

20. Carl

Caroline and I were on one of the early morning walks we took together, exercising the dogs from the kennel where she worked.

It had become our routine after Fridge died. Caroline insisted she needed my help with the dogs, but we both knew she was only doing it for me.

At first, we'd walked together in companionable silence. Mercifully, she didn't offer meaningless platitudes about Fridge dying doing what he loved, or say how heroic he was, or how brave and honourable.

But as time went on we'd begun to talk about all sorts of things together. In fact, I'd started to enjoy her company so much that sometimes I'd go to the kennels just to hang out with her. Something about watching her with the dogs as they followed her every move, obeyed her every command, made me feel calm. Caroline was gradually teaching me how to be around dogs.

This particular morning she was busy feeding the dogs some treats. Out of the blue, she suddenly asked me, 'Do you think people like us can be good parents?' She stared at me.

I knew that by 'people like us' she meant people who have been in care. We'd talked about it in the past. Talked about being mixed-up kids who grow into mixed-up adults who do their best to pretend they're not. But we'd never talked about having families of our own. I didn't say anything.

'Jobbo's been talking about children,' Caroline went on. 'I know how much he wants them, and I do too, I really do. But, Carl, I'm scared. What if I'm no better than my own mum? What if I have a kid who's as good and decent and wonderful as Jobbo, and I mess them up.'

It was something that had crossed my own mind from time to time. I'd always felt like I'd let my brothers down, not fought hard enough for them. Who was to say I wouldn't do the same with my own children?

But listening now to Caroline say those words out loud, I suddenly knew, without a shadow of a doubt, that if someday I was lucky enough to have children, I would never let any harm come to them. I would be there for them in a way that neither of my parents had ever been there for me.

I knew that with an absolute certainty because, like Caroline, I knew how rubbish it felt when they weren't.

I looked at Caroline. 'Yes,' I told her. 'Yes, I believe we'll be there for our kids. We'll know how to be good parents when it's our turn.'

'I don't know,' she said, unconvinced. 'I always thought my mum loved me but then when my stepdad came along everything was about him. The first time I told her he'd hit me, she didn't believe me. The second time, she said it was my fault, that I must have provoked him. That I should show more understanding for how much pressure he was under at work. After that, I stopped telling her.

She stopped walking then and looked at me, with tears in her eyes.

'What if it's in my DNA, Carl? What if I'm like my mum?'

Behind her I could see a camel train passing the camp's eastern entrance. The moment Caroline saw it, I knew she would squeal with delight. She always did – even though, every time, I told her they were almost certainly transporting harvested opium.

I put my hands on her shoulders. 'Caroline, you'll be an incredible mum.'

'Do you really think so?' She looked doubtful.

'I know so. Look at how you are with the dogs, with all your friends, with me. You're the most patient, kind, protective, loving person I've ever met. You even love camels.'

'Camels? Where?' She spun her head around to look at them. 'Did you know that camels can completely shut their nostrils during sandstorms.'

'You're so weird,' I said, and we both laughed.

Assami waved to us in the distance.

'What are you two laughing at?' he asked as he got closer to us.

'How weird she is,' I told him.

'Don't you listen to him, Miss Caroline,' he said. 'He is very bad mannered, and not at all gentlemanly.'

'That's true,' I admitted.

Caroline hugged Assami hello, then reached into her rucksack. 'For your children,' she said, holding out three bags of Haribo she'd bought that morning in the camp shop.

Assami placed his right hand over his heart and nodded gently. 'Thank you, from the bottom of my heart.'

Assami and I hugged Caroline goodbye and left to get ready for our patrol.

I wish I'd known it was the last time I'd see her. I would have hugged her for longer. I would have held on to her for dear life.

21. Sarah

Danny was waiting for me outside the hospital when I finished my shift. He was behaving oddly, even more agitated than normal, pacing up and down.

'Hey you,' I said, coming out of the doors.

The minute he looked up, I knew something was wrong.

'Caroline,' he said. That was all he needed to say.

I knew she was gone.

We clung to each other for a long time. I couldn't stop Danny shaking. I could feel his heart racing against my chest, and his cheek, next to mine, felt clammy.

It felt unreal, that Caroline could be gone too. Caroline with her neat plaits and immaculate uniform. Her kind brown eyes, with little flecks of yellow that looked like they were gold in the sunshine.

Caroline was one of those perennially upbeat people who couldn't bear to see others feeling sad. She told me once, after I'd watched her cheering up one of the other nurses, that she just wanted the whole world to be as happy as she and Jobbo were.

I think it was more to do with having known so much unhappiness herself, and not wanting others to have to suffer like she had. But either way, she spent an awful lot of time worrying about everyone else.

Caroline was the one person who knew the truth

about my feelings for Carl. She saw me break down that time in the hospital, after he'd been injured on patrol, but she was too tactful to ask me directly.

Instead, she waited until we were in the gym together, a couple of weeks later. 'How's Danny doing?' she asked gently.

I stared ahead at the monitor on the running machine so I didn't have to meet her eyes. 'Things haven't been right between us for a while,' I admitted.

I told her how my feelings for Danny had changed, even before I'd got to Afghanistan. That I'd wanted to talk to him, but that he seemed fragile, was struggling enough with the tour.

It was so exhausting, pretending everything was fine, that for a moment I felt relieved to have told someone. But then I immediately felt guilty for betraying him.

'I can't bear to make things worse for him,' I went on. 'Besides, I love him still, a part of me always will. I don't want to hurt him.'

We had both stopped running by then, and Caroline turned to face me.

'People don't get to choose who they fall in and out of love with. Good people stick with things, with relationships, because they think they ought to. But Sarah, if being out here has taught me anything, it's that life is short – happiness, love, it's there to be seized. And love shouldn't be about obligation.'

Her words came back to haunt me now, on the night of her death.

Had she been shot? Blown up? For a moment I felt

as if I'd been blown apart too, as if I was no longer there. But I was. I had to be. For Danny. Pulling away from him, I took a deep breath and held out my hand. 'Come on. Let's get some tea.'

It was one of those crazy Afghan sunsets where the sky turns ice-lolly pink and orange and purple. I used to think they were beautiful, but that night the sunset just felt sinister, as if we were all on the set of an apocalyptic horror movie. Which, in a way, we were.

With each new death, every harrowing patrol he made it back from, Danny had retreated more and more into himself. Now, losing Caroline too, I feared he would disappear even further.

He stared at me trustingly as we turned to walk towards the mess, and that's when I saw them.

Carl and Assami, knocking on the door of Rose Cottage.

A shiver ran through me. Rose Cottage was the morgue.

The powers that be must have thought that calling it Rose Cottage would make it less upsetting every time an announcement had to be made about the morgue. But they were wrong. Calling it that didn't make it any less horrific for any of us. A morgue's a morgue. Naming it after a romantic flower doesn't hide the stench of death and formaldehyde that hits you the second you step inside.

Danny tightened his grip on my hand. The sight of them was so desperately moving. Carl adored Caroline. Assami did too. He used to bring her tubs of delicious-smelling sweet rice dishes his wife, Habiba, made to thank her for the sweets she bought all the time for his children.

Assami was hovering protectively at Carl's side, his hand on Carl's shoulder. I had a sudden urge to run to Carl. For me to be the one to comfort him, not Assami.

But at that precise moment Danny slumped to the floor beside me. He buried his head in his hands. 'It's our fault,' he moaned.

His hair was covered in a smattering of dust. I reached down to brush it away. Then I sat down next to him, put my arm around him and pulled him close.

He started to cry. 'It's our fault Caroline's dead.'

'What do you mean?' I asked gently.

He told me that, although it hadn't been confirmed, the word spreading around camp was that her death was due to a friendly fire incident.

I wanted to cry then, too, but I knew I couldn't, not in front of Danny. But I could be angry. Not the sort of anger I felt when something upset me at work, which it often did. Not even the sort of anger I had felt when Dad left.

This was different. This was a visceral fury that had been curdling inside me for days, weeks even. All this death. Not only our soldiers but death on all sides.

Just yesterday we'd treated a 35-year-old farmer who had lost his legs driving his tractor over an IED. And last week a five-year-old girl had been badly burned in a bomb blast that killed both her parents.

Caroline's death – a needless accident, if Danny was right – seemed to sum up the pointlessness of it all.

'It's not fair,' Danny was saying. 'None of it. Fridge and Squadron and Tom – and now Caroline. What happened to Sarge too. All of it. I was so sure when I came here that we were doing the right thing, that we were the good guys. But death is death, isn't it? No matter what side you're on.'

I reached out to him but he became more agitated, and pushed me away.

'It never occurred to me that I was a bad person before. I always just assumed I was good. Good enough, at least.'

'You *are* a good man,' I said, kissing him. He tasted of salt and dust.

'Then why am I out here, killing people?' he asked.

I tried to reason with him, but he wouldn't listen.

'When I'm out on patrol I feel this sickening dread that I'm going to be next, and I pray that it won't be me, that it'll be someone else instead. But who does that? Who prays for one of his mates to get killed instead of himself? A monster, that's who.'

Night had fallen by then, its thick black veil hiding Danny's face. I thought of the day he first asked me out. How innocent we both were, how much we'd changed since then, and felt overcome with sadness.

'You're not a monster,' I told him.

'Don't ever leave me,' he said, shaking. 'You're the only thing that keeps me from thinking I'm a terrible person. Because if you're with me, I can't be that bad, right?' He smiled weakly. 'Please don't ever leave me, Sarah. I need you.'

I felt myself freeze.

Caroline was right, love shouldn't be about obligation. But at the same time, how could it not be?

'I won't ever leave you, Danny,' I said. 'I promise.'

22. Carl

Caroline died of a single wound to the chest and abdomen.

Two patrols had left the camp that morning. The first patrol, the one Caroline was in, came across a policeman washing at a stream in preparation for prayer. They mistook him for a Taliban fighter and fired a warning shot.

It's impossible to know why they took that first shot, other than to say things can look very different when your nerves are strung out sky high.

Did the policeman jerk forward, as if reaching for something?

Did he stumble with nerves?

Was he reaching for his clothes or a weapon?

A second patrol, looking down at the very same scene from a different vantage spot, heard the warning shot and assumed they were under fire.

They fired back, killing the soldier who had fired the warning shot.

And Caroline.

Like the rest of us, Jobbo just couldn't believe it.

He couldn't bring himself to go and see her body in the morgue, but he couldn't bear the thought of her being alone.

'I've got this,' I told him. 'I'll stay with her until they fly her home.'

'I will too,' Assami said, stepping forward. 'It will be my honour.'

He took a step closer to Jobbo, bowed his head and put his hand over his heart. 'Your Caroline, she was such a wonderful woman. It will truly be my honour.'

Jobbo looked up at him, his face streaked with tears, and nodded.

'She did not deserve this,' Assami went on. 'And neither do you, my friend.'

The sergeant who opened the door to us both at the morgue couldn't have been kinder, but a chill ran through me when he led us through to a spartan white room with a couple of gurneys and a wall of cabinets.

Staring at them, I felt a terrible weight of grief inside me. All those ghosts. All those devastated families waiting for them back home.

The sergeant nodded to a label on a cabinet at the bottom right, and pulled over a couple of chairs for us to sit on.

'I'll leave you to it.' He withdrew quietly.

Assami started to pray and, angry as I was with God right then, the sound of him chanting was comforting. It felt good to know that, even in death, one of us had Caroline's back.

After a while, he stopped.

He took my hand in his. 'I am praying to the angels,' he said.

'What angels?' I asked, suddenly curious to know.

Maybe the angels in his world would make more sense to me than the ones in mine.

He smiled. 'The Questioning Angels, Munkar and Nakir. They come to the grave to interrogate the person who has died, to see if they have led a good life.' He shook his head. 'But I do not think Caroline will suffer the interrogation in the grave. She has led a good life.'

'If there *are* angels, how can they have let this happen to her?' I asked bitterly.

'I cannot answer that for you, my friend,' Assami said, and he bowed his head again in prayer.

I cried then. I couldn't help it.

Because Caroline had led a good life. But life hadn't been good to her.

And death had come far, far too soon.

Home

2011

Poppy #4

It started raining the day after I got back from Jenni and Cherub's, and it hasn't stopped since. Fierce, slanting rain that falls apocalyptically from a forbidding, cigarette ash-coloured sky.

By the time I get to the tattoo shop I'm completely drenched, water trickling down my back and pooling on the mat beneath my sodden boots.

Barry laughs when he sees the state of me.

'Come on through,' he says. 'Let's get you dried off.'

It's warm and cosy in his room, with the fan heater blasting away in the corner.

I take off my wet clothes and dry myself with the towel Barry holds out for me, then I lower myself on to the bed.

'Ready?' Barry asks.

'All set.'

The sound of the rain that I've done battle with all week on the waterlogged moors sounds almost soothing in here as it taps rhythmically against the window.

It's funny. I know how much it's going to hurt. But even so, I'm glad to be here. Relieved to have nothing to think about other than the person who has brought me to this room.

The person who has been on my mind all week.

'Music?' Barry asks.

'"Sweet Caroline",' I say. Of course.

Hers was the most futile death of them all. An accident. A shot fired by someone on her own side.

That morning – the morning Caroline had asked me if I thought she would make a good mother – just before Assami and I left, his mobile phone went and he stepped away from us to take the call.

'Where's all this soul-searching coming from anyway?' I asked her.

Caroline turned to look at me. 'Can you keep a secret?'

Now, I wonder: did I do the right thing by saying yes?

There have been so many times over the last few years when I've asked myself that. When the burden of it has felt like a dead weight tugging at my conscience.

I told her she had to go home, that it wasn't safe for her to be out there, but she begged me not to say anything, insisted that she wanted to tell Jobbo first.

Instead, I should have made her listen to me.

'Don't worry,' she said, kissing me on the cheek. 'I promise I'll tell him today.'

She never got the chance.

If only I'd gone straight to her bosses, told someone, anyone, then they would have ordered her to go straight back to England, and she never would have gone out on that patrol.

I've longed to tell Jobbo. A part of me wanted him to be angry with me. But what would have been the point? It would only have increased his heartbreak.

Jobbo's hair literally turned white with grief after Caroline died. I never used to think that was a real thing. I thought it was something that only happened in fairy tales. But it is a thing, I know that now, because within six months of her death his once brown hair was completely white.

'Sweet Caroline' has long since stopped playing when Barry finally holds the mirror up for me to look at his latest work.

Another beautiful, vibrant red poppy, its petals unfurling across my back.

In the end I did keep Caroline's secret. Well, almost.

This new poppy, unlike the others, has a tiny, pale green bud hovering below it. A poppy and a bud.

For Caroline and her unborn baby.

23. Sarah

Annie's hair is white now. It looks like candyfloss, the sort Danny always used to buy whenever we caught the bus to Barry Island to spend the day at the seaside together.

Sitting at the kitchen table, I watch as she sieves flour into a bowl and then throws in a lump of butter. She rubs the flour and the butter between her fingers.

'How was work today, love?' Annie asks.

I think of the twenty-year-old lad rushed in after a motorbike accident. Shrieking alarms telling us he had gone into cardiac arrest. The panicked dash to his bedside, the rush to attach sticky pads to his skin. Defibrillator paddles slamming on to his chest, shocking his heart back to life.

The smile of pure relief on his mum's face when I told her he was going to be all right. I wish, more than anything, that I could make Annie smile like that. That I could do something, anything, to help Danny.

'Busy,' I answer. 'Did I tell you Vihann's wife is expecting again?'

'Is she? Ahh, that's lovely news.'

Annie adds sugar and sultanas to her mix as she chats. She has been making Welsh cakes for so long, she doesn't need to weigh any of the ingredients, just spills what she instinctively knows to be the right amount into her ancient cane-coloured mixing bowl.

The bowl is chipped at the edge but Annie won't hear of replacing it. It used to belong to her mum, Granny Gwen, who worked as a cook in a nearby stately home and taught Annie to make Welsh cakes.

'They're such a nice couple. Will that be their third?' she asks.

'It will.'

We sit in happy silence as she cracks an egg into the bowl and then, a few minutes later, lifts the doughy mixture on to the floured kitchen surface before energetically rolling it out.

I've always loved watching Annie bake, but never more so than now. There is something comforting in the soothing repetition of her actions, of knowing exactly which ingredient will be added next.

The sense of control, and the welcome distraction from anything else, both of our minds completely absorbed in the here and now. Neither of us glancing up at the kitchen clock, wondering where Danny is, when he might come home, what his mood will be like when he does.

He and I used to eat Annie's Welsh cakes fresh from the pan, still warm, after school. No one in the house will eat this batch. I'll discreetly put them in a tin later and take them in to work.

They are nearly done now. Annie is stamping her crinkled cutter into the dough and, one by one, lifting the little doughy discs on to the griddle. The second the last one goes on, she looks up at the clock. Her expression – relaxed while she remained absorbed in her task – returns to a worried frown.

'Tea?' I ask.

She nods gratefully, and I get up to put the kettle on.

Poor Annie. The skin on her once-rounded red cheeks is paper thin, like the rest of her. She hasn't eaten properly since Danny got back. Not since that first Remembrance Sunday.

He had been home a week and the service in the local church was being held in his honour. Annie had invited everyone to a special lunch at theirs afterwards, to celebrate his safe homecoming.

I was afraid it might be too much for him.

'He's just tired,' Annie said, when I tried to talk to her about it.

I explained how worried I was about him. How anxious he had been in Afghanistan.

'He'll be fine,' she insisted. 'He's been through a lot. He just needs to readjust. To know he's safe.'

On the Sunday, Annie got up early to prepare the lunch. She peeled the vegetables and set the table with her best tablecloth and her best china. Just before we set off for church, she put the roast in the oven.

But no one sat down for lunch that day.

The vicar, who had known Danny all his life, talked movingly about a time for love and a time for hate, a time for war and a time for peace. He smiled at Danny as he said that those who had returned deserved peace, and he called on us all to pray that they would get it.

Then a little boy, his bright orange hair specially combed for the occasion, picked up his trumpet and walked to the front of the church. He raised the trumpet, took a deep breath, and began to play the 'Last Post'.

Danny's hand, clasped in mine, began to tremble. He turned to look at me, and I saw it in his eyes.

I'd seen eyes just like his in the camp hospital. The eyes of men so frightened, they had retreated into a place where no one could reach them. A place from which they couldn't be rescued.

I thought of Danny back in camp, the 'Last Post' playing at the eerie sunset vigils, staring at the Union flag draped across coffins being carried on to the RAF C-17s. I remembered the times when he had been the one doing the carrying.

Shouldering the coffins of Fridge and Squadron.

And then Caroline's.

Jobbo buckling as he tried to hold up her coffin. Carl shooting out an arm to steady him, while Cherub and Danny struggled to hold the coffin level behind them.

'It's okay,' I whispered as the trumpet's sound poured through the church, squeezing his hand. 'You've seen terrible things that you're not going to forget overnight. But everything's going to be okay. You're home now.'

But the truth is that Danny, the old Danny, never really did come home.

Does that make it better? That I yearn for a life away from him. A life with Carl.

Or worse?

24. Carl

It's burning like a bastard this morning. The whole thing feels feverish.

Barry told me to take an antihistamine if it got too uncomfortable, or to get some hydrocortisone cream from the doctor, but I like the pain. It makes it feel like a worthy tribute to them.

To Fridge and Squadron.

To Tom.

To Caroline and her baby.

I stare at the after-care leaflet Barry gave me on my first visit.

CONGRATULATIONS ON YOUR TATTOO!

It will last forever. But the health and appearance of your tattoo depend on how you look after it in the first few days. Poor care during the healing process may result in infections, flaking or fading. So give it some TLC!

Leave the dressing on initially for a few hours, to absorb any fluid or excess ink. Wash your hands with soap before removing the dressing. When you do take the dressing off, fluid will ooze out. This is blood, plasma (the clear part of blood) and some extra ink. It's gross but it's normal, so don't worry!

They're not wrong. It is gross. It is also, as they predict it will be, red and sore. Awkwardly, I reach behind me to wash the tattoo with fragrance-free soap as the leaflet advises. As I rinse my hands, the water in the basin slowly turns red with ink, as if I am washing off blood.

I pat it dry and apply a layer of Aquaphor lotion, remembering the words of the leaflet.

No matter how badly you want to slather ointment on to soothe it, don't put on too much! The tattoo needs to breathe so the skin can regenerate. Too much ointment will clog pores and cause other problems.

Putting on the cream, I feel vain and ridiculous – I've never used cream in my life. I imagine the ribbing I would get from the lads if they could see me. But Barry was insistent. He says the cream will improve the tattoo's final appearance, so I do what I'm told.

This is being done in their memory, so I need to take care of it, respect it. Not do what I really want to do – which is to run outside and drag my back across the bark of a tree like a bad-tempered bear.

I feel the lines inked into my skin as I rub in the lotion, then I put the bottle down and stare at the tattoo in the mirror. It's raised and cracked, and there are dried, coloured, peeling chunks waiting to drop off that don't even look human; they look like something a snake or a lizard would cast off. A sign, apparently, that the skin is healing.

It's still itching, in spite of all the lotion. I was already dreading the thought of having to see Sarah at this afternoon's wedding dance rehearsal. And now I'm going to have to contend with this.

Mercifully, I'm spared any more torturous thoughts about seeing Sarah – and having to dance in front of an instructor – by the sound of Maggie letting herself in downstairs. I hear her voice and then Roz's, and I happily listen to them gently bickering while I finish my packing.

By the time I get downstairs the dogs are hoovering down their breakfast, their metal tags clattering against the sides of the bowls, and there's a cup of tea ready for me on the kitchen table.

'Fancy some scrambled eggs, sweetheart?' Roz says.

She nods at the fresh loaf and eggs she must have picked up on the path from the farmer's wife. They sit temptingly on the kitchen table.

I shake my head.

Maggie stoops down to pick up Mr Jones and spots my overnight bag. 'Ready for your secret mission?'

The dogs start barking at the sound of the taxi driver beeping at the top of the lane.

'Got to go,' I say, swallowing down a mouthful of hot tea from the mug that Roz insists I drink.

She takes the mug off me and presses something else into my palm. 'For you,' she says. 'The forecast says it's going to freeze tonight.'

It's a hand-knitted red woolly hat, and I love it. Not the style – I hate to think how ridiculous I look in it – but I love that she made it for me. That someone thinks I'm worth worrying about.

I pull it down over my ears and reach over to kiss her on the cheek.

'Thank you,' I say.

Maggie laughs. 'Well, if you are a spy, they won't need satellite images to see you coming if you're wearing that.'

I take it off the minute I get into the cab. But then I find myself repeatedly reaching into my pocket to check it's still there. I rub the soft wool between my fingers and feel better.

I can do this, I tell myself.

I can do this for Jenni and Cherub.

But I notice that my hands, as they hold on to the wool of the hat, are shaking.

25. Sarah

The noise wakes me with a jolt and it takes me a couple of seconds to get my bearings.

Danny's house. The sofa. I must have dozed off as I waited with Annie for him to come home.

I hear the noise again, a crashing sound coming from the kitchen.

Annie is already out of her armchair. A coiled spring of anxiety and relief.

'Danny?' she calls out. 'Is that you, love?'

Another crash, and this time I hear the sound of china smashing on to the floor.

Annie makes it to the kitchen first and raises her hands to her cheeks in alarm.

Danny is staggering by the sink, a bottle of vodka swaying in his hand, filthy faced and filthy drunk. Annie's precious mixing bowl – which I carefully washed last night and left to dry on the draining rack by the sink – is in pieces by his feet.

'It's okay, Sarah,' Annie says, holding an arm out to stop me going into the kitchen. 'It's just a bowl.'

I look at her exhausted face, see the tears in her eyes.

'But it isn't just a bowl, is it?' I say, suddenly furious. 'Look at the state of him. Look at the state of *us*.'

I know I shouldn't be this angry. I know it's not fair.

It's Danny's chronic PTSD that drives him to drink. And it's the drink that triggers his moods, stops him caring about his behaviour, his appearance. About us.

But I can't help myself, I'm so tired. Tired of all of it.

Everything I've seen, all that pain, all that loss.

Putting my life on hold.

Watching Danny wrestle with his demons. Staying out all night, with people who couldn't care less about him, while we wait anxiously at home.

I feel like a doll that has had all the stuffing pulled out of her.

'Please, Danny,' I beg. 'Please stop doing this.' I start to cry. 'Please let us help you.'

Annie puts her hand on my shoulder.

Danny is staring at us both but his face is blank, as if he has no idea who either of us is. He makes as if to reach for a weapon he no longer carries, then, staggering, he lunges forward.

I rush in front of Annie and grab his arm. 'Please, Danny, don't –'

He throws me against the wall. 'I don't need your fucking help,' he yells, and stalks upstairs.

Annie crouches down beside me. 'Are you okay? Has he hurt you?' She starts to sob. 'I'm so sorry, Sarah, I'm so sorry.'

I register her face in front of mine and I hear her talking. But I don't see her or hear her.

Because suddenly all I can think about is seeing Carl tomorrow at the dance rehearsal.

Danny is ill, I know that.

We've been together a long time, I know that too.

But for all our history, all his pain, I also know I can't do this any more.

26. Carl

The inside of the community centre is every bit as run-down as the outside. The wood-chip paper on the walls is stained with tobacco, and a strong smell of disinfectant grips the back of my throat.

But it's warm and bright. Jenni is practically doing somersaults with happiness, and it's hard not to let her excitement rub off on me.

'This is gonna be a pure belta,' she says, beaming at me.

Her stepmother, Eileen – the ex-cruise ship dancer, and our teacher for the day – nods her unnaturally bronze-coloured face in my direction, then opens the door to the hall.

'Right, then,' she says in an accent that sounds just like Jenni's. 'Let's see what you've got.'

I sneak a glance at Sarah. She looks every bit as terrified as me. She seems tired too, now that I look more closely at her, with that faraway expression on her face. It's the one she used to have in Afghanistan when she was worried about something – usually Danny.

Danny.

Has something happened?

I feel guilty all of a sudden for not ringing her after that weekend at Jenni and Cherub's. I did think about it – just to check if they were both okay. But then I told myself I'd embarrassed Sarah enough with the near kiss. The last thing I wanted to do was to overstep again and make her feel even more uncomfortable.

'Showtime!' Eileen cries, dramatically flinging her leopard-print fur coat on to the stage behind her. 'The dance I'm going to teach you is to a song called "Young At Heart".' She is staring right at me as she starts demonstrating the moves.

Her leg is going backwards and forwards, then she's stomping her heel on the floor and clapping like she's doing some sort of Irish jig. She does it again, and I swear her legs are made of elastic. Then she turns to face us.

'Easy!' she cries. 'That's all there is to it!'

I'm not sure whether to laugh or cry.

A deafening blast of music bursts out of the speakers. I look over my shoulder to smile at Sarah. But then Eileen starts belting out instructions like a sergeant major and I don't have time to worry about Sarah any more as I frantically try to imitate what she's doing.

At first everything I do is wrong. I use my right leg when it should be my left, and by the time I realize and make the switch Eileen is using her left leg again. Everything is too fast, my arms are waving madly, and my feet feel like they're trying to dance through setting cement.

Jenni and Cherub look like they've done this a million times before. They actually look like they're enjoying themselves.

But then I see Sarah. She has stopped dancing and is bent over, her hands clutching her knees.

'No,' she says. 'No, I can't. I'll never be able to do this.'

'For pity's sake,' says Eileen, coming to stand between us. 'You two are hopeless.'

I like the sound of 'you two'. Knowing Sarah is struggling as much as me makes me relax. We're in this together.

'Breathe deeply,' barks Eileen.

I do as I'm told, taking great lung-filling gulps of air.

'Now, watch me. It's all in the way you carry your upper body.'

At this I look at Sarah who is trying not to laugh.

Exasperated, Eileen shows us the steps again, and we repeat them . . .

And repeat them . . .

And repeat them . . .

Until it clicks.

My clumsy legs seem to be dancing on their own.

And suddenly I feel a lightness of step that I haven't felt since we touched down in Afghanistan.

27. Sarah

Eileen tells us to take it from the top, and just as she hits 'play' Carl's strong hand grabs my arm. He looks at me as if he is asking permission. I nod, and he takes my hand and holds it tight.

His bright blue eyes lock on to mine and immediately the room feels charged, as if it is spinning away with just the two of us in it. A sort of twinned energy flows through us. We are completely one. Even our breathing is in time.

I get so caught up in the two of us dancing together that I am barely even aware of Jenni and Cherub being in the room. With Carl smiling at my side, and sunlight flooding the hall, I could dance all afternoon.

'Yes! That's it,' yells Eileen happily.

It is, I think to myself. *This is it.*

A peacefulness washes over me. My shoulder – which has been throbbing non-stop since Danny flung me against the kitchen wall – no longer hurts. I don't feel exhausted from lack of sleep. Or bitter at the thought of Danny sleeping off his hangover, knowing that when he wakes he won't remember a thing.

I don't feel angry or hurt or anxious or taken for granted. I just feel happy. And, for the first time in a long while, I dare to feel optimistic. I tell myself there has to be a way for me to leave Danny without turning my back on him and Annie. I just need to talk to her. Tell her how much I love them both – that that will never change. I just can't keep on pretending Danny and I are still a couple.

Then I'll talk to Carl, make him understand that things with Danny are over. See if there is a chance for me and him.

Swirling and swaying, I tap my feet and lose myself in the rhythm of the music.

But then, all too soon, it's over. Eileen announces she has to be somewhere else, wraps herself dramatically in her enormous fur coat, and disappears out of the door.

'Drink?' Jenni suggests. 'We could go next door to the clubhouse and grab one? Dad's got the kids, so there's no rush to get back.'

'Definitely. I'm up for it.' Carl grins.

High on adrenaline still, the four of us walk through the community centre and out into the adjoining club and bar. The room is packed, a Friday night buzz in the air at the promise of the weekend to come.

For a moment Carl looks overwhelmed but then Cherub, who has noticed his expression, takes charge. He finds us a table to sit at, then goes to the bar to get a round in.

Carl starts to relax.

Cherub returns with a tray of drinks. 'So,' he says, after taking an enormous gulp of beer. 'Who knew Carl was such a talented danzetore?'

'Danze what?' Jenni splutters as her gin and tonic goes down the wrong way. She makes a strange gurgling sound.

'Danzetore. Snakehips. Twinkletoes.' Cherub laughs.

'Shut up,' Carl says, laughing too.

'I'm serious,' Cherub counters. 'Those legs of yours would look amazing in a pair of ballet tights.'

'He's right,' Jenni joins in. 'You were quite the compelling spectacle on the dance floor.'

'Eileen clearly thought so,' Cherub adds.

Carl puts down his pint and thrusts his shoulders back. 'It's all in the way you carry your upper body,'

At which point we all laugh even harder.

'You do have a magnificent upper body,' Jenni says, reaching out to pat his chest.'

'She's clearly drunk,' Cherub says, pushing her gin and tonic away from her. 'She doesn't know what she's saying.'

And so the evening wears on.

The events of last night melt away as I remember how it feels to laugh with friends. To relax. Tease one another, knowing no one will take offence when none was meant. Lash out for no reason.

I'm so tired of it all. I try not to be, but I am. I'm tired of having to be so careful all the time. Mindful of what I say. Of what I do. Of what we watch, where we go, who we see. And I'm tired of being tired.

Carl stands up to go for another round of drinks. But there are so many people around us, and we are squashed together so tightly, he loses his balance and sits back down. He puts his hand on my thigh to steady himself.

'Sorry,' he says, but he doesn't move his hand. He sits there for a moment, staring at me.

Blood fizzes through my veins and my cheeks feel as if they are on fire.

'Are you getting those drinks, or what?' Cherub yells over the chatter around us.

Carl smiles at me and squeezes my thigh. It is the faintest squeeze but it makes me feel intoxicated.

'On my way,' he says. He turns, and I smile.

I watch his back as he disappears towards the bar.

Suddenly he stops dead in his tracks.

I know, without him having to turn around, that something is wrong.

28. Carl

The song that's been chosen to start tonight's Sixties Disco is 'Black Is Black'. Its familiar opening chords are drifting through from the dance floor in the hall next door.

It's one of the many songs Danny used to play back in our Camp Bastion tent on that mad old-fashioned record player of his. He talked endlessly about music – about the power of songs to transport you to other places and create different moods.

We used to tease him about it, but he was right, wasn't he? About the power of song? Because how could this be anything other than a testament to him? How can this not be a sign? That of all the millions of other sixties songs, they chose to launch tonight's disco with this particular one.

A minute ago, I was buzzing. The beers had worked their magic, loosening me up, and I was enjoying having a laugh with my old friends. Being with Sarah felt okay. Good, even. She looked happy, much brighter than she had before we started dancing, and I found myself thinking that maybe there could be something between us.

But how can there be? Sarah is with Danny.

Listening to this song he loved, I feel a familiar heaviness spread through me, the distinctive tug of shame and guilt.

Instead of going to get drinks, I start to push my way through the crowds eagerly making their way through the bar to the dance floor. I stumble towards the exit.

With an angry shove, I push open the doors and find myself back in the porch where I met Cherub just a few hours ago. The words 'Newcastle UNT' are spray-painted across one wall, while a thick layer of cigarette butts, crisp packets and empty beer cans pool around my feet.

'I'm guessing whoever wrote that took one of your English classes,' I'd said, and Cherub had laughed and kicked a can at me.

I'd felt comfortable, happy, and I try now to pull myself back to how I felt then. I take a series of deep breaths, an exercise Brian taught me the first time I'd sat in his office.

An icy wind burns my cheeks. I pull my collar up around my neck and rub my hands together for warmth. Then I remember Roz's red knitted hat and reach into my pocket, feel its soft wool beneath my fingers, and smile.

It's okay, I tell myself as I pull the hat down over my ears. *Everything is okay.*

'You look like something out of Wallace and Gromit.' A familiar voice behind me.

Sarah pulls the hat off my head, squeezes it in her hands, and laughs. 'Are you okay?' she asks gently. 'I saw you freeze, back inside. I came out to check on you.'

I lean back against the wall of the porch and rake my fingers over my head. Even after all this time I'm taken aback by the length of my hair. I still expect to encounter the brush of stubble I used to feel on my shaved scalp when I was in the army.

'I'm sorry,' she says.

Puzzled, I turn to look at her. 'Sorry?' I ask. 'What for?'

'For what happened at Jenni and Cherub's,' she explains. 'I shouldn't have led you on.'

I knew this was coming, but still it hurts to hear her say it out loud.

Sarah stares at me steadily. She really does have the most startling green eyes.

I look away, at the floor, kick an old crushed can between my feet, anything but look into Sarah's beautiful eyes, as she explains to me the precise reasons why she doesn't want to be with me.

'I mean I wanted to, I really wanted to.'

My face whips round to look at hers again.

She hesitates, searching for the words. 'The thing is . . .' She takes a deep breath.

She wanted to?

'What's the thing, Sarah?' I ask impatiently. I can't help myself.

'Danny.'

As soon as she says his name, my heart sinks.

Danny.

Danny is the reason Sarah and I can never be together. I already know that. It's why I'm out here shivering in the cold, unable to kick back with my mates inside. Because he is my mate too. Why do I keep losing sight of that?

Sarah starts to talk again.

179

'Anyway, I did love Danny. Do love Danny,' she corrects herself. 'It's just that Danny, well, he isn't Danny any more. Not really. And I never felt for him the way I feel about you. I wanted to tell him. Ages ago, when I first got out to Afghanistan. We were already such different people, had grown so far apart. But he was so pleased to see me, I couldn't bring myself to do it straight away. And then, after Fridge . . .'

She pauses, meets my gaze. 'You remember, he started getting anxious. And, well, the time, it just never felt right. And now . . . how can I tell him now? Leave him now?' Her eyes fill with tears.

It makes my heart actually hurt to see Sarah cry, to think of her being scared, or hurt, or lonely. I hold out my arms and pull her towards me.

She buries her head in my chest, and it feels so good. I breathe her in. Every bit of me wants to kiss her, make things better for her. Tell her she's right. Danny isn't Danny. That it's okay for us to be together.

But it isn't, is it? Because Danny *is* Danny.

And she's right. How can she leave him now? I can't be the reason she does.

I pull away. Her face as she looks up at me is so achingly beautiful, her eyes so beseeching, I have to summon all my strength to do what I know I need to do. Say what I have to say.

'But he is still Danny. And you're still his girl.'

I look up at the dark sky. Even the moon seems to be staring down at me accusingly.

I take a deep breath. 'I'm one of the only people alive

who understands what he's been through. What we've been through together. And mates like that are meant to have each other's backs. I promised him once that —'

The doors to the exit fly open and a gang of giggling middle-aged women in miniskirts stagger outside. They stop to stare at us as they light their cigarettes, then totter off into the night, hooting with laughter.

When I look back at Sarah, she has the same expression I used to see on my mum's face when yet another man had let her down, and I hate myself. I always told myself I would be different, I would be better than all those men. But I'm not, am I?

This isn't Sarah's fault. She didn't make Danny ill. And yet here she is, bound to this life with him. I wish more than anything that I could make it better for her. Tell her everything is going to be all right. Hold her in my arms again and never let her go.

I reach forward to brush away a tear from her cheek, and for a moment I let my thumb rest on the curve of her jaw. This is it, I tell myself. All it can ever be.

She is shivering now. I take Roz's hat out of her hands and pull it down over her ears. She looks adorable in it. Irresistible.

'I'm sorry Danny's in a bad place,' I tell her. 'And I'm more sorry than you'll ever know that he hurt you. And that we can't . . .'

There are no more words.

29. Sarah

He doesn't finish the sentence. He leans forward, kisses my cheek and is gone. There is a burst of music and chatter as he opens the door to the bar and then, as it closes behind him, nothing.

Even with Carl's hat on it's bitterly cold. For a minute I hold my face up to the sky and let the freezing gusts of wind blast against my cheeks. Then, knowing Carl will be gone by now, I make my way back inside.

I stand where I watched Carl stand earlier. I was worried for him, but I needn't have been. Carl plainly doesn't need my concern.

I order a shot of tequila, and suddenly Jenni is at my side.

'That's my girl,' she laughs.

I down one and then another, and then I grab her hand and pull her into the middle of the dance floor. I spin around to the beat and lose myself in the sea of heaving, happy bodies.

After a while, Jenni signals that she needs the loo. We make our way off the dance floor, past Cherub – who is pogoing with a gang of shaven-headed lads in leather jackets – and into the Ladies.

'What's going on?' she demands. 'And don't even think about telling me everything is all right. Don't get me wrong, I'm happy to knock back tequilas and dance with you all night long. But I'm curious to know why Carl has gone home early with a face like thunder, pretending he has a headache, and you're drinking shots in a manner that suggests a carefree abandon you and I both know you don't possess.'

She finishes applying her lipstick, then turns to look at me.

'So?' she demands.

So I tell her. I tell her everything.

About the real extent of Danny's illness. About the trip to casualty, and the litany of other injuries, and how many times I've been desperate to tell her but couldn't bring myself to.

About what happened last night. How tired I am of it all, and how much I hate myself for being tired of it because I know it's not Danny's fault.

And then I tell her about Carl. About the drunken near-kiss in her kitchen, and the feelings I've had for him ever since Afghanistan. About how I'd stopped having those sorts of feelings for Danny even before I'd got out there.

Finally, I tell her about the humiliating rebuff I've just received from Carl on the community-centre porch.

She listens to it all without saying a word, other than to occasionally tell whoever is banging on the door to the Ladies to bugger off.

When I finish, she puts her arms around me and holds me for a long time.

'I'm so sorry. I'm so sorry that you've had to go through all of this on your own.'

And hearing her say that makes me cry. Tears of relief.

Relief at no longer having to keep secrets from my best friend. And relief that she hasn't judged me for admitting to having feelings for Carl.

'Come on,' she says, wiping the big black smudges of mascara from under my eyes with her thumbs. 'Let's get you home.'

She leads me out of the Ladies toilets, plucks Cherub from the middle of the dance floor – where he is now swaying to the music alone – and bundles the three of us into a taxi.

Back at theirs, Cherub heats up some oven chips and we share another bottle of wine. Then we dance around the kitchen to 'Young At Heart' until, finally, Jenni declares it's time for us all to go to bed.

By the next morning Jenni has a plan.

She sits on the edge of my bed holding out two paracetamol tablets and a glass of water.

'Right,' she says briskly. 'You have to talk to Danny. And if not Danny, then his mother. You owe him – and her – that much. But, Sarah, you don't owe him anything more. I feel sorry for him, I really do. But you only get one life, and you can't live it in the shadow of someone you're afraid of. He has seriously hurt you in the past. What if he does something really awful to you? Something even worse.' She sighs. 'The fact is, this isn't a healthy relationship any more. You need to explain all that to Annie.'

She pauses for a moment, allowing her words to sink in.

'As for Carl,' she says, changing tack. 'If you want my opinion?'

I swallow the tablets and nod.

'Last night wasn't about him humiliating you. It wasn't even about him walking away from you. It was about him doing the right thing by Danny. The decent thing. Carl's a soldier through and through. He's all about their code of honour to one another.'

Her words make sense, but they offer little comfort.

'He's wracked with guilt for not saving Fridge and Squadron,' she continues, 'and I'm guessing he feels guilty about betraying Danny, in the same way that you do. But, Sarah, no one can say you haven't tried with Danny. No one could have done more. And falling in love with someone else doesn't make you a terrible person. It makes you human.'

'Really?' I ask.

There is a crash next door, followed a moment later by loud wails.

Jenni leaps off the bed. 'Cherub,' she yells, opening the door. 'You're supposed to be minding the boys.' She looks back at me and smiles. 'Really,' she says.

With that she is gone. As the door slams behind her I sink back against the pillow and close my eyes, waiting for the paracetamol to kick in.

Jenni's right. Carl was always honourable and dutiful

in the way he looked out for the others. I know he felt responsible for them all. I saw it after Fridge's death – how much he blamed himself for not being able to protect him. Squadron too.

But there was more to it with Danny. It went beyond a sense of duty. Carl treated him like a younger brother. And suddenly it comes back to me. What Carl said last night.

Something about making a promise to Danny.

What promise?

Afghanistan

2008

30. Carl

One night, when I was getting close to the end of my last tour, Sarah came to see me.

She was due home the following day and was worried about Danny. She didn't know where he was. Would I help her find him?

'I'm going back to England tomorrow but I can't leave without knowing he's okay,' she said. 'I'm sorry to put this on you, but I won't be here and I'm worried about him.'

As she spoke there was rising emotion in her voice.

I swung my legs over the bunk and stood to face her. She looked exhausted; there were bruised purple crescents beneath her eyes, which I'd never noticed before, and her skin was pale.

'When did you last see him?' I asked.

'This morning. We were having breakfast together, but then a message went out on the tannoy for medical staff to report to the hospital, so I had to leave. I haven't seen him since.'

Now that I thought about it, I hadn't seen him all day either, which was unusual. With Fridge and Squadron gone, Cherub was spending whatever spare time he could with Jenni. And Jobbo mostly wanted to be on his own, so Danny and I often hung out together.

We played volleyball or football, worked out in the gym. Sometimes we gamed or watched a movie. We rarely talked, and never about anything significant. All the things we'd seen, all that chaos and danger. Where would we even start?

'How did he seem at breakfast?' I asked Sarah.

'Okay. Maybe a bit more fidgety than usual, and he wasn't eating. But you know how he is – he's permanently on edge these days.'

Sarah was right. Danny was permanently on edge. But then we all were.

Just that morning, five British troops had been killed in double blasts while out on patrol. Three others were killed yesterday by a hidden roadside bomb. Eight dead in two days. I wasn't sure what victory meant any more. But I was pretty sure this wasn't winning.

Sarah stared at me, and I realized in that moment that no matter what I'd told myself that first time I'd met her in the canteen, and no matter how many times I'd reminded myself since, every time she smiled at me, every time we exchanged a glance, even though she was with Danny, I would always have feelings for her.

I knew I could never be more than a friend. But still, I wanted to be there for her, to help her. I wanted to make her feel better. To make her smile.

'Don't worry. He's probably in the gym or caught up in a game of Xbox.'

A flicker of relief crossed her face.

'Are you okay?'

She smiled, a smile that didn't quite reach her eyes,

and nodded. A strand of hair that had worked itself loose from her ponytail fell across her face. I longed to reach out and smooth it back into place.

'Thank you, Carl,' she said.

There was something so touching in the way she said my name, something so trusting in the way she looked at me. Maybe it was because she had come to me for help, had shown faith in me at a time when I had none. Or maybe it was just that I had lost so many people, and so many others were dying every day, that I felt raw, exposed.

Whatever it was, I felt a palpable closeness between us. A connection that seemed so real to me in that moment that I was sure, if I reached out, I would have been able to touch it.

'Right,' I said, clearing my throat. 'You check the mess and the canteen. I'll head to the gym and do a quick circuit of the camp perimeter.' I smiled what I hoped was a reassuring smile. 'Try not to worry. I'll find him.'

She smiled too, and then she turned and began to walk in the direction of the canteen.

For a heartbeat I let myself watch her. Just a heartbeat. But I knew I would always remember how she looked in that moment, still wearing the too-baggy uniform that seemed as if it belonged to somebody else.

It wasn't until she had gone that I realized I might never see Sarah again. Tomorrow she would be going home, and soon Danny would follow her.

They would build a new life together. A life after war.

Setting off to look for Danny, I wondered what that life would look like for me. I couldn't even begin to imagine.

I found Danny sitting alone in the Afghan village. Built as a replica to give us a feel of what to expect when we went out on patrol. At night, deserted, its food stalls empty and bread ovens unmanned, it felt almost ghostly.

'Hey,' I called out to him.

He didn't look up.

I lowered myself down on to the dusty ground next to him. 'Everything all right?' I asked.

His head was in his hands, so that when he spoke his voice sounded muffled.

'Do you ever wonder why us?' he asked.

I shuffled closer to him, put my hand on his shoulder. 'Why us what?'

'Why you and me are still here, when Fridge and Squadron and Caroline and all the others ... while they're gone?'

Luck guilt, they call it. Dumb luck that we survived and they didn't. I wondered about it all the time. Still wished that it had been Fridge who had made it back, instead of me.

Danny's hands were shaking. I thought of something Cherub had said when someone made a joke about the chances of us making it back from our last patrol.

'Probability compression,' he'd said, out of nowhere.

We had all looked at him blankly. 'What's that, Professor?' I'd asked, and everyone had laughed.

'Basically, it means you don't want to be the last bloke to die, so you get more and more superstitious as the tour goes on,' he explained.

It made sense.

'I do wonder,' I answered Danny, covering his hands with mine. 'Especially now, now that we're nearly at the end.'

He looked up at me then, and I could see he had been crying.

'It doesn't make any sense,' he said. 'None of it. But surely it has to mean something, right? That we survived. Somehow we owe it to them to make it mean something. To live a full life. Carl, I so want that life to be with Sarah. It's all I've wanted for as long as I can remember. A simple life, nothing fancy. Just a house, kids, you know?'

Nothing fancy. And yet what Danny was describing was what we all wanted. If we made it back home.

'But she's going home tomorrow,' he continued, 'and I'm scared to be out here on my own. I'm scared that, without her to remind me what my old life looked like, I'll forget. Forget who I am, forget what being normal is. I feel like I'm hanging on by a thread.' He was becoming more agitated. 'And Carl?'

'Yes,' I answered gently.

'What if I don't make it back?'

I squeezed his shoulder. 'You *will* make it back.'

He stared at me, his eyes wild. He looked more scared than he'd ever looked before.

'You'll make it back, Danny,' I said. 'Back home to be with Sarah. I'll make sure of it. I promise.'

It was that simple. Because friendship – love – is simple. It's about putting someone else's happiness above your own. Danny's happiness. And Danny's happiness meant Sarah.

That night, I promised Danny that he would make it home to be with her. That he would have the family life he craved with Sarah. I would make sure of it.

I hadn't been able to save Fridge, or Squadron, or Tom, or Caroline. But I might just be able to save Danny.

So I made him a promise.

Danny became my project.

My mission.

Home

2011

31. Sarah

I pick up the plate of untouched food that sits on the table beside Danny's armchair. A bacon, lettuce and tomato sandwich – his favourite, or at least it used to be his favourite, I don't know any more.

I don't know anything that goes on inside his head. The flashbacks, the paranoia, the anxiety. The uncontrollable rage that makes me too scared to be in the house alone with him now.

Upstairs I hear Annie running a bath. The ever-present radio is burbling away in the background, keeping her company.

'He had a bad night,' was all she said when I called in this morning.

A bad night means anything from nightmares to chronic headaches, dizziness or chest pains.

Poor Annie looked shattered.

'Why don't you have a bath?' I told her. 'I can sit with him for a bit. My shift doesn't start until lunchtime.'

'Danny? Danny?' I urge. 'Can I get you anything else?'

When he doesn't respond, I take the plate into the kitchen, scrape the uneaten food into the bin and load the plate into the dishwasher. I look around the kitchen for any jobs I can do to help Annie out. But everything is spotless, as usual, so I dig my laptop out of my bag and settle down at the kitchen table to scan the news.

There's a story about a suicide bomb in Kabul. I automatically click on the link, drawn in by the photograph of a soldier standing in front of the remains of a burnt-out vehicle.

I scan the headline: SIXTEEN DEAD IN KABUL SUICIDE BOMBING.

Then I start to read the story beneath, about Taliban fighters threatening a bloody wave of suicide attacks and raids against international troops.

And that's when I hear him behind me. Deep, heavy, ragged breaths that turn my heart to stone. I reach forward to close the laptop.

Gently, I remind myself, *no sudden movements*.

But I can tell from his laboured breathing that it is already too late. I know he saw it – the photograph of the soldier standing amid the detritus. The aftermath of a bomb.

I know, too, from the endless medical journals I've read on PTSD and its triggers that Danny's heart will be racing. That when I turn to look at him there will be a film of fine sweat on his forehead. His mind will be in the grip of a flashback so vivid he might as well be the one standing in front of that burnt-out vehicle.

I can't even call up to Annie, because the sound of me yelling may reinforce the threatening and dangerous place his mind has already taken him to.

How could I have been so careless? So stupid.

I think of the 'crisis plan' his doctors discussed with us.

The list of instructions they gave us that Annie painstakingly wrote out in capital letters and stuck on the fridge door. I must have glanced at it a hundred times.

Try to stay calm.

Gently tell him that he is having a flashback.

Avoid making any sudden movements.

Encourage him to breathe slowly and deeply.

Encourage him to describe his surroundings.

The spiderweb threads of hope I glance at every time I open the fridge. As if, by memorizing these instructions, I will be able to help him. Pull him back to the present and take away his pain.

Slowly, I turn around. Danny is pacing up and down in front of the kitchen table.

'Sweetheart,' I say gently. 'It's okay. You're having one of your flashbacks. Let's take some deep breaths together.'

He doesn't hear me. He has disappeared into the dark recesses of his mind, and no amount of gentle encouragement from me is going to persuade him he's not in the Afghan hell where he thinks he is.

But I have to at least try. 'Danny, it's okay,' I say again. 'You're having one of your flashbacks,' I repeat. 'Let's take some deep breaths together. Can you do that for me, sweetheart?'

Even as I say the words I can almost hear the demons in his head mocking me. *Deep breaths*, they scoff. *Is that all you've got to come at us with?*

Danny's head swivels towards me. His eyes are

burning with rage. I shudder to think what horrors those demons are tormenting him with.

'Sweetheart,' I say, slowly getting up from my chair. Danny doesn't move, and I inch slowly, so slowly, towards him. 'That's it,' I say. 'Nice and steady.'

Carefully, I hold a trembling hand out towards him. But when my fingers touch his, he leaps back as if I have given him an electric shock.

His face is so angry. Danny's face. A face as familiar to me as my own, but that is not the face before me now. His grey eyes, once so gentle, burn with a fiery hatred. His chapped lips are curled back, his teeth bared.

For the first time I see that his overlapping front tooth is chipped. How did that happen? When? It seems inconceivable to me that I haven't noticed this before. How could I not know? This man whose face, whose every freckle, every contour, I know by heart.

The slight crook in his nose from the impact against another player during the schools' rugby final we all travelled on the coach to Cardiff to watch.

The pitted chicken pox marks above his lips and on his chin.

The sunken shrapnel scars on his cheeks.

Fleetingly, I think of Carl's face on the night before I left Afghanistan, the night I couldn't find Danny, when I already knew there was something wrong with him. I remember how Carl had looked at me with such exquisite tenderness.

Danny is making a strange growling noise now. He swallows, and then swallows again, as if he has something stuck in his throat. His eyes flick over my face. He looks panicked, frightened.

'Danny,' I try again.

But this just makes him worse. Whatever it is, whatever dark, horrible memory he is locked in, I realize there is nothing I can do but let it run its course.

I feel a deathly calm descend on me.

Agitatedly, Danny rubs his hand down his face and I think of Carl again, his hand on my face just the other day, brushing away my tears as we stood together in the porch of the community centre.

I try to remember the feeling of being safe that comes over me whenever I'm with Carl, and I start to cry. Tears of longing for Carl, but for Danny too. For the man Danny used to be.

I search his eyes, his face, his lips, but I don't recognize anything about the man who stands before me. I tell myself that's for the best, because this is not the real Danny.

The man raising his fist above my head is not Danny. Not really. Whatever happens next, it's not his fault. I've got no one to blame but myself. I should never have opened my laptop. I know what his triggers are, and none are more incendiary than visions of the war he fought in.

Danny's breaths are even shorter now. What is it that he sees? I wonder. What has made him clench his fist above me? It hovers there, as if in slow motion.

My heart is pounding. I don't want this. I don't want any of this any more. I want a life. I want to live.

Fight or flight, I tell myself. *Fight or flight*. I turn to run.

But I don't even make it past the table before he catches me.

The pain blasts inwards from the point of impact on the side of my head, and I feel myself fall, hard, on to the kitchen floor.

There's a strange noise in my head, a sort of high-pitched whining, and the pain is coming from all directions now.

Blinking furiously to try and keep everything in focus, I see something glinting in front of me. It's a small, jagged piece of china, a shard from Annie's broken mixing bowl. I try to reach for it but my arm won't move.

So I lie there, staring at my useless hand lying splayed in front of me, listening to the ringing in my ears.

My eyes search for the shiny fragment of the bowl, but I can't see it any more.

I can't see anything.

Poppy #5

*The smell of the ink. The sound of the machine. The familiar
sensation of the needle brushing against my skin. I thought that
this time, having the last poppy tattooed on my back, I'd feel
excited. Exhilarated, even.*

*But as Barry goes to work there is no adrenaline rush, no
state of welcome catharsis as I let my mind drift beyond the pain
to what brought me here. I'm too agitated.*

*'Everything okay?' Barry asks. 'You seem . . .' he chooses his
words carefully, 'not quite yourself today.'*

*He doesn't say much, Barry, but he doesn't miss much
either. Ever since that night after the dance rehearsal, I've
been questioning what Sarah told me about her and Danny.
That things were over between them before she even got to
Afghanistan. That she'd just never found the right time to
tell him.*

It always seemed so black and white to me. Sarah was with

Danny. So I couldn't be with Sarah. It didn't make me happy, but it did make sense.

But now? Now I'm doubting all of it. Because is it right that she stays with him when she wanted to end things such a long time ago? Is it fair that she's only staying out of a sense of loyalty and obligation because he got ill?

I should have been more understanding. More honest — told her that I felt the same way she did, but I felt honour-bound to keep the promise I made Danny. If only I hadn't been so bloody proud.

'I've been too hard on someone,' I tell Barry. 'I should have been kinder, more honest.'

There's a rustle of paper as Barry adjusts the acetate stencil on my back. Then he switches off the gun for a moment. 'But you still could, right? Reach out to them, I mean, tell them what you just told me.'

Barry turns the tattoo gun back on and I take a deep breath, square my shoulders and bury my head in the pillow again. I listen to the words of the song. Today it's 'Brothers In Arms' by Dire Straits.

Listening to the lyrics as Barry works on the tattoo usually makes me feel better. I wait for the song to transport me back in time to a place before the pain and sadness that brought me here. I wait for the rush of happy nostalgia.

But the lyrics don't bring me any comfort today, because I keep turning over the words Barry just said. About me still having a chance to reach out.

That's exactly what Assami would have said. He actually did say that to me once, when he was telling me about a row he'd had with his brother. It was his wife, Habiba, who made him say sorry.

'She is very wise, my wife,' he told me. 'She understands that men can be proud but that pride is a curse. Never be too proud to reach out to someone, Carl.'

Assami himself reached out to me in a letter, two months after I got back. I'll never forget the words he wrote.

I am devastated. You were all brothers to me. You promised me.

The insurgents – they have scores to settle. It is a matter of honour to them that we are hunted down, but I know that you know this.

So many failed promises. I do not understand. It is hurting me inside that you have turned your back on me and my family. I pray every day that you will come, but still I hear nothing.

I trusted the British one hundred per cent. Why do they take so long? Do they not care? Do you not care either? I feel so betrayed.

Assami wasn't just an interpreter, he also carried out crucial intelligence work for us, listening in on Taliban radio communications so he could warn us about ambushes and hidden IEDs.

Recalling his words now, I feel sick to my stomach. I remember one of the last conversations I had with him in camp. He was about to head into a local village to see if he could pick up any intelligence on the Taliban.

'It's too risky,' I told him. 'Too many villagers know that you work for us as it is. Any one of them could tip off the Taliban. This isn't your job. You're here to translate for us. Not to put your life at risk by acting like some secret agent, trying to find out which patrols they're going to target.'

But Assami shook his head, waved away my concerns. 'I am one of you now. If they target you, they target me. Besides, I know that if and when the time ever comes that I need your help, you will be there for me. The British army will help me.'

The song finishes but Barry doesn't reach out to put another track on. With his usual canny knack of sensing that I might want to talk, he says, 'Just so you know, we tattoo artists, we're like men of the cloth when it comes to listening. Your secrets are safe with us.'

His voice is warm and trusting, and something about having my face down on the pillow – so I don't have to meet his eyes, or risk his judgement on things I should have done better – persuades me to open up.

So I tell him about Assami and everything he did for us. All the lives he saved. And how ashamed I am that after all the promises top brass and the government made, when it came to it, none of us were there for him.

I wasn't there for him.

While I talk Barry picks up the tattoo gun again, but this time I don't register the pain. There is too much adrenaline flowing through me as I tell him the story of what happened to Assami.

How one of the people in his village tipped off the Taliban about where he lived. How at first they taunted him with intimidating phone calls. But then one afternoon they grabbed Assami's son Mustafa, snatching him from where he was playing on the street and bundling him into a car.

I know all this, I tell Barry, because when I first got Assami's letter I went to a reporter who had met us both back in camp. He'd interviewed me about Fridge's death and he gave me his card, told me to get in touch if ever there was anything he could do for me.

'I went to him,' I tell Barry, 'because when I wrote to my old unit they fobbed me off, told me they were doing all they could, that I should be patient. But it's hard to be patient when someone you care about is in danger.'

'I get that,' Barry says.

'He was great,' I tell him. 'The reporter I mean. Really sympathetic. He knew another reporter based in Afghanistan who visited Assami's house and managed to piece together what happened.'

'What about your friend's son,' he asks, 'the one who got snatched? Was he okay?'

'They held a knife to his throat and told him they were going to kill his father for being an infidel and feed him to the dogs. Then they slapped him around and shoved him out of the car while it was still moving.'

'My God,' Barry says. 'They did that to a kid?'

'A kid who was the son of an infidel,' I explain.

'Then what happened?' he asks.

'Assami went to the British embassy. He told them that he had worked for the British army for five years. He told them what had happened to his son –'

'I don't think I want to know what happened next,' Barry says quietly.

I take a deep breath. 'The embassy told him there was nothing they could do. They said that because they had paid him for his services they didn't have any obligation to help him. They told him to move. It must have been around that time that he wrote to me. He knew he was running out of options, and he was desperate to protect his family. That's when he went into hiding. He had been gone only a few days when the Taliban tracked down his brother, tortured him until he gave them Assami's address.

'The next morning, while his brother was still fighting for his life in hospital, masked gunmen with AK-47s arrived in a convoy of three four-wheel-drive trucks outside Assami's safe house. They pulled him from his bed and dragged him, handcuffed, outside into the streets. They wanted to make sure that everyone saw what they did to "spies." Then they shot him.'

My gentle friend with the knowing brown eyes. A man who knew right from wrong, who loved his wife and still read his children bedtime stories. Who wanted them to grow up in a better world and took a chance on us so that they might.

I think of Habiba. Her kind, gentle face. She came to the camp once. Security wouldn't let her past the gate but she insisted on waiting there while Assami came to fetch me. She spoke no English but she held out a basket of cookies she'd baked.

'We make them to celebrate Nowruz, our new year,' Assami explained. 'She says she wants to give them to you personally, to the man I talk about all the time.'

The same man who let him down. Who let them all down.

Unexpectedly, I find myself crying. Barry reaches behind him for a box of tissues but I wave them away. Embarrassed, I swipe my hand under my eyes to wipe away the tears.

Barry gives me a moment to compose myself, then he lays a hand on my shoulder and I feel a swell of affection for this gentle, considerate man.

'We're done, my friend,' he says. 'And I can't think of a more fitting tribute to Assami. To all your friends. Are you ready to see it?'

Standing with my back to the mirror, I study the image staring back at me. The five beautiful scarlet poppies – and the one tiny bud – that cascade down from the top of my shoulders to my waist. The outlines are so smooth, the poppies so realistic, it's perfect.

'D'you mind if I take a picture for my hall of fame?' Barry asks.

He points to the wall behind him. It's covered in Polaroids of his other customers with their tattoos. Other stories to tell. He takes two pictures and gives one to me. I watch as the picture of my poppied back emerges, as if by magic.

'Thank you,' I say, looking at the floor. I'm so overwhelmed by what I am feeling, I don't know what else to say.

I reach for my wallet, but Barry pushes it away.

'Your money's no good today.'

I protest, but he is adamant.

'For all of them,' he says. 'I won't forget them, and I won't forget you.'

32. Sarah

'Can she hear me?'

It's Carl. I recognize the distinctive northern burr in his voice. He sounds upset.

'I think so, pet.' Jenni is using her nurse's voice, soothing, reassuring, kind.

'Can *who* hear you?' I want to ask, but the words won't come. They're floating right in front of me but my mind can't seem to string them together.

My mouth feels dry. So dry. Did I drink too much last night?

I try to open my eyes but, like my tongue, they refuse to work. No matter how much I will them to open, they stubbornly resist.

And then the pain hits me. An intense pounding inside my head and around my eyes. I lie still, hoping that if I stop trying to talk and open my eyes maybe the pulsing agony will go away.

I swallow but the dryness in my mouth, like the pain in my head, doesn't go away. It's too much.

I'm relieved when the darkness comes for me again and pulls me back under.

The soft tread of soles on a polished laminate floor, curtains being swished backwards and forwards against a metal frame, the whir of a machine right by my side.

I recognize the regular rhythm of a monitor beeping in the background, instinctively know the precise sound its alarm will make if any of the patient's vital signs change. The noises are comforting and familiar. It dawns on me that I must be at work.

But why am I asleep in bed if I'm at work? Whose vital signs am I listening to? I don't understand.

Then the pain hits me like a wave crashing into my forehead. My throat feels raw. But this time there is something else too. I'm afraid. I don't know what of. But whatever it is, it's real and it's powerful, and I know I have to get away from it. I let myself sink back into the darkness.

Whatever this is, I'm not ready to face it yet.

His voice is low at first, mumbling even, but then it gets stronger.

It's Carl, and I can tell that he's angry. Really angry. Is that why I feel afraid? Did Carl do something?

The fear is back. I have to tell Jenni to get help. But the words still won't come, my eyes still won't open.

I try to move my hand. If I could just reach out to her, then maybe I could get her attention. The pain is so bad, I gasp. But I can't let myself drift away again. I have to do this. I have to warn Jenni.

My fingers slowly come back to life. I'm about to summon the energy to lift them up, but then Carl lets out a long, shuddering sigh.

'Jesus,' he says.

He doesn't sound angry any more. Just sad. Very sad.

'How could I have let this happen to her?' he says.

My hand immediately relaxes. Whatever has happened to me, it was nothing to do with Carl.

'You didn't,' I hear Jenni say. Her voice is pacifying, but she is upset now too.

'If anyone's to blame, it's me.' Mum's voice. She sounds distraught. 'I was on my way to be with her, but I didn't make it in time. I didn't get to her in time.'

Mum starts to cry, and my mind swims with confusion. Mum would never do anything to hurt me. I want to reach out to her, tell her not to cry, but when I try to lift my head, the pain is excruciating.

I immediately fall back on the pillow, defeated.

'Where is Danny now?' I hear Carl ask.

My eyes spring open at the mention of his name, and suddenly I remember all of it.

His dark eyes.

The strike to the back of my head.

Falling dazed on to the kitchen floor.

Pain ripping through my head. Everything blurring.

Annie screaming my name, begging me to stay with her.

The police, the ambulance. The trolley being pushed down a corridor at speed.

Danny.

It all makes sense now. The sound of a pump delivering liquid into veins. My pump. My veins. My vital signs.

Carl runs his hand through his hair and as he does, he glances towards me.

His eyes light up. 'Sarah! She's awake! Look, she's opened her eyes!'

Suddenly his face is swimming directly above mine. I feel his breath on my cheek.

'Sarah. You're awake. Sarah,' he says, speaking my name with such sadness. 'Sarah, I'm so sorry. I'm so, so sorry. I'm never going to let anyone hurt you ever again.' He reaches down and softly strokes my hair. 'Are you okay?'

Mum and Jenni move to the opposite side of the bed. Mum takes my hand in hers.

She is still crying. 'Thank God,' she says. 'Thank God.'

But I'm not looking at Mum. Or Jenni. I'm looking at Carl. Gently, so gently, he takes my hand in his. 'You're safe,' he whispers to me. 'You're safe now. Everything's going to be okay.'

My eyes are locked on to his and I can't bear to tear them away. I'm too scared to blink, for fear that if I close my eyes, when I open them again he will be gone.

My mind is foggy, my brain blurred, but I absolutely understand that if Carl isn't here, if I lose sight of him for just one second, I won't feel safe any more. And even though I can't speak, I know he understands.

Tears streak down his cheeks. 'I've got you, lass, I've got you now.'

33. Carl

It tears me apart, seeing her in that hospital bed. She looks so tiny, so fragile, I would do anything to swap places with her. For it to be me lying there with my head wrapped in a bandage, my face swollen and bruised.

I deserve to be. I was so caught up in doing the right thing by Danny that I turned my back on Sarah. But what about doing the right thing by *her*? Why didn't I think about that?

I was walking back to the van after getting my latest tattoo – on a high after talking to Barry – when my phone rang.

It was Cherub. No doubt with more instructions from Jenni about my best man duties, I thought.

'Hey,' I said happily.

'Hey, mate,' he said.

I knew immediately it was bad news. I'd heard that tone of voice too many times before. The only question was who.

My thoughts are chasing round and round in my head now. I should have protected Sarah from Danny, and I'm burning with an uncontrollable rage at him for doing this to her.

But Danny's mind is destroyed. It must be, because

the Danny I knew would have struggled to do to the enemy what he's just done to Sarah.

I will make it up to her. No matter what she thinks of me now – and I pray it isn't as bad as some of the things I've thought about myself – I will make it up to her. I will never let him hurt her again.

Jenni and the nurses, even Sarah's mum, keep telling me I need to rest. But there's no way I'm leaving her side. What if she wakes up and needs something. A painkiller or a drink or something to eat? What if she's too hot or too cold? Worse, what if she's scared? Or has a nightmare?

No, I have to be here to protect her, to make her feel safe. So I'm staying here for as long as it takes, watching over Sarah, willing her to get better.

I run a hand through my hair, shifting my cramped limbs in the chair next to her bed, in danger of nodding off. I glance across at Jenni, and Sarah's mum, keeping a vigil on the other side of the bed.

Suddenly I'm aware of the tiniest movement.

Did I just imagine it?

I detect another slight movement, and I lean in to be sure. I dare to hope.

'Sarah! She's awake! Look, she's opened her eyes!'

It's late at night. Jenni has gone back to see the kids, and Sarah's mum has popped home for a shower and a change of clothes.

The poor woman looked exhausted. She's a nice lady. Asked me if there was anything she could get for me.

'I'll get some fruit and some fresh juice for Sarah and one of those chocolate muffins Vihann tells me she loves. And what can I get for you? You must be absolutely starving.'

Her being nice to me made me feel like a fraud. I don't deserve it.

I said as much, but she told me not to be silly. 'You're here for her now,' she said, putting her hand on my shoulder. 'That's all that matters. You promise you won't leave her until I get back?'

I promised.

I think of Assami keeping me company, that long night we watched over Caroline. How he told me about the angels Munkar and Nakir coming to the grave to interrogate the person who has died, to see if they have led a good life.

I won't let them visit Sarah. It isn't her time yet.

I stare at the stitches on her forehead from where she hit the ground with such force she knocked herself out. I can't stand to think about it, about how afraid she must have been, about the moment of Danny striking her.

So even though she is asleep, I tell Sarah a story. A story to occupy my mind, one that Assami used to tell his children. It's about Neem, a half-human boy who must drink a special medicine from a dragon's cave to become whole. Assami told it to me on the way back from a patrol once. It had been a rough night, and my nerves were shot to pieces, but listening to his deep, melodic voice calmed me – as I imagine it must have calmed his children when they couldn't sleep.

Maybe Sarah will like it? Maybe it will calm her too?

So I stroke her hand and tell her about Neem, who not only conquers his fears of the dragon in order to get the medicine he needs but also learns to understand the dragon, and help the dragon, and save the people it's been frightening in the process.

When I finish telling the story, Sarah opens her eyes.

'Hey,' I say, 'you're back with us.'

She opens her mouth to say something but the words won't come. I reach for the glass of water and carefully hold the straw in her mouth as she takes tiny, hesitant sips.

Seeing my look of concern, she smiles, or tries to smile. Only one half of her mouth curls upwards. The other half, the half that must have hit the tiled floor when she fell, is still too swollen to move. Looking at it, my eyes fill with tears.

'I'm so sorry,' I tell her.

When she speaks, it's barely a whisper. 'It's not your fault,' she says.

I shake my head. 'I should have listened to you at the community centre when you told me you'd stopped wanting to be in a relationship with Danny a long time ago. If I had – if I hadn't been so concerned about looking out for him – you might not have gone back to him, and none of this would have happened.'

'You were just looking out for your friend,' she says, her voice hoarse.

'I should have looked out for you. Told you it was okay to leave, if that's what you wanted. Offered to help with Danny. Sarah, I've been such a coward.'

She smiled her crooked half-smile. 'You're the bravest person I've ever met.'

I shake my head. 'Sarah . . .'

I want to tell her that all this time the reason I haven't been in touch is because it was too hard to see her with Danny. That ever since that morning in the canteen, I've had feelings for her. That after listening to Barry I was going to ring her and tell her to leave Danny, but I never got the chance.

I'll regret that forever.

But I can see that she is fighting to keep her eyes open, and this isn't about me or my feelings. This is about Sarah. She's all that matters.

'It's okay,' I tell her. 'You sleep, I'll be right here when you wake up.'

She forces her eyelids open one more time, looks up at me with those beautiful green eyes of hers. 'Tell me another one of Assami's stories,' she says. 'I like listening to you talk.' And then she drifts off.

Being careful not to hurt her, I bend down and kiss her lightly on the forehead. Then I sit back in my chair and start to tell her another story.

34. Sarah

When my head hurts, or I can't sleep, or a vision of Danny standing in front of me, his arm raised above my head, comes back to haunt me, I close my eyes and think of Carl.

I imagine he is talking to me, telling me another one of Assami's wonderful stories. I hear his reassuring northern accent in my head, and suddenly I don't feel anxious any more.

My favourite story is the one about Fatima. Her life is beset with what she thinks are disasters. But after a long journey that takes her through Morocco to the Mediterranean, Egypt, Turkey and China, Fatima realizes that these terrible things that have happened to her are what eventually make her feel fulfilled.

I picture myself, like Fatima, in the bustling souks of Morocco, swimming in the warm blue sea of the Mediterranean, or staring at the pyramids in Egypt. I imagine how amazing it would be to take a tour of the Blue Mosque in Istanbul, or walk along the Great Wall of China.

Whenever I think of myself doing any of these things, Carl is always by my side. We are laughing or swimming, or he is holding my hand, making sure I don't trip, or fall, or swim too far away. Holding me steady. Keeping me safe.

The sound of shrieking wakes me with a start. For a moment I can't place where I am, but then I take in the swirling ocean night light by my side, the soothing blue dolphin wallpaper, and the basket of cuddly toys at the end of the bed.

I am at Jenni and Cherub's house.

In the bedroom next door I hear Cherub roar, and then the sound of his footsteps and more shrieking and giggling as he chases scampering little footsteps across the floor.

My body – which had flooded with adrenaline – relaxes. I listen to the sound of their laughter, and I smile. This is such a happy house. It's why I wanted to come here after I left hospital. I couldn't bear the thought of going home, of being two streets away from Danny's house.

No, there would be too many reminders of our life together.

Of Danny.

I know the police arrested him after the attack, but I imagine he is back home now. Still drunk. Still angry.

At least I assume he is. No one talks to me about him, and that suits me fine. I'm not ready to deal with how I feel about Danny yet. I know he still needs my help, and I will always be there for him. But only when I feel stronger. When I get better.

With my friends I stick to safe subjects like the weather and the kids and the wedding. Jenni, bless her, offered to cancel, but I told her not to be so ridiculous. Getting better for the wedding in two weeks' time is the goal I've set myself.

'For pity's sake!' I hear Jenni's voice on the landing outside. 'Will you lot keep the noise down? Poor Sarah is trying to sleep.' The door opens and she puts her head around it. 'Honestly,' she says, 'the air strip at Camp Bastion was quiet compared to this place. Are you okay? Can I get you anything?'

'I'm fine,' I tell her. 'I like the noise.'

'Well, let me know if it gets too much. I'll go and get you a bowl of soup.'

Lovely, wonderful Jenni. She has taken such good care of me these last few days – and my mum, Jenni insisted she come and stay too.

I can hear Jenni outside my door now, asking Mum if she'd like a bowl of soup too.

My poor mum is in pieces about what happened to me. She still can't look at my face without bursting into tears. 'I should have protected you, darling,' she sobs. 'I should have been there.'

Dad was devastated too. He came to see me in the hospital with a crazily lavish bunch of flowers. He told me how sorry he was. For everything. Not just about what had happened with Danny, but about letting me disappear from his life.

'I've wanted to contact you ever since I heard you went to Afghanistan,' he told me. 'I just never knew what to say – which seems ridiculous now, because now I know exactly what to say, and that is how very proud I am of you. And how sorry I am that this has happened to you.'

He promised he would make it up to me, and he and Mum even managed to have a civil conversation.

'It feels good to finally forgive him,' Mum said to me as we sat in the back of Cherub's car on the drive up here. 'It's time for a new start for all of us,' she said, squeezing my hand.

From the minute we got here, Mum, Jenni and Cherub have guarded me like the Crown jewels. If I so much as put a foot out of bed, Jenni tuts and immediately tucks me back in again.

'Rest,' she orders in her most matronly voice.

'Rest,' my worried Mum echoes at her side.

'Rest,' Cherub says. 'Or Carl will never let me hear the end of it.'

Carl.

He rings every day to check on me. To ask if there is anything I need. Anything he can do for me. Often there will be a dog barking in the background, or Maggie will say something, and I hear a lightness in his voice. Today, when he rang off, I heard him laughing at one of the dogs.

It makes me happy to think of him laughing. It's too painful to picture him sitting next to my hospital bed; his anguished expression, the pity in his eyes as he took in my swollen face.

By the time I was discharged, he looked completely exhausted. No wonder! All the time I was there, day and night, he absolutely refused to leave – insisting on sitting at my bedside.

Like a sentry keeping guard.

35. Carl

Maggie points at her dad's black suit lying on the dinner table.

'Go and try it on,' she orders. 'You can't go to the wedding in jeans.'

She's right. I grab the suit, carefully pick my way out of the kitchen without stepping on Mr Jones, who has taken to falling asleep in the most inconvenient locations – he is currently lying on his back in the middle of the doorway – and head upstairs to try it on.

The suit has been sitting there for nearly a week, but I've always hated shopping and trying on clothes.

The only time I ever bought anything was if I was tagging along on one of Fridge's shopping trips. He'd be posing in front of the changing-room mirror, batting away compliments from a gaggle of assistants, while I'd be praying for a hole to open up and swallow me.

Squadron hated shopping for clothes, too, but only because he was so tall he could never find anything to fit. I smile at the memory of him emerging from a changing room on Fridge's stag weekend in a pair of comically short trousers.

'You look like the Incredible Hulk,' Fridge had laughed.

'You mean buff and muscular with the abs of a God?' Squadron had retorted. 'Anyway, who cares what you think? You're on your stag weekend, and you want to go shopping when right now we could all be in the pub.'

'I don't *want* to go shopping. But you two will never get into a club tonight in what you're wearing now. You dress like a couple of teenage tech-bro nerds. A look which, incidentally, neither of you are remotely handsome enough to pull off.'

Squadron had looked at his sad pile of scruffy clothes on the changing-room floor, and growled, 'Well, don't just stand there, go and find me some trousers that fit.'

God, I miss those two. I ache for their company, their gentle and not so gentle teasing. I long to tell them about everything that has happened. Ask their advice.

I wish they were coming to the wedding too. This is the first party I'll ever have been to without Fridge to back me up. He loved to party. He was always the first person to the bar, the first person on the dance floor. The last person to leave.

Sighing, I look down at myself in the suit. It seems to fit, but I have no idea how it looks. Clothes are strictly functional as far as I'm concerned – one of the great advantages of being in the army was never having to waste a moment's thought on what you were wearing. The welcome anonymity that came with being kitted out, head to toe, in camouflage.

My wardrobe now consists solely of sturdy boots, jeans, a couple of chunky, warm navy sweaters that have seen better days, and a bunch of checked shirts. One uniform swapped for another.

The thought of going shopping without Fridge or

Squadron makes me feel indescribably sad. With luck, I won't have too – the suit looks okay to me – but for once I want to look more than okay. I want to do Jenni and Cherub proud.

There aren't any long mirrors to look at myself in, so I go downstairs to see what Maggie thinks.

She looks up from the kitchen table and bursts out laughing.

'What?' I ask.

'You look like a bouncer.'

I pick my Leeds United bobble hat up off the table and pull it down over her face. 'What would you know? You have no class.'

She pulls off the hat and looks me up and down.

'Does it at least fit?' I ask.

'It fits.'

I head back upstairs and change quickly, feeling relieved to be back in my normal clothes. Then I set off for the farm with the dogs, to chop some wood. My head is bursting with thoughts of Fridge and Squadron.

And Sarah.

Thanks to Maggie, I'm now worrying about looking like a knuckleheaded bodyguard the next time I see her.

Chopping wood. Honest labour. That will calm me down.

Elsa skitters obediently along the frosty lane beside me. Poor Mr Jones, with only three legs, skates along as best he can behind her. He has never seen frost before, and he's struggling to stay upright on the slippery cobbles. I've only just put him down and I'm already desperate to pick him up again, but I'm mindful of the vet's advice to let him make his own way, not to be overprotective.

I still find it hard to look at where his fourth leg should be. It's a good job I'll never know the bastard who did that to him.

'All right, Jonesy,' I say, encouragingly. 'You've got this.'

Mungo, every bit the ex-military dog, marches dutifully behind them both. He's very grand, Mungo, and very serious. It's hard to believe we took him in because the army said he was too skittish to be reliable. I haven't seen a murmur of skittish behaviour.

They were about to have him put down – I read about it in the local paper shortly after I got back from the dance rehearsal. I rang them up just in time and drove straight over to pick him up as soon as Sarah left hospital.

I've been grateful for his silent companionship ever since. Two worn old soldiers together.

Now we've reached the farm, Mungo sits obediently on command.

'Good boy,' I tell him, patting him on the head. 'Look after the rest of the patrol for me.'

Knowing they're in safe hands, I wander into the shed. I grab the axe and a heavy log, and carry them back outside. I place the log in the centre of the old tree stump and adjust my grip until it's just right.

Then I stand up straight, like I'm on parade, and

swing the axe high into the air above me. I love this bit. The moment when I bring the blade down and the log easily splits in two.

Swing. Cut. Swing. Cut.

It's such a simple act, yet so satisfying, because for those few minutes my mind is completely clear of anything else. Not suits or Sarah or Danny or any of the others. I'm entirely focused on my grip, on feeling the arc of the axe as it curves behind me, and keeping my eyes on the exact spot where I want the blade to land.

When I'm done, my back aches like it used to when I'd got back from an exercise, and my mind is in a good place again. I feel tired and content.

I drop off some freshly cut logs at the farm. The farmer is long since dead, and it's just his wife, Ettie, on her own. I know she gets lonely, because she always thinks of another story to tell me about him, or something she needs help with, when I say I need to get going.

Today I stay and chat for as long as I can. I gratefully accept the eggs and freshly made bread she always insists on giving me in exchange for the basket of logs.

'Go on with you now, pet,' Ettie says. 'And mind how you go, it's icy out there.'

Darkness is edging in as I wander down the lane to the cottage. Maggie will have gone home by the time I get back, and I think of Ettie, like me, alone in her remote house.

I've got so good at telling myself that's fine, more than fine, because I have Maggie and Roz and the dogs.

And if that's all that's written for me, then I'll make my peace with that.

But I'm done pretending it's what I want. I want a house that's a home. Where, when I open the door, Sarah is inside waiting for me.

36. Sarah

'Is everything okay?' the hairdresser asks. 'I'm not hurting you?'

Her face radiates concern. It's the same look I've seen on everyone's face since the moment I woke up in hospital.

In a second, Jenni is at my side. 'You okay, pet? Has she hurt you? We don't have to do this.'

'We are definitely doing this,' I tell her. 'Have you seen the state of my hair?'

Jenni forces a smile. 'Go easy on her,' she says to the hairdresser for the third time.

The poor girl looks terrified as she picks up the hairdryer and points it towards my head. You'd think she was handling a loaded gun.

I reach out and pat her arm. 'Honestly, I'm fine,' I tell her. 'Do whatever it takes to make me look presentable.'

She moves behind me, gently wrapping different sections of my hair around a giant curling brush and holding the dryer above it. As she lifts the hair back from my face, I stare at myself in the mirror.

The pale, shrunken image that stares back doesn't look like me. I find myself assessing the reflection in the same way I would a patient.

The fluid retention beneath the left eye has almost

gone. The contusion has progressed from the vivid purple indicative of an angry, fresh bruise to blue – a sign that it's healing. Beneath my right eye, the contusion is already yellow and green. In a few days, it will be gone.

Criss-crossed lines, pink and raised above the rest of my skin, sit squarely in the middle of my forehead. Fibrous structures formed by my body to mend the wound.

The scars are so fresh, they look as if they've been drawn on with a marker pen. Jenni, who carefully took the stitches out yesterday, reassured me that these scars will fade in no time.

If I were treating a patient, I would have said the same thing. I would have told them to moisturize and massage the area for ten minutes a day.

But I know that even if I do this, even if I use the most expensive of skincare oils, I will still carry these scars for life.

My mum cried when she saw me. She thought she was being kind, a couple of hours later, when she said she'd been looking online and there were all sorts of treatments for facial scars now.

She told me about chemical peeling and dermabrasion and laser treatments. 'Micro-needling is meant to be very effective as well,' she said.

My poor mum. She's desperate to help, to put things back to how they were before. To make my scars disappear, so she doesn't have to be reminded of me being hurt – and what she sees as her failure to protect me.

She doesn't understand, none of them do. Not even Carl, who is staying in the same hotel and popped his head around our door a few minutes ago to ask if there was anything we needed.

I watched as he registered my face, then flinched and looked away. It was just a moment. By the time he looked back, he had composed himself. But he couldn't hide the pain in his eyes. Like Jenni and Mum, he blames himself.

What none of them realize is that to me the scars aren't ugly. To me they are heroic. They bear witness to love and loss. The love I once held for Danny, and the loss – because although what he did to me was terrible, it has made it easy for me to walk away. For the first time in a really long while, I feel free.

Suddenly, the room falls silent as the hairdresser turns the hairdryer off and lays it on the dressing table in front of me. She stares at the scars on my forehead, then tactfully arranges my hair to cover them.

I smile and thank her. 'See,' I call out to Jenni, 'I won't ruin the wedding pictures after all.'

Jenni looks up and smiles. She is currently sitting on a chaise longue, soaking her feet in a small tub of soapy water while sipping a glass of champagne, and staring at a chart of nail varnish colours.

'The most beautiful bridesmaid in the world.'

I pad over to the chaise longue in my hotel slippers and sit next to her.

'What do you think?' she asks, holding out the chart. 'Classic nude, soft blue, or lavender?'

'Classic nude,' I say at the exact same time as the manicurist tells her the soft blue.

'It'll make your wedding ring and engagement ring pop,' she adds as she lifts Jenni's foot out of the tub and dries it with a towel before laying it on her lap.

'And it'll be your something blue,' I add.

The manicurist smiles. 'Exactly!'

'Soft blue it is, then,' says Jenni, reaching out and putting an arm around me. 'Now, is there any way you can stop my feet from looking like a pair of old potatoes?' she asks the manicurist.

The woman begins to aggressively file the dry skin on Jenni's heels with what looks like a giant cheese grater, while Jenni pours me a glass of champagne.

'To you and Cherub,' I say, as an excuse to knock back the whole glass. I need something to take the edge off the ordeal of having my make-up done.

I needn't have worried. Like the hairdresser, the make-up artist is considerate, tactful, gentle. And miraculous. When, after forty minutes, she spins me around on the stool to see my reflection in the mirror, for the second time that day I don't recognize the face that stares back at me.

Glossy lips, long, fluffy lashes and smooth, glowing skin. The bruises are hidden beneath concealer and foundation, the scars invisible beneath a carefully arranged sweep of hair.

Jenni comes to stand behind me. 'You look beautiful,' she says. 'Are you absolutely sure you're up to this?'

I nod. 'Absolutely sure.'

She grins. 'In that case, please will you do me up?'

The make-up artist holds out the dress, and Jenni gently pulls it over her head. The hairdresser immediately fusses around, touching up her hair, as Jenni pulls down the sleeves.

It is the most beautiful vintage forties, ivory cream, long satin dress. I found it for her in a specialist shop in London, and it arrived while I was recovering at their house last week. Jenni cried when she opened the parcel and unwrapped the dress, and she has tears in her eyes again now.

'I can't believe you found this for me,' she says, doing up the tiny buttons on the front.

'It's perfect,' I tell her.

It really is. I step back to admire her.

It is everything I could wish for her. Magical and romantic and full of promise, as if somehow its previous owners are whispering to her, willing her to be as happy as they were on their Big Day. Other girls, other times, but filled with the same love and hopes as Jenni.

I reach forward to do up the last satin-covered buttons at the top of her back, then Jenni turns and holds up her hands so I can do up the matching buttons at her wrists.

'What do you think?' she asks, uncharacteristically nervous.

'I think,' I say, 'that you look absolutely stunning.'

The make-up artist is holding Jenni's fur stole. I take it from her, gently drape it across her shoulders and tie the ribbon at the front myself. I think of her brushing my teeth for me while I was in hospital, when I couldn't make it to the bathroom on my own, and am suddenly overcome with emotion.

'I'm so lucky you're my friend,' I tell her. 'I love you.'

'I love you too,' she says, and we both smile.

We have been through so much together – war, death, heartbreak, sadness. So much sadness. But standing here, looking at Jenni in her beautiful wedding dress, I realize I feel hope.

I don't have to worry about Danny being here and being drunk and getting violent.

Or Danny not being here.

Right now, for the first time in so many months, I don't have to worry about Danny at all.

37. Carl

I smile at the sight of her toothbrush sitting in the glass on the shelf above the washbasin. At the shocking-pink hairbrush next to it, matted with long strands of Sarah's golden-yellow hair.

Then I spot her perfume. I take the lid off and hold the bottle to my nose. The unmistakable smell of Sarah, all citrusy and gorgeous. It's so immediate and wonderful, it's as if she's standing right next to me.

And then I see the bottle of painkillers next to a glass of water, and my smile vanishes. I pick it up and turn it over in my hands. The tiny tablets rattle as they ricochet off the orange plastic container.

The pills Sarah has to take because she's in so much pain from being attacked by Danny. An attack that should never have happened – that I should never have allowed to happen.

I poked my head around the door to the bridal suite earlier, to see if there was anything they needed, and she told me she'd forgotten her tablets, asked if I'd grab them for her and held out her hotel-room key card.

The bruising and the scars, they looked so painful still. A bitter reminder of how much I've let her down.

Sarah must have read my mind, because after she

handed over the card she kept her hand on mine and her touch was like magic. For a brief moment everything inside me, all the noise, all the regret, fell silent.

She smiled. 'I'm okay, I promise.'

Staring at myself in the bathroom mirror now, I fear that Maggie was right, I do look like a bouncer. I feel ridiculous.

The new, crisp white shirt feels stiff and uncomfortable, and I don't know what I was thinking buying a real bow tie instead of a clip-on one. There's nothing for it, I'm just going to have to get Cherub to redo it for me.

I hold up the cuffs of my shirt to look at the cufflinks again – cufflinks with my initials on, which Cherub gave me this morning to thank me for being his best man.

It's the most expensive gift anyone has ever given me.

My phone rings, chirping noisily in the hotel bathroom, and makes me jump. It's Cherub. He's downstairs in the lobby.

It's time.

Cherub fidgets anxiously as we wait in the pews at the front of the church.

'You've definitely got the rings?' he asks for the third time.

'I've definitely got the rings.' I smile and put a reassuring hand on his shoulder. Then I turn to the back of the church.

Jobbo, who is posted by the door to signal Jenni's

arrival, nods briefly. I, in turn, nod at Jenni's nephew Maddock, who solemnly nods back and presses 'play' on the CD player.

'She's here,' I tell Cherub, and we both stand.

Then, for all my nerves, for all Cherub's nerves, we both start to laugh as the sound of 'You Sexy Thing' by Hot Chocolate echoes through the high-ceilinged church. I should have known Jenni wouldn't go for the traditional wedding march. There is nothing traditional, nothing ordinary, about Jenni.

Everyone turns to look at her as she walks down the aisle, but my eyes go straight to Sarah. Her beautiful face, dancing in and out of the shadows of the candlelight.

Then Jenni arrives next to Cherub, and there is a loud click as her nephew turns off the CD. Her face, beaming up at Cherub, is bathed in the jewelled colours of the stained-glass windows behind her so that she literally looks radiant.

Cherub grins back at her, and his hands that have been twitching since the minute we left the hotel are suddenly, miraculously, still.

The church is packed – maybe a hundred people or more, all with their eyes trained on the four of us.

I expected to feel nervous. I'm not used to big crowds any more. I'm not used to the attention. But seeing Jenni and Cherub so happy, being aware of Sarah standing so close to me, I don't have anything left in me to be nervous. For the first time I can remember, I'm too busy being happy.

The vicar clears his throat. 'We are gathered here today,' he begins.

Then it all happens very quickly. Before I know it, I'm handing over the rings and Jenni says, 'I do,' and Cherub says, 'I do,' and they promise to love each other for better, for worse, for richer, for poorer, in sickness and in health. 'Till death us do part.'

Everyone claps and cheers as the vicar announces they are man and wife, and tells Cherub he may kiss the bride.

I cheer along with them, because suddenly those words mean everything.

The organ starts up and Cherub and Jenni walk down the aisle. Sarah smiles and slips her hand in mine, and we take our place behind them.

I rub my thumb across her knuckles for reassurance and then we follow the newlyweds out of the church. As we step outside, I notice that alongside the clusters of roses and ivy that make up the arch of wedding flowers over the entrance, there are poppies too.

Bright red, beautiful poppies.

'Look!' says Sarah, happily. 'It's started to snow!'

She takes a deep breath of the icy air and reaches out her hands to touch the snowflakes. But I'm not looking at the snow, I'm looking at her, and I can see that she is shivering. She is wearing a white fur wrap and I reach over to pull it more closely around her shoulders.

I'm hit with a sense of déjà vu; not for something that actually happened, more of a feeling. A feeling I used to have when we were out on patrol in Afghanistan. The urge to make sure everyone had the right kit. An instinct to protect them all. To bring everyone home safe.

Dear God, I whisper silently, *let me keep Sarah safe from now on.*

Up ahead, Jenni and Cherub are supposed to be posing for their official wedding pictures. The photographer is impatiently trying to get them to stand still and smile for the camera, but neither of them is listening.

Jenni is waving her arms around in the snow, while Cherub is laughing and holding out his hand for her, and I think that is the wedding picture the photographer should be taking. The real Jenni and Cherub. They don't need forced smiles or clichéd poses – because just look at them.

The perfect, happy newlyweds.

The chair scrapes behind me as I stand up and tap the side of my glass with a fork. The room dutifully falls silent.

'Those of you who know me know I've always been more a man of action than a man of words,' I say. 'But today is a very special day, and words are called for. So here goes.'

I delve into my pocket and take out the carefully folded piece of paper on which I wrote my speech the very day Cherub asked me to be his best man. I've rehearsed it so many times that the paper is worn at the edges and coming apart at the folds.

'Firstly, I'd like to say how beautiful the bride looks,' I read.

At which point Jenni, already on her way to being very drunk, stands up. 'I really do,' she says, then she curtsies.

Everyone cheers.

'And the bridesmaid.'

Sarah smiles, and there are more cheers.

'Cherub is . . .' I begin.

The room goes silent. Words and letters dance on the page in front of me. I know every word by heart, but these words don't come from the heart. They don't come close to saying what I want to say. I screw up the piece of paper and look directly at Cherub.

'. . . brave and strong and good and generous, and there for you when the chips are down.'

He has his arm around Jenni, and they are both staring at me intently.

I go on. 'I used to pride myself on being all of those things, but lately I've come to see that I'm not. That being strong is about more than brute strength. It's about being the sort of man Cherub is. Don't get me wrong – he does have brute strength.'

Everyone laughs.

'There was plenty of that on display in Afghanistan. I was lucky to have Cherub by my side. He looked out for me. He looked out for all of us. He brought me home. Cherub is so much more than just a good soldier. He's a good man. A good teacher. A good dad. And I know he'll make one hell of a husband . . .' I pause.

The room is completely silent. Even the children are quiet.

'Jenni's pretty amazing too, by the way,' I add.

Everyone laughs as she stands up and does another curtsey.

'All of which is to say, I'm so honoured to be Cherub's best man. I would – I did – trust him with my life. I know Jenni can trust him with hers. I love you both.'

There is a chorus of 'ahs', and I feel myself go red.

'To Cherub and Jenni, and to absent friends,' I say, raising my glass.

Everyone stands up and the room erupts with echoes of, 'To Cherub and Jenni, and to absent friends.'

Before anyone has the chance to sit down, the first bars of 'London's Burning' by The Clash come screaming through the loudspeakers.

'Uh oh,' says Jenni, before downing her champagne in one. 'The DJ's gone rogue.'

A bustling team of staff have moved the tables to the edge of the room, and Eileen – who looks even more orange than the last time I saw her – taps me on the shoulder and tells me it's time for the dance.

I walk over to where Sarah is sitting chatting to an old couple, and I hold my hand out for her.

'Ready?' I ask.

She nods.

'Excuse me,' she says to the old couple. Then she clasps my hand and gets to her feet.

'Are you feeling okay?' I ask. 'Have you taken your tablets?'

'I have,' she smiles and then adds, when I raise my eyebrows, 'really. Let's do this.'

I lead her to the centre of the dance floor. Eileen nods at Jenni's nephew, who has both hands dramatically cupped over his headphones. He takes one off to give her a thumbs up, and the first bars of 'Young At Heart' start to play.

Jenni and Cherub walk hand in hand on to the dance floor, to a round of applause.

I take my jacket off and throw it to the side. Eileen catches it and winks at me, and someone wolf whistles. Then the four of us start to dance in unison and a loud cheer goes up.

Noah and some other kids totter on to the dance floor and start trying to copy us, and then Eileen joins in and a few others too.

I lose myself in the dance, my body twisting and tapping and clapping, and when it finishes, I pick Sarah up and swing her round, and then I immediately put her back down in case I hurt her.

Then Billy Idol's 'White Wedding' comes on, and I'm worried the DJ is going to be in trouble again. I watched Eileen actually clip him around the ears earlier, then stand over him while he switched the song from 'London's Burning' to 'You To Me Are Everything'.

But Cherub just takes his bow tie off and starts pogoing, jumping up and down on the dance floor like a man possessed. Then Jenni joins in too, flinging her arms in the air. I remember her dancing like this in the NAAFI bar in Camp Bastion the night she met Cherub.

243

Her dad starts doing the exact same arm moves, and I realize where she got her dancing skills from.

And there they all are – grannies, soldiers, ex-soldiers, teenagers, little kids – all dancing, laughing and happy. Noah tugs my trousers and I scoop him up and swing him around. By the time I put him down, Sarah has vanished.

I turn to look for her and see a bunch of old army buddies knocking back flaming sambucas. They gesture for me to come and join them, but then I spy Sarah out of the corner of my eye. She's falling into a chair next to the old couple she was talking to earlier.

I make my way over. 'Let's get you out of here,' I say, crouching down beside her.

'I'm fine,' she insists.

But her face tells a different story. She is struggling to keep her eyes open and she is rubbing her temples as if her head hurts. The make-up that has hidden her bruises all day is starting to wear off, and suddenly she looks just as vulnerable as she did when she was lying in that hospital bed.

'That's an order,' I say, but gently, and she smiles and holds out her hand.

I slide my arm around her and lead her into the lobby. She leans into me, resting her whole body against mine, as we wait by the lift.

'Remind me what floor you're on,' I say.

She looks straight ahead and swallows. 'Is it okay if I come back to your room? I don't think I'm ready to be on my own.'

'Of course,' I tell her, helping her into the lift.

We get out on my floor and, still with my arm around Sarah, we walk slowly to my room. I fumble with the key card, swiping it again and again, but my big hands feel clumsy and I can't get the card to work.

Sarah laughs. 'Give it here,' she says, and immediately, effortlessly unlocks the door with one easy swipe. 'After you, Jason Bourne,' she says and laughs again.

I must have heard Sarah laugh before, but I can't remember it sounding like this. Or experiencing this warm, mysterious feeling of joy that is spreading through me, making me want to laugh too.

Laughter. It has been in such short supply for so long. But that isn't what makes the sound of Sarah's laughter so magical.

It's the sound of listening to someone you love laugh.

And I don't ever want it to stop.

38. Sarah

The door closes behind us and we stop laughing. For a moment, we just stare at each other. The pulsating sound of Donna Summer's 'I Feel Love' drifts up from the disco downstairs.

The air between us feels charged, and I barely notice the throbbing in my head that just ten minutes ago felt unendurable.

His eyes scan my face with concern. I've always felt so safe looking into those eyes. In hospital, and before that, on my very first day in Camp Bastion. I feel safe staring into them again now.

'Can I get you a glass of water?'

I nod, sitting down on the edge of the bed while he takes a bottle of water from the minibar and pours me a glass.

'Here you go,' he says, holding it out for me. He takes my tablets out of his jacket pocket, twists the cap and shakes two into the palm of his hand.

His skin brushes against mine as he hands them to me, and a thrill of desire shoots through me. 'Thank you.'

He is still looking at me as I swallow the painkillers, but I don't want him to look at me with concern. I want him to look at me with the same intense longing that I feel for him.

I turn my face away and reach down to undo my sandals.

'Let me,' he says, kneeling down in front of me.

The satin straps are thin and the buckles fiddly in his huge hands, but his fingers as they work are sure and steady. He gently slides the sandals off, then he closes his hands around my ankles and leaves them there. It is as if he is anchoring me to him.

I don't ever want him to let me go. Afraid to meet his eyes, I stare down at the thick carpet, letting my hair fall over my face. I don't shake it away. Carl is so close to me, I feel conscious of the ugly scars on my forehead.

But just as I am thinking about them, Carl reaches up, brushes my hair off my face and tucks it behind my ear. I shake it free. Let it fall over my face again.

'It hides my scars,' I tell him.

Gently, ever so gently, he reaches up a second time, and draws my hair back. But this time he keeps his hand on the side of my head, holding my hair firmly away from my face.

'I want to see your scars,' he says. 'I want to see you.'

As my eyes meet his, I am struck all over again by how incredibly handsome he is. His deep blue eyes, the colour of my hospital scrubs, his crazy expressive eyebrows. His mouth. Without thinking, I reach forward and trace my thumb across his lips.

He kisses my fingers. 'You're beautiful. All of you. Scars or no scars. And you never have to hide them from me. You never have to hide anything from me. All that matters is that you're here. You're safe.'

247

He kisses my fingers again, then he takes the glass out of my hand, gently places it on the floor, and leans forward. He kisses me on my forehead, on my scars.

I think of how the puckered skin must feel beneath his lips and, embarrassed, tilt my head to one side, but he tenderly threads his fingers through my hair and coaxes me back again to face him.

He keeps his hands there, holding the sides of my head for a few moments, before leaning forward and kissing the scar tissue a second time. He kisses my eyelids, the end of my nose and then, finally, just as I am dizzy with anticipation, his lips are on mine.

His mouth feels warm and wonderful, and I close my eyes and kiss him back, slowly at first, but then it changes into something more urgent. A deep, searching, needy kiss. Because Carl is the one. The one who can make me feel like me again. Make all the pain stop.

I want to give myself to him completely.

But then Carl pulls away and rocks back on to his ankles. 'I'm so sorry,' he says. 'Your poor head. You must be in so much pain.'

His face, as he searches mine, is distraught. It's the same look he gave me when he backed away from me outside the community centre, and as he sat by my side in hospital.

He gets to his feet, runs his hands through his hair, his eyes no longer on mine.

This can't be happening again. He can't be pulling away from me again. I can't bear it. 'Carl,' I step towards him.

He backs away. 'You don't understand,' he says.

'Understand what?'

From somewhere deep in his chest, he lets go of a long sigh. 'I'm so sorry. I'm so sorry for all of it. I told myself I was doing the decent thing. I told myself you were Danny's. That night – that night after the dance rehearsal – I never should have walked away. I should have been there for you.' He looks at me again then. 'I was so preoccupied with protecting myself that I turned my back on you, let you walk straight back into his arms. Let him hurt you. I should have protected you from him. Forgive me.'

'If you forgive *me*,' I tell him, reaching up and putting my arms around him. 'For hurting you at Jenni and Cherub's. That night, I wanted to kiss you more than anything. The only reason I didn't was because I felt guilty. I felt guilty about Danny. Guilty for never having felt for him what I felt, what I feel, for you.'

I kiss him. 'It isn't your fault that he hurt me. It isn't really his, either, but it doesn't matter any more. Danny and I are done. I should have been brave enough to end things a long time ago.'

He loops his arms around me. 'You're the bravest person I know,' he says, kissing the top of my head.

I'm not brave at all.

There will never be anyone who means as much to me as Carl.

I can live without Danny. But I cannot live without Carl.

39. Carl

I want her so much it takes my breath away. I lean back to look at her, rub my finger across her scars. And then I remember – my own scars, or sort of scars. I pull away.

'I need to show you something.'

She looks at me quizzically. 'Okay,' she says, slowly sitting back down on the bed.

Suddenly nervous, I pull my bow tie loose and throw it on the back of the chair. I loosen the cuffs of my shirt, fumbling as I unfasten the cufflinks. I put them on the table, then I undo the buttons and throw my shirt on the back of the chair too.

I look at her one more time, then I slowly turn around so that she has a clear view of my back, praying that when I turn back to see her face again, she will still be looking at me like she is right now. That she won't be disappointed. That she won't have changed her mind.

Squaring my shoulders, I stand still. I focus my gaze on the polished wooden hotel door with its laminated fire instructions pinned in the middle. I stare and stare until my vision is blurred.

When I first started having the tattooing done, I didn't really think about anyone seeing it. It was only ever meant for me. It definitely never crossed my mind that Sarah would see the poppies.

What if she hates tattoos? Danny didn't have any – is that why? Not knowing what she thinks is agony. The clamouring voices in my head start up their chatter again.

She hates it. Of course she hates it. The voices shout louder and louder until, after a few minutes, I hear her get up off the bed and walk slowly towards me. She stops. Oh God, she's going to leave.

She must be about to. Because otherwise she would have said something by now, wouldn't she?

She is so close I feel her warm breath on my neck.

Still, she says nothing.

Then her hand is on my back. Her fingers start to map the outline of each poppy, and her touch is like a soothing ointment, healing old wounds. I take a deep breath and close my eyes.

The tips of her fingers work slowly, deliberately, as they trace the shapes of the flowers. Her touch, as she reaches the centre of my back, is so intensely pleasurable that I gasp out loud. I want to spin around and take her in my arms, but I daren't move for fear of breaking the spell.

It's as if, until this moment, nothing has ever truly felt real.

'They're beautiful,' she says.

I feel her hands on my shoulders as she gently turns me to face her. I smile at her with relief, and she smiles back at me.

'Five poppies,' I tell her. 'One for each of them. Fridge and Squadron and Tom and Caroline and Caroline's –' I break off, unable to say the words. 'And Assami.'

I lift her chin so that she is looking straight at me. I look into her eyes. Eyes that burn with the same desire that burns in mine.

Sarah slowly spins me around again, and this time I feel her lips brush against my skin as she kisses each poppy in turn. Every kiss is tantalizingly soft and slow, so that by the time she puts her hand on my shoulder and turns me to face her, my whole body is aching for her.

'They're beautiful,' she says again.

'You're beautiful.'

Sarah walks backwards, leading me by the hand, and sits down on the edge of the bed. Somewhere downstairs George Michael starts to sing 'Careless Whisper'.

We listen for a moment, then Sarah smiles and holds out her arms.

'Come here,' she says.

I sit down next to her and she reaches forward to kiss me. I kiss her back. I want her like I've never wanted any girl before, but suddenly the weight of that longing, the strength of the love I feel for her, makes me pull back.

Feeling her body pressing into mine, I think of her leaning against me for support as we waited for the lift. Her body is still fragile.

'Are you sure?' I ask. 'I don't want to hurt you.'

'The only way you'll hurt me,' she says, 'is if you stop.'

She gets up from the bed and stands in front of me. She pulls the straps of her dress over her shoulders and lets it fall to the floor. Then she just stands there in her lacey silk underwear, looking at me, daring me to make the next move.

I take a deep breath, feel the rush of air being sucked into my lungs, then slowly let it out again. She is unbelievably, exquisitely beautiful.

Getting up from the bed, I step towards her, my heart beating more wildly with every step I take, until it feels like it used to when I was out on patrol, high on adrenaline, and afraid of what might happen next.

I put my arms around her neck, feel the softness of her skin next to mine.

Pulling away slightly, she twists her arms behind her back to release her bra, but I get there first and hold my hands steady for a moment before unfastening it myself.

Then I lift her into my arms and lay her down on the bed. Slowly, I run my fingers up her calves, her knees, her thighs, until I reach the slippery silk of her knickers. I leave them there for a moment, feeling her skin beneath the fabric, before pulling them down and dropping them on to the floor.

I stand, step out of my boxers, then climb on to the bed. Carefully, I lower myself on top of her, and as my body closes over hers, I feel a pull of desire so low and so deep inside my body I ache with the intensity of it.

I've never felt this before. But whatever it is, it's controlling me now.

Looking deep into her eyes, I move a wispy strand of hair away from her face, kiss the scars on her forehead, then the bruises beneath her eyes. Then I kiss her neck, her chest, her stomach.

I keep kissing her until I reach the inside of her thighs. I hear Sarah murmur. I want to make her feel special in a way I never have with any of the women I've taken to bed before her.

With them, I realize, I was only ever going through the motions. Sex was something that was no more meaningful than an exercise drill.

Magazine release.

Pistol grip tight.

I never meant to be a git. I just didn't do intimacy. I never knew how. Never wanted to. But this? This feels easy. This feels amazing.

Slowly, I kiss my way back up her stomach, her breasts, her neck, savouring every moment, before she pulls me towards her, and I mumble how beautiful she is before my mouth finds hers.

The first touch of our tongues is slow and tender. I run the tips of my fingers over her stomach, searching out the contours of her body, and the kissing becomes more intense.

I reach down to touch her, move my fingers between her legs and let them linger at the top of her thighs. I feel her shuddering beneath me and know she is ready.

'Is this okay?' I ask before I slide into her.

She smiles, nods, then bites her lower lip and wraps her legs around me, urgently pulling my body against hers. Her muscles tense. Every bit of me wants to be deeper inside her, to let go of everything. I try to hold myself back, to go slow, but she arches her back and shivers, and when I hear her moan again it's too much.

I move up and down inside her until my brain lets go of all the fear and confusion. For once, my mind cuts me some slack. It makes room for me to focus on feeling good.

Sarah cries out, and as she does, I close my eyes and let the wonderful thrill of release rush all the way through me. And finally, I understand. I understand what it is to completely abandon yourself to someone.

To love someone.

I think of all those hearts I have been careless with in the past. I will never be careless with Sarah's.

Afterwards, I roll on to my back and she lies with her head on my shoulder, one leg flung over mine. Her arm is draped across my chest as if it's the most natural, casual thing in the world. Sarah's arm. My chest.

She is here. In my bed. In my arms. Her hair tangled over my chest.

I breathe her in, the ridiculously lovely smell that is Sarah. I tell myself to remember this, like I trained myself to do as a child when Mum was on good form.

Then I dare to hope that I don't need to control my thoughts, school my emotions, because there will be other nights like this. Nights when I take it for granted that she is lying next to me and that we are together.

She is breathing deeply, her cheeks are flushed.

'There's never been anyone like you,' I tell her.

Because there hasn't.

She kisses me.

Suddenly I'm exhausted, but I'm fighting every urge to sleep, blinking to stay awake. Because never, in all my days on this earth, have I ever come close to feeling as happy as I feel right now, and I don't want it to end.

We lie there for a while, our bodies folded together. Then she reaches up to kiss my cheek before settling her head back down on my chest. She runs her fingers over the scar on my stomach.

'I remember this scar,' she says, reaching down to kiss it. 'I remember changing the dressing . . .' She pauses. 'I wanted to tell you then –'

My mind flicks back to that bleak Christmas morning, waking up to the new reality that Fridge was dead. To Sarah changing the dressing on my stomach. Her fingers as cool and soft as they are now.

'Tell me what?' I ask.

'How much you meant to me, how relieved I was that you survived.'

She rests her hand on my cheek, and I reach up to press my own hand down on top of hers.

'But then the moment passed,' she continues. 'I could tell you were in pain, even though you insisted you weren't, and you were so heartbroken to have lost Fridge, the time didn't feel right to say anything. I checked back in on you at the end of my shift, but you were fast asleep. So I went back to the mess to meet up with Danny, and that's when I saw for the first time that something wasn't right with him.'

A shadow crosses her face, and I kiss her hand.

'The weeks passed,' she continues. 'He got worse and worse, and he needed me more and more. And then Squadron died, and then Caroline. There were so many times I wanted to find you and tell you. But as the weeks wore on, Danny relied on me more. I didn't know how to leave him.' She kisses me on the lips. 'I should have left him. I should have told you.'

I should have told her too. That night before she left the camp, when she came to ask me to look for Danny with her. I should have told her then.

I pull her close and hold her tight.

All that time we've lost. All that pain we could have avoided.

40. Sarah

He didn't sleep for long, and I didn't sleep at all. I just lay there, listening to the distant disco and the occasional whoop and shout of drunken wedding guests staggering about in the corridor outside.

When eventually everything falls silent again, I imagine all the mini dramas being played out behind the closed doors. All those hidden worlds. All those secret midnight murmurings. I wish that everyone could be as happy as I feel now. A new, all-consuming, dizzying happiness that I want the whole world to share.

It feels like a thing of wonder, having Carl lying asleep next to me, what we've just done.

I think of all the times I had sex with Danny. Fumbling teenagers in the early days and, later, illicit trysts on camp. Sex on camp was technically banned, so it could only ever be a rushed affair, snatched in the dark behind tents and trucks and empty hangars.

Danny never touched me like Carl has done tonight. I thought he loved me. I thought I loved him. But the truth is, I've never felt as loved and as wanted as Carl makes me feel.

All those nights in Wales lying next to Danny, unable to sleep, worried that he would wake up, angry and afraid, from another nightmare. Trying to talk to him, to help him, but being forever locked out. They were the loneliest nights of my life.

I don't feel alone any more.

My body is perfectly folded over Carl's. My head on his chest and my knee across his legs. I can feel his breath on the top of my head. I run my fingers up and down his arms.

Across the peaks and valleys of his muscles. Across the hairs and freckles and the deep, smooth groove of a scar below his elbow. I know how he got most of his scars, but I don't know how he got this one.

I can't bear to disturb him but I'm bursting for the loo. I wait for as long as I can, but when I can't wait any longer, I gently lift his arms off me, and creep out of bed.

When I get back from the bathroom, Carl has rolled over on to his side, one enormous arm dangling over the edge of the bed. He looks so peaceful.

I climb back under the sheets behind him. I stare at his back, at the violent red of the poppies that seem to grow out of his skin.

I kiss his back, his beautiful, poignant tattoos, and suddenly he is awake. He turns to face me. He brings his face next to mine and we kiss. A long, wonderful kiss. He wraps his hands in my hair and pulls me closer to him.

My skin fizzes beneath his touch, and I feel a rush of longing that makes me bold. I climb on top of him and guide him inside me. He rests his hands on my hips and I watch his face beneath me, a jigsaw of emotions – of vulnerability and grizzled worldliness, of endearing anxiety and a dangerous wolfishness. All waiting for the last piece, so they can be put back together. Be whole again.

There is longing and intensity – and love too. I can see it in his eyes. There is no going back for us now. There is nothing I will not do, no hurt I will not inflict, if it means I can be with him.

I lean down to kiss him, but he gently pushes me back.

'I want to see you,' he says.

We look at each other for a long moment. I watch his eyes take me in, register the frown of concentration between his eyebrows that have always expressed so much more than the words being spoken.

He reaches a hand up and slowly, torturously slowly, traces his fingers up my stomach until they reach my breast. I watch his fingers move over my skin, feel as it turns to goosebumps and dances with pleasure beneath his touch.

When he starts to circle my nipple, gently massaging it, my groin begins to throb. Then, when I already feel like I might die with pleasure, he reaches between my legs with his other hand.

He is toying with me now, touching me then stop-ping until I can't bear it. I take a deep, shuddering gasp and, as he touches me again, close my hand on top of his to keep it there.

I reach down again to kiss him, and this time he lets me, one hand on the back of my neck, pulling me tightly against him. I push my body on to his, pressing my hips into him.

His breath beneath me is ragged, urgent, like mine, until finally, the most intense sensation of pleasure shivers through me.

41. Carl

Afterwards, she slowly traces over the poppies again. For so long it has seemed impossible that I could be this happy. But here I am, drunk on the sheer elation of being with Sarah.

Sarah, who is so close that I can feel the rise and fall of her chest on mine. Sarah.

'It's so beautiful,' she says. 'They were all lucky to have known you. To have known someone who would do this for them, to celebrate them. You were a good friend, and you're a good person.'

Her words hit me like a physical blow.

I have tried to be. I have tried to honour Squadron and do good. I have tried to be the loyal soldier we all trained to be. But if I was all those things, then how come my comrades are dead. And how come Sarah is lying next to me with a face covered in angry red scars?

Like I said in my best man speech, I used to think I was a good man. But now I'm not so sure.

Sitting upright in bed, I pull away from her and push my fingers through my freshly barbered hair.

'I don't think I am,' I say.

She sits up next to me. 'I don't understand.' She looks puzzled and hurt.

I can't bear her looking at me like that, but at the

same time I can't have her thinking that I'm this great guy. The tattoos were never meant to be a showcase for *me* being a hero.

What a good bloke I am for remembering my friends. Christ, is that what people are going to think? Is that what Sarah thinks?

It was for *them*. It was my way of saying sorry to them for not being there. For not being a good friend.

'If it hadn't been for me,' I tell her, 'things I did, things I didn't do, things I should have done differently, they would all be alive now.'

'That's not true,' she says, reaching out for my hand.

But I brush it away and shake my head. 'It is, it *is* true. For starters, Fridge shouldn't even have been out there. He signed up after me, when the war was big in the news. Ange was furious. Billy was a baby – she couldn't understand why he would leave them. But he got it into his head that it was his duty to the country, but more especially to me.'

Sarah sits up, pulls the sheet around her.

I go on. 'Fridge was working as an apprentice carpenter with his dad, and he would have just got on with his life if he hadn't seen me with all my new army mates, having a great time. "I can't let you take all the glory," he joked when he got back from enlisting. Selfishly, I was thrilled, because it meant that he would be with me. That we would be going on this adventure together.

'But the truth is, I had nothing to lose. I was excited to be running away. But Fridge, he had everything to live for. Amazing parents, a wonderful woman who loved him, and who he loved back, and a baby son.'

Sarah reaches out to take my hand – which is trembling – and this time, I let her.

'Ange was furious,' I tell her. 'She said that it was me who had sowed the restless seed in him. I'd made him think there was adventure to be had out there with his mates, good to be done in the world, when there was more than enough good to be done at home, with his family.

'The day we buried him, I remembered what she'd said. Just before she threw her handful of soil over the coffin, she looked at me, and I saw in her eyes . . . Sarah, she was so angry.'

'But, Carl, that was just the grief talking. You can't possibly be held responsible for what happened to Fridge. I didn't know him for long, but I knew him well enough to know that he was a strong-minded man who made his own decisions.'

She brings my hands to her lips, kisses my fingers.

'Carl, Ange may be heartbroken for losing her husband, but that doesn't mean it's your fault that he's dead.'

My thoughts are spinning now.

Fridge lying dead on the ground.

Ange, the children, Michael and Kathleen, so dignified at his funeral. So gracious and kind to me always.

I've never been brave enough to talk about his death with Michael and Kathleen. Is it too much to hope that Sarah is right? That they think this was Fridge's choice and his alone?

I shake my head. 'Sarah, even if that were true – and I know in my heart that it isn't – there are still all the others who I couldn't save either.'

I need her to know. I need her to know the truth about why I had these tattoos done.

And when I start to tell her, I find that I cannot stop.

42. Sarah

The words spill out of him in a rush. Cupping his cheek, I wipe away his tears but I don't even think he realizes he is crying.

He tells me about the policeman who wasn't a policeman – the sniper who killed Squadron. And the explosion that killed Tom.

I remember both those nights. Shifts where every time the trauma doors opened I was gripped with a terrifying fear that the body lying on the trolley would be Danny – or Carl.

Gently, I try to interrupt, to tell him once again that none of this was his fault, but he immediately closes me down.

'Maybe I wasn't technically responsible, but if I'd stuck closer to Squadron, seen what the shooter was about to do, or been the one to go ahead instead of letting Tom . . .'

He spits out the sentences like machine-gun fire, toxic bullets of pent-up hurt and rage and guilt.

'And then there was Caroline,' he says, and his shoulders stiffen. 'She was pregnant.'

Something inside me goes cold. The tattooed poppy with the tiny bud next to it.

'I've never told anyone that before,' he says as fresh tears slowly begin to fall down his bristly cheeks.

I say nothing. I just hold his hand. Feel the grip of his strong fingers.

People who are dying relax when you hold their hand. My first matron told me that. I have felt it so many times, sitting next to a patient's bed, their hand in mine, while I stroke their palm. As if by magic, their breathing steadies, and their body relaxes.

But Carl's body does not relax. It remains rigidly alert.

I think of poor Caroline. There wouldn't have been time for anyone to hold her hand – not Jobbo, or Carl, or Cherub. Lovely Caroline who only ever wanted to help people, who adored her fiancé and her friends and the dogs she looked after.

'She told me, that morning,' Carl says, pulling his hand away from mine and pressing the heels of his fists into his eyes, angrily wiping away the tears. 'What was I thinking?' he goes on. 'I never should have let her go back to work. I should have told someone. It would have been easy. There are strict rules in the military, banning mothers-to-be from serving in a war zone. They'd have sent her straight home.'

He is right. I was shocked at how many women were sent home from Afghanistan after finding out they were pregnant. Around a hundred. One soldier actually gave birth while I was working out there.

The delivery was such a joy, all of us clamouring to help, to be part of a new life coming into this world instead of watching yet another body being carried out. When a team of paediatricians were sent out from the

UK to escort her and the baby home, a couple of days later, I felt bereft.

No more staring at that beautiful baby boy, at his perfect golden crown of hair, his tiny feet and his fat pink fists as he happily punched them in the air.

Jobbo would never know the joy of staring at his and Caroline's newborn, cradling the baby in his arms, as that exhausted but elated soldier had done. Crying and laughing at the same time at the miracle that lay in front of her.

Poor Jobbo. I talked to him at the wedding reception earlier. He was sweet, as always, with the same kind eyes, but he looked defeated. There was none of the old joy and bounce about him that I remember.

He chatted about his job, told me that he 'couldn't complain', although we both knew that he could. That the awfulness of what life had hacked away from him gave him the right to complain for the rest of time. Later, I saw him standing at the bar alone, drinking whiskey.

I imagine him asleep in his hotel room now, with only the ghosts that haunt him for company. I think of how much worse it would be for him to know, to understand that he has lost even more than he thought.

But even if he knew, he would never blame Carl.

Sweet Carl, who has carried the burden of Caroline's secret for all this time. Who has somehow twisted her and all his other friends' deaths into being his fault.

'Carl, listen to me.' I turn my body so that my face is in front of his. 'None of this is your fault. Caroline, like

Fridge and Squadron and Tom, knew what she was doing. They all knew the risks they ran, understood that the ultimate price of being out there might be their deaths. We all knew that –'

I break off, holding his gaze with mine. Desperate to reach him.

'And Carl, they were all so proud of what they did. Not one of them would have changed anything. Yes, we all have to live with their loss, and that's heartbreaking, but death is the price you pay for war. A war that wasn't your fault, any more than their deaths were.'

He stares back at me, his eyes pools of dark despair.

'But what about Assami? I have a letter to prove that's on me. The others may, have been casualties of war. But the interpreters, they were only casualties because we let them be. We turned our backs on them.'

His voice stutters with anger. He's struggling to get the words out.

'Assami understood he was at risk for helping us. He knew the Taliban would hunt him down to make an example out of him. But he always thought that we'd be there to protect him.'

I think of Assami, and I see his dark eyes – so black he looked as if he had eye liner on – his thick dark moustache and long, frazzled grey beard. He used to drape his arm around Carl protectively and whisper conspiratorially into his ear. Every time he laughed, he threw his head back and clapped Carl on the back.

They adored each other.

'I wasn't there for him, even though he wrote to me

begging for my help. None of us were. We betrayed him. And all the other interpreters. Assami knew by then they would come for him, that it was just a matter of time. Imagine how that feels – knowing you are being hunted down by the most brutal, bloody, unforgiving fighters in the world.'

'I can't,' I reply honestly. 'But I do know that if there was anything, anything at all, that you could have done, then you would have done it. It was the government that didn't do enough to protect them, not the soldiers. Everyone understands how angry you all are that more wasn't done to help them. To bring them and their families over here.'

He looks at me. 'His family, Sarah. His wife and three children. I don't even know what became of them. I would have done anything –'

'I know you would,' I cut him off. 'Carl, these decisions are made by people we'll never know, for reasons we'll never understand.' I kiss him. 'But what I do know is that the people who make those decisions don't have an ounce of your bravery, or loyalty, or goodness. And certainly not your guilt, although they're the ones who should be feeling it.'

He looks pitifully relieved, and my heart fills with love for this decent, honourable man who's been made to feel that he has failed by a system that has failed him.

'I was worried if you knew . . .'

But he doesn't finish the sentence, because I reach forward and kiss him. For a moment he resists, but then he kisses me back. He traces my scars with the tip of his thumb.

'Caroline said this thing to me once about letting down my shield, letting people in. I made a joke of it at the time, but now I know what she meant. She meant this.'

I pull him into me and hold him.

He clings to me and I cling back, holding on tightly to this broken man who has turned his back into a form of self-expression because he doesn't know any other way to explain how he feels about the people he's loved and lost.

Who carries an impossible burden of guilt he does *not* deserve to carry.

Who has been kicked so many times by fate he simply lies in wait for the next blow.

Who thinks because he has never been loved before that he doesn't deserve to be loved now.

He has demolished the elaborate wall he built up around himself, he has trusted me, and I understand now why that has been so hard for him.

I run my fingers through his hair and kiss the top of his head.

I close my eyes and when I do, I see his eyes, the vulnerability in them when he turned to me after showing me the poppy tattoos.

I will never betray that trust. I love him, and I will show him how much he does deserve to be loved.

43. Carl

When I wake up, Sarah is still asleep beside me. For a few minutes I let my body rest against hers, listen to the gentle rhythm of her breathing, and allow myself to dream of what it would be like to wake up like this every morning.

They say love makes you vulnerable. Lying here naked in Sarah's arms, I understand what that means. I have never opened up to anyone like I did to her last night. Never felt like I feel this morning.

There have been other women of course, but none like this. They were only ever possibilities of love. If I'm honest, they weren't even that. Always carefully chosen so they wouldn't want anything more than one snatched night of affection.

Sarah is so much more than a possibility. For the first time ever, I've found myself wanting to talk, really talk, to a woman. I've felt able to be myself. As if being myself just might be enough.

I see how lonely I've always, always been. And how exhausting that loneliness is.

Carefully, I unlace Sarah's fingers from my shoulder and stare at her sleeping face on the pillow beside me. At the dark bruises under her eyes and the vivid pink scars on her forehead.

I couldn't stand to lose Sarah. It's the only way I can square it with what I've done to Danny. Knowing what he did to her – surely, whatever loyalty I once felt for him is cancelled out by his actions?

But then, maybe the reason he is what he is, did what he did, is down to me too. Should I have spotted it when we were in Afghanistan? Should I have taken better care of him?

Last night we talked about so much, but we didn't talk about him. Still, no matter how much I try to block him out, his face keeps creeping back into my consciousness.

Is it possible that I was so destroyed by the deaths of Fridge and Squadron, so desperate to get back on to the battlefield, to wreak my revenge on the enemy who had taken them from me, that I didn't look out for the kid standing right next to me?

I've always told myself that I kept my promise to him – I got him back to Sarah. But I never considered what state I brought him home in. Should I, could I, have been more careful?

I creep out of bed and pull the curtains back a chink to marvel at the silent, glistening white world outside. The snow is still falling, like little feathers floating past the window.

People bundled up in colourful scarves and thick winter coats pick their way along the street below, delighted by the crisp, untouched snow beneath their feet. I long to get out there with them. To lace up my boots and stride across the moors. I know that's the only way I can get my head together. Properly order my thoughts.

Somewhere in the corridor a door opens and closes, footsteps tread quietly past our room.

'What time is it?'

I turn, watch Sarah rub at her eyes, then I pad back to the bed and sit back down beside her. I put my arms around her, kiss the top of her head. I know I should talk to her about Danny but I just can't bring myself to.

Because what if it is my fault? What then?

'Early,' I say. 'It's just gone seven.'

She sits forward and grins. 'Fancy breakfast in bed? I'm starving.'

We order full English breakfasts with extra toast and croissants on the side, fresh orange juice and coffee.

'I've been thinking,' says Sarah, biting into a slice of thickly buttered toast and marmalade.

'It's hard to take you seriously when you have marmalade on the end of your nose.' I laugh, reaching forward to wipe it off.

She wrinkles her nose adorably and I can't help but kiss her.

'I've been thinking,' she says again, 'and I have no idea where we'd start, or if it would even be possible, but could we look into finding out what happened to Assami's family? To Habiba and the kids. And if we find them, maybe there's a way we could bring them over here?'

My heart feels as if it has skipped a beat. Does she

mean it? Does she think that's actually something we could do? How?

Sarah reads my mind.

'I'm not exactly sure how, but I have all this money sitting in an account that I never use. Dad sends me a ridiculously generous cheque every Christmas. Guilt money, Mum calls it, for never spending any time with me. Anyway, I never wanted to use it. It didn't feel like it was mine somehow. But ever since he came to see me in the hospital, I've been thinking about him, about us.

'Dad went to one of those fancy schools where everyone always knows someone who can help. He's a lawyer with lots of powerful contacts. He asked me to give him a chance to help. This could be it.'

I let all this sink in. Sarah would do all this for me. Well, not for me, for Habiba and her children. But yes, for me too.

After Assami died, I had so wanted to look for them myself, but I didn't know where to start. I had no money, no contacts. I talked to the reporter and he told me that without resources, without government backing, it would be almost impossible. But now, with Sarah's dad, maybe . . .

'But it's your money,' I tell her. 'I have some savings, but not much.'

She waves her hands dismissively. 'It's never felt like my money, which is why I've never spent it, but I can't think of a better way of using it. And I don't have to feel guilty about it, because Mum's finally made up with Dad too.'

She takes a gulp of tea. 'In fact, I was actually thinking of setting up some sort of charity to get families in danger out of Afghanistan. Ever since I heard what happened to Assami, I've wondered what happened to his children, to Habiba. I remember that time she came to the camp and brought you biscuits. Caroline gave one to me later, said how lovely she seemed. Carl, what if we can help her? And if not Habiba, then we could at least help other families who are living in hiding from the Taliban. What do you think?'

Excitement floods through me at the prospect of being able to do something for those families. People the rest of the world seems happy to forget. And to be doing it with Sarah too.

'I think it's an amazing idea!' I tell her.

'That's settled, then,' she says, reaching forward and helping herself to another piece of toast.

44. Sarah

Outside, the snow is still falling after breakfast, coating everything in its magic white carpet. Lying in bed with Carl, watching it together, I am overwhelmed by a cosy feeling of belonging. It's as if I'm lying at the warm centre of the universe and no piece of me ever wants to let him go.

His hair, cut specially for the wedding, is as short as it was when he was in the army, but there are flecks of frosted grey around his temples now that weren't there then.

The eyebrows are still wild and unruly, and I can't resist the temptation to reach out and run my fingers over them to smooth them down.

He frowns, making them knit together, and I laugh. Then he grabs my fingers and kisses them.

'We better get a move on,' he grins. 'Cherub said they'd be leaving at about eleven, and I want to give them a proper send-off. I'm going to hop in the shower.'

I follow him into the bathroom, borrow his brush to clean my teeth, and admire his broad, tattooed back as he steps into the shower. Last night he was so nervous about showing it to me, afraid that I might think it was a mistake.

Looking at it now, I think how beautiful it is. How

wonderful it would be to wake up to it every morning, fall asleep lying next to it every night. I feel so blessed and privileged that he trusts me enough to have shown it to me. To be part of such a special secret.

Like yesterday, getting ready for the wedding, witnessing Jenni's excitement, I feel a flush of hopefulness. At the prospect of being with Carl, of having the chance to get to know Dad again, of working with both of them to help the people I couldn't help before.

I'm still haunted by the local Afghans we treated in the camp hospital. Innocent bystanders caught up in a situation beyond their control. We'd patch them up in the hospital as best we could, give them a meal, then send them back to their homes to pick up the pieces of their broken lives.

To homes, I knew, that were often unheated and without running water. What became of them? I wonder. We may have saved their lives, but what sort of life lay ahead for them?

A life like Habiba's and her children's, lived in fear, in hiding from the Taliban? And hiding was the best-case scenario. I couldn't bring myself to imagine the alternative – where the Taliban found them and punished them, like they had Assami.

With Carl and my dad's help, maybe we have a chance to help them. And maybe others too.

Spitting my toothpaste into the sink, I watch Carl in the mirror. Suddenly an image of two mini-Carls, with mad, curly dark hair and twinkly, cheeky eyes, roaring into our bedroom on Christmas morning, pops vividly into my head.

Two chubby little boys in matching checked pyjamas. The image is so vivid, it feels like an actual memory rather than a fantasy. It's as if I already love them.

Danny, before he got ill, talked about us having children. One boy and one girl. I used to listen to him talking about them, but those children never once felt real in the way these two little boys do.

I think of Danny now and a shudder passes through me. A shudder of pity for a life crippled by PTSD. I don't know if he will ever be as happy again as I was last night. As I am right now, buoyed up by the idea of a future with Carl at my side.

He turns, sees me watching him, and smiles. Then he beckons for me to join him. As I open the door he pulls me inside and folds me in his arms.

'Is the water warm enough?' he asks.

But he doesn't need to because, as always, when Carl touches me, my body is flooded with warmth. I nod, and he pushes my wet hair out of my eyes.

My God, this business with my hair. It's something he's now done a handful of times, either holding it back from my face with the palm of his hand, or both hands, or tucking it behind my ears.

Each time he does it, it feels like an act of such intense sexiness and affection – exactly how love and longing should feel – and I know I don't ever want to go back to a life without it.

He starts to hum 'It's Beginning To Look A Lot Like

Christmas'. Christmas is just two weeks away, and suddenly there is only one person in the world I want to spend it with.

'What are you up to, this Christmas?' I ask.

'Nothing much. Just me and the dogs. Although I'm busy training Mr Jones to pull a cracker, so it won't be as tragic as it sounds.'

'Well, I wouldn't want Mr Jones not to have an audience.'

Slowly, his face lights up as it dawns on him what I'm suggesting. 'So you've got room for one more?'

'Of course! I better get a tree. A tree – and Mr Jones pulling a cracker. It's going to be a magical Christmas.'

He tells me it will be the first Christmas tree he has ever bought, and my heart twists with affection for this wonderful man, who has had so little in his life so far. I want to make it up to him, to give him everything.

I picture myself with Carl in the Yorkshire of my imagination, all tearooms and pubs with roaring fires. And hot buttered toast and market squares and Yorkshire puddings and flat caps and chimneys. And dogs. And Carl.

I'm not due back at work until the new year. Vihann insisted. He was so upset when he came to see me in the hospital, he buried his face in his hands, unable to bring himself to look at mine.

I tried to protest at the time. Because the weeks seemed to stretch before me like a cruel prison sentence, with no idea how to fill it. But now, now I never want this moment in time to end.

45. Carl

Time stands still on the moors. It always does. The steep, unchanging paths, the endless expanse of heathered moorland that sprawls ahead of you like the rolling deserts of Afghanistan.

Nothing ever changes. Nothing but the seasons, that is. Today the ground, when I get back from the wedding, is shrouded in snow. A pristine white blanket that sparkles beneath the winter sun, daring me to march across it.

The dogs greet me, happy and excited to have me home. I slip on the warm parka Maggie has decided is hers, pull Roz's red hat over my ears and set off. Sarah gave it back to me this morning and it smells of her perfume. I breathe it in and smile.

'Come on, you lot,' I call to the dogs.

They streak straight past me the second I open the gate.

And off we trek, the freezing ground crunching beneath us. Mr Jones is very suspicious of this strange new powder, cautiously rolling from side to side before standing up with a wobble.

Mungo, serious as ever, stops only to keep an eye on the little dog's antics, while Elsa runs in gleeful circles around the pair of them before dashing up to me and burrowing her snow-covered head into my thigh.

'I know, lass,' I laugh, picking up a clump of snow, rolling it into a ball, and throwing it in front of me for her to chase.

I think of the snowball fights Fridge and I used to have as kids. For once, a happy memory and I bask in it, smiling to myself at the thought of the snowman we once built and dressed in the very parka I'm wearing now. Michael laughed when he saw it, although he made us take the parka inside and hang it on the kitchen radiator.

I must ring him, I think.

Maybe even invite him and Kathleen over on Christmas Day to meet Sarah.

Half an hour later, with Mr Jones nestled happily in my arms, we head back to the cottage. I catch sight of it up ahead of us and it looks as if it's been coated with a white frosting, like something out of a fairy tale. I picture us all cosily inside on Christmas Day.

I think about the sparsely decorated council flat of my childhood. My bedroom with three beds in it long after Adam and Scott had gone. It was always cold, even in the middle of summer.

No wonder I always longed to be at Fridge's. It wasn't just that his house was warm, I realize now. Or that he had a big telly and a climbing frame and a fridge permanently full of food – although all those things were great.

It was that his house had a beating heart. Happy things happened inside it. Things like birthday parties with entertainers dressed up as cowboys, and Easter egg hunts, and Bonfire Nights, and summer sleepouts in the garden in a tent that came free with tokens Fridge collected from boxes of Weetabix.

Could this cottage have a beating heart too, if Sarah was here with me? I rented this place six months ago, when the business took off. I needed somewhere that backed on to countryside, somewhere with space for the dogs to play in, and the moment I walked down the steep cobbled path and saw the yellow front door, the ivy that clothes the front of the cottage like a vest, I knew that I'd found it.

Upstairs, it's nothing to write home about – just two bedrooms and one small box room. Only one – mine – has a bed in it. The others have become dumping grounds for laundry, giant sacks of dog food, and old boxes.

But I wasn't interested when the estate agent showed me the bedrooms. Or the bathroom with its dated avocado-coloured bath. She kept apologizing for the 'seriously dodgy patterned tiles' in there, too, but I didn't care. Because I'd already made up my mind.

I knew I wanted to rent the cottage the minute I set foot downstairs. Because downstairs is amazing.

There's a grey flagstone floor throughout, worn shiny with ancient footsteps, and a big kitchen with a walk-in larder – or 'food cupboard', as Maggie says.

'A larder?' She laughed the first time I called it that. 'Were you born in 1912?'

The kitchen also has an old cream, very temperamental Rayburn that is older than me and makes more noise than a ship's engine room. Depending on its mood, I can watch my soup boil dry in a couple of minutes or resign myself to it not being warm until the next day.

Maggie goes on about how rubbish it is, and it drives Roz mad whenever she comes over and tries to cook something on it. But I like it, because at night it keeps me company.

Ever since my stay in the camp hospital, I don't like the sound of quiet at night. I'm scared of what I may hear. Lying in bed and listening to the old beast whistling and putt-putting with the effort of keeping the cottage warm comforts me.

The living room is just off the kitchen. It has a real fire and one of those Victorian bay window affairs, like a box that juts out from the wall of the house.

One of the first things I did when I moved in was take down the old flowery patterned curtains so I could see the moors, uninterrupted. The views extend beyond the drystone walls to the roofless ruins of an old smelting mill that sits in the top right-hand corner of the valley's U-shaped curve.

The mill is only visible on a clear day. On other days, the views close in with the weather. The rain lashes against the windowpanes and the wind bounces off the walls. Or, like today, snow pads silently down, covering the moors in a giant pearly eiderdown.

I love them all.

Sitting in here with whatever motley collection of dogs I'm looking after lounging around in front of the fire, for all the world as if it was their very own gentle-man's club, I stare out of the window. 'Like Old Father Time,' Roz says.

Then there is the real fire. Maybe it's because our flat was always so cold when I was a lad – who knows? – but I love everything about it. Even going up to the farm on cold mornings to chop wood, then carrying it back down and filling the log basket ready for the evening.

And when darkness starts to fall, there is the whole ritual of scrunching up old bits of paper, pushing them between the logs with a handful of kindling, and then watching, satisfied, as they burst into flames.

Back in the army, the other lads would talk about feeling homesick and I would pretend I felt it, too, but I never did. I never understood what they were talking about. I signed up because, back then, I had no home to leave behind.

But I understand now, because in this cottage, in this living room, I feel safe. I don't have to be on my guard. There's no one jumping out in front of me, no sudden movements that might set me off in a panic.

No noise but the sound of wind soughing in the chimney or wood crackling in the fireplace.

As I open the front door and usher the dogs inside, I hope, with all my heart, that Sarah will love it here too.

46. Sarah

I hate being back in Wales. Everything reminds me of Danny. In the taxi on my way back from the station after Jenni and Cherub's wedding we drove past our old school, his rugby club, the pub, the park, the shops, his house.

I scanned the shadows of each and every one of them, nervously looking for signs of him. It's irrational, I know. Mum assured me that he was staying at home, that Annie's brothers had moved back in with her to take care of him. But still, I can't face the thought of running into him.

It doesn't help that Mum has to work to make up for all the time she took off while I was in the hospital, so I'm alone in the house for most of the day.

'I'll be fine,' I reassured her. 'I'll keep myself busy.' The minute she left the house I double-locked the door.

For the last two days I've done nothing but lie on the sofa and watch back-to-back Christmas movies, but today I'm looking forward to wrapping all the presents I ordered online.

For once, I've spent some of Dad's money. I rang him when I got back to talk about my plan with Carl to track down Habiba. He was so helpful and kind, promised to do everything he could.

When I offered to use the money he's sent me over

the years, I could tell he was hurt that I'd never once spent any of it on myself.

'But that money was for you,' he said. 'It made me feel better to think that at least I could provide for you financially. That you'd have a bit of money to spend on anything you wanted.'

So I decided to take him at his word and spend some of it spoiling the people I love – the people who, in their own way, have all spoiled me.

Firstly, I ordered an enormous hamper from Fortnum & Mason for Jenni and Cherub, as a small thank you for taking such good care of me when I came out of hospital.

I also arranged for two bikes for Noah and Toby, with giant teddy bears sitting on the saddles holding bags of chocolate coins, to be delivered at the same time.

Along with the hamper for Jenni and Cherub, I ordered another one for Carl, filled with brandy butter, mince pies and a Christmas pudding. All the traditional festive treats. For once in his life, I want him to be completely spoiled.

It's due to be delivered on Christmas Eve morning, so hopefully it should be there when I arrive in the afternoon. Plus a case of champagne, and a box full of squeaking reindeers and repulsive-looking pure meat sticks – which the man from the pet shop in town assured me the dogs will love. But that still leaves plenty of parcels to be wrapped. A gorgeous red cashmere cardigan for Mum, as a thank you for not making me feel guilty about not spending Christmas with her. And a giant scented candle that smells of clementines and cinnamon for her sister, my Aunt Lily, who she's arranged to spend the day with in London.

For Annie I chose a gold chain with alphabet charms – the letters 'D' for Danny and 'J' for Joanna, his sister. I bought one for my mum, too, with the initials 'S' and 'E' – for Elizabeth, her name.

I even bought something for Dad, for the first time since he left. A beautiful hardback copy of *Treasure Island* – the book I remember he used to read to me when I was little.

There was something heart-warming about choosing and wrapping a present for him after so long. For Carl too. I run my hand across the soft navy-blue cashmere jumper I picked out for him. Thick cable knit; I imagine it keeping him warm on his dog walks. Along with a pair of red cashmere gloves and a matching scarf that will go with his ridiculous red bobble hat – the one he pulled down over my ears to keep me warm, the day of the wedding dance rehearsal.

But the thing I'm most excited to wrap, the present I'm most excited about, is a box of decorations. Carl told me that this will be the first time he's bought his own Christmas tree, and I wanted to find some beautiful decorations to make it special. These are exactly what I was looking for, without even knowing quite what I had in mind.

I'm about to start wrapping them when the phone rings. A thrill fizzes through me at the thought of hearing Carl's voice. But it isn't Carl, it's Danny's mum.

'Sorry to bother you, love,' Annie says. She sounds frightened.

'You're never a bother,' I tell her. 'What's up?'

'It's Danny,' she says. 'He's gone missing.'

My stomach drops like a stone. 'I don't understand,' I say. 'I thought he was with you?'

Annie starts to cry. 'He was, but I left him with my brother while I went to the supermarket. He went to answer the front door, to sign for a package, and when he went back into the living room Danny had gone. I should never have left him – just like I should never have left you.'

'Oh, Annie, it's not your fault,' I tell her.

But she starts to cry even harder. 'It's so cold out, Sarah, and he's been gone for twenty-four hours. I can't stand the thought of him being out in this weather. Can you think of anywhere he might be?'

I think of all the places where we've found him, drunk and passed out, over the last couple of years. A neighbour's caravan, the rugby club changing rooms, the building site, a skip, the police station.

But none of those occasions had been in weather like this. When I went out this morning to get some milk with Mum, everything was coated in a heavy frost.

'He'll turn up. You know what he's like, he'll have found somewhere to bunk down. Any minute now, you'll get a phone call from one of the neighbours to say they've seen him.'

'But, Sarah, it's so cold outside, no one will spot him

288

because they're all at home, keeping warm. What if he's hurt or trapped?' A sob catches in her throat.

'Don't worry,' I beg. 'I'll head into town, do a trawl of his usual pubs.'

I sit back down at the kitchen table to lace up my boots. Out of the corner of my eye, I see them, glinting in their box: six glass Christmas tree baubles with beautiful hand-painted poppies on their sides.

Before Annie rang, I was feeling so happy. I've never had so many Christmas presents to wrap. So many people in my world to love, to love me, to make life feel less precarious.

And now, just like that, the feeling has gone. In its place is an ominous sense of foreboding.

47. Carl

A bad feeling passes over me, the sort of feeling I used to get back in Afghanistan when we were out on patrol and someone was unaccounted for – someone I had let out of my sight.

'Everything okay with your mum and dad?' I ask Maggie.

She looks up, puzzled.

'Yes, why?'

'Just it's a busy time of year,' I say, aware of how ridiculous I sound, and telling myself to stop being so stupid.

It must be the thought of Sarah arriving tomorrow. Wanting everything to be perfect for her.

'Right,' I say to Maggie, grabbing my keys and coat. 'Time for some last-minute shopping. You okay to hold down the fort?'

'You? Shopping?' she asks incredulously. 'It's a Christmas miracle!'

She's right. I hate shopping. But right now I'll do anything to stop myself from dwelling on the gnawing anxiety in the pit of my stomach.

I ruffle the top of Elsa's head and head out.

Miraculously, the van starts on the first attempt. And even more miraculously, just as I'm pulling into Otley, another van, identical to mine, flicks its indicator on and drives out of a parking space right in front of the market. I reverse in smoothly and turn the engine off.

Maybe someone up there is looking out for me, after all.

First stop, the cheese shop. I spend ages marvelling at all the different colours and sizes and shapes of some-thing I've never given any thought to before in my life – other than to ask for an extra slice of it on a burger.

I don't know what to choose, because I have no idea what Sarah likes. I don't even know if she likes cheese. In the end, I pick out a lump of Wensleydale, which is Fridge's dad's favourite – he always has it in his sand-wiches, with a dollop of Branston Pickle – and some Stilton, because I hear the woman in front of me in the queue tell the shopkeeper it wouldn't be Christmas without it.

Waiting in line to pay, I think about getting to know what food Sarah likes; the idea of us shopping together, like this, then cooking dinner. Not that I've ever cooked before in my life. Imagining this new life with Sarah, I start to feel calmer.

Next, the off-licence – and this time, I know what she likes. Red wine. Pinot Noir, to be precise. That's what she always drinks.

After buying the wine I go to the supermarket, where I pick up fresh coffee, vegetables, a box of satsumas, some nuts and a medium-sized turkey. Then I put the turkey back and swap it for a large free range one.

I'm not even sure this turkey will fit in the oven, or if

the Rayburn will behave itself for long enough to cook it, but I don't want to risk there not being enough. Besides, we can use the leftovers for sandwiches on Boxing Day – like Fridge's mum always used to.

Then I remember that Fridge's mum used to put chestnut and sausage meat stuffing in the sandwiches, and I go back and put some of that in my trolley too. And pigs in blankets that are helpfully stacked in piles next to the stuffing.

And a tub of shop-made gravy. For a fleeting moment I remember the time in Bastion, the day Fridge died, with all of us talking about how to make gravy before we headed out on patrol.

Now, as then, I realize I wouldn't know how to make gravy if my life depended on it. I'd totally forgotten about that conversation, but thinking about it now, it makes me happy to remember Fridge boasting about how good his mum's gravy was – to know he had a happy memory floating about in his head that day.

I stop off at the electrical shop, where I buy some white Christmas tree lights and mulled wine scented candles in tins. And then, on a whim, I pick up a huge bunch of lilies and red berries from a metal bucket outside the florist.

Just as I'm heading back to the van, I catch sight of the small jewellery shop on the edge of the market square. There are a couple of awkward-looking guys, clearly undecided, staring hopelessly at the window. But when I look through the glass, I glimpse what I want immediately. A tiny pair of sparkling star-shaped earrings.

The bell above the door rings out with a festive chime as I enter the shop.

I point to the earrings, and while they're being wrapped, I pick out a silver friendship bracelet for Maggie, too, and a little horseshoe-shaped brooch for Roz, because she always says that horseshoes bring you luck. I get one for Fridge's mum too.

When I emerge from the shop, the ice-white Christmas lights hanging from the lamp posts around the square have been turned on, and there's a brass band playing 'Oh Come, All Ye Faithful'.

There's an old boy in uniform collecting for the Salvation Army, and I think of Cromwell's army gathered here, all that time ago, and the loved ones they had left at home. I wonder how many made it back to them for Christmas.

I stuff a tenner into his tin. When he says, 'God bless you,' I feel like an extra in some cheesy BBC Dickensian Christmas story, but I don't care.

'And you,' I reply happily, and I wish him a Happy Christmas.

On the drive home I stop off one more time to pick up a tree. I pay the extra for a Nordmann Fir, because the lad selling them says their needles won't drop. I pick the bushiest and the heaviest and heave it into the back of the van. Its branches spill over the driver's seat so that, as I drive back to the cottage, I feel like I'm sitting in the middle of a pine forest.

The tree's spicy, woody scent manages to overpower the van's usual aroma of wet dog, and it makes me smile as I drive.

It's the smell of Christmas future, not Christmases past. It's the smell of possibility . . .

This time tomorrow, Sarah will be here.

48. Sarah

The towering inflatable Santa outside Danny's house lurches from side to side and raises his enormous swollen hand, as if in greeting, as I push open the front gate.

When we first moved to Wales, that first Christmas we spent here – and all the others since, apart from the one when we were both in Afghanistan – that enormous Father Christmas has always welcomed me into Danny's home.

Looking at it now makes me feel unbearably nostalgic – for who Danny was back then, who we both were, and for what we had. Because in spite of everything that has happened since, there is no denying how much we meant to each other.

I remember teenage Danny flinging open the door, the first time I came here, the grin on his face as he pulled me inside. I looked around in wonder. We lived just three streets away, in an identical terraced house – yet our homes could not have been more different.

At ours, everything was tasteful and pared back; sprigs of holly carefully arranged in front of the rows of bookshelves, a Christmas candle burning on top of one of the antique tables. A stylish wreath, freshly made by the local florist out of mixed spruce, eucalyptus and ivy berries, was hanging on the front door.

At Danny's house, the wreath on the front door was made of brightly coloured pompoms that he and Joanna had made when they were little. Inside, there were neon reindeers, and stars, and strings of lights and tinsel on every available surface – even the TV had tinsel draped around it.

It was, by some distance, the most welcoming house I had ever set foot in.

On Boxing Day, it felt as if the whole town dropped in for drinks, with a constant trail of happy, tipsy guests squashing themselves into the living room and drinking a glass – or two, or three – of Danny's uncle's famous punch. Helping themselves to food from a table groaning with leftover turkey, reinvented in pies and curries and a coronation salad, along with home-made mince pies and heaving tins of chocolates.

It was our second Christmas, my second as Danny's girlfriend, when Mum splashed out and bought Annie a karaoke machine. She wanted to do something generous for this woman who had made her – and me – feel so welcome.

Annie was over the moon, not that she got her hands on the mic that day, because Danny immediately claimed the karaoke machine as his. He spent all day belting out songs, making people dance around the living room with him, insisting they join in.

Where did he go? My gentle, generous Danny? The boy with the enormous heart who never wanted anyone – me, his aged aunts or his elderly neighbours – to feel left out.

I stare at the front door now. I don't want to give Annie the bad news that I haven't managed to find him. That no one has seen him in any of his usual pubs. The landlords were all sympathetic but busy. No, they hadn't seen him. Yes, they would keep a lookout for him. Yes, they would definitely call if he came in. I smiled and left them to serve the hordes of Christmas revellers pressing against the bar.

A sudden gust of wind catches the inflatable Santa again. I take one last look at his face, pray that his talismanic presence will guide Danny safely home, and ring the bell.

Annie flings open the door, just as Danny did all those years ago. But there is none of the happiness that spilled out from inside her home then.

Her face falls when she sees I'm not Danny. 'Nothing?' she asks.

'Nothing.' I close the door behind me, take off my wet coat and boots.

Annie shakes her head.

'We'll find him,' I tell her.

I think of Carl promising to find him for me, that night in Camp Bastion, and realize just how long it is that poor Danny has actually been lost. Alone in a hostile world, crippled by PTSD.

I tell Annie to put the kettle on. 'You make tea, and I'll make a list of all the places we've checked between us, and then we can start driving around the ones we haven't. Sound like a plan?'

She bites her lip and nods.

'Mum's on her way, she'll help too.' I hold out the present I wrapped for her. 'And this is for you, to put under the tree.'

'You shouldn't have,' she says, and starts to cry. 'I'm so glad you're here. I know we have no right to ask anything of you, not after what happened. Thank you, Sarah. It means the world.'

I hug her. 'I'll always be here for you, Annie.'

She squeezes me tight. Over her shoulder I see Joanna hovering in the kitchen doorway. She smiles when she sees me looking at her.

'Joanna! It's so good to see you. How's university?'

Poor Joanna. She looks wrung out with worry too. She used to be such a wild teenager – all red hair and school detentions and inappropriate boyfriends – but ever since Danny got home, she's gone out of her way not to be another cause of worry to her mother.

She started to work hard at school and got into university to study psychology. Last time I saw her, she told me that she wanted to do her dissertation on PTSD, become a therapist.

'Uni's good,' she says before nervously going back to chewing her nails.

'Right, then,' says Annie. 'Let's make a start on this list. There are some freshly baked Welsh cakes in the kitchen too.'

Of course there are, I think to myself sadly.

The phone rings in the hallway, and suddenly we all freeze.

Annie looks at me. She looks terrified.

I put a hand on her shoulder. 'Go on,' I urge her. 'I'm right here.'

She picks up the receiver. I hold my breath.

'Yes, this is she.'

Every inch of me goes cold.

And then Annie grins.

'Thank God,' I hear her say. 'So he's okay?'

She nods at me and the world that, just a moment ago, felt as if it was on mute bursts back into glorious volume. Much as I hate Danny for what he did to me, and as scared as he has made me feel, I don't ever want anything bad to happen to him. We have shared too much. For good, for bad, a part of me will always love him.

'Where is he?' I ask, the second she puts the phone down. 'Who was that? Is he okay?'

'The hospital,' she says. 'He was brought in drunk, with no ID on him. He's only just woken up and told them who he is. They're keeping him in overnight, for observation, but we can go and visit.'

Even as she says this, she is reaching for her coat. I watch Joanna tug off her slippers and shove her feet into a pair of boots, but I find myself unable to move.

Danny is in the hospital where they took me. Much as I want to know he's okay, I can't . . . I can't go back there. It's too soon.

'Are you okay?' Joanna asks. She has learned to read faces for clues to people's moods. She looks concerned.

Annie spins round, takes one look at me, and gently pulls me down on to the bottom of the stairs. She squeezes in next to me and puts her arm around me.

'I'll get a glass of water,' Joanna says and disappears into the kitchen.

I turn to look at Annie. 'I don't think I can go and see him in there,' I tell her. 'I'm so sorry. It will just remind me . . .'

Annie hushes me, clasps my hand in hers. 'You have nothing to be sorry for,' she says. 'I totally understand.'

Joanna appears in front of us and holds out a glass of water.

The glass trembles in my hand, and when the doorbell rings I jump so violently that water spills on to my legs.

'Sweetheart!' says Mum, sweeping into the hall and falling to her knees in front of me. 'Are you okay?'

Mum and Annie talk, then Mum leans down and scans my face with concern. 'Come on, let's get you home,' she says, hoisting me to my feet.

The last thing I hear Annie say to Mum as we leave is, 'We're fine. Really. You've both already done so much. And besides, for once we know exactly where Danny is. He's safe. We can all get a good night's sleep tonight.'

Outside, the air is crisp and cool. I feel freezing and yet somehow hot at the same time.

'Is everything okay?' Mum asks.

I look at her anxious face and see the same

vulnerability I saw in Annie's. The vulnerability that comes with loving someone. All this time I've been worrying about Danny. But also, without realizing it, I've been worrying about Carl.

Because I really, really couldn't stand to lose him.

49. Carl

The doorbell rings.

It's Roz dropping off the Christmas cake she offered to make for me and Sarah.

'It's incredible!' I tell her as she lifts the lid on the box for me to peek inside.

She blushes. 'Well, hopefully it will taste all right,' she says modestly.

'Thank you, Roz. Thank you for everything.' I step forward to hug her. 'Have you got time for a cup of tea?'

'I haven't, love,' Roz says. 'I need to get to the pantomime.'

'Of course!' I say. 'How could I forget?'

Maggie and Roz have done nothing but talk about the pantomime for the last six weeks.

Roz's son, Archie – Maggie's older brother – is in charge of lighting and has a front-row perspective on all the gossip. This morning, Maggie was telling me they all thought Peter Pan, who is dating Tick-Tock the Crocodile, was having a fling with Captain Hook. At least I think that's what she said. I lost track halfway through and started to think about Sarah being on her way here, this time tomorrow.

'You sure you won't change your mind and come?' she asks.

'I'm sure,' I tell her, unable to think of anything worse. 'I've got a few things to sort out.'

'All right, love, see you soon.'

'Give Peter Pan my love,' I tell her. 'And thanks again. For the cake. It's perfect.'

After she's left, I get myself a beer and take another look at the cake. The white icing is so smooth it could have been done by a professional. But I don't think any shop-bought cake could have been decorated as beautifully as this one.

On top of the icing Roz has drawn a perfect nutcracker soldier, using black icing for his moustache, belt and boots, and yellow icing for his buttons. His jacket is the same vivid red as the tattooed poppies on my back.

And next to him, his yellow-haired dancing doll stares up at me expectantly. Her hair is the same colour as Sarah's, and I can't wait to show it to her tomorrow. I can't wait for her to be here. Full stop.

I move the lilies to one side, to make room for the cake, then I go next door to light a fire. As I sit down I notice a solitary present under the tree.

It's wrapped in brown paper with little green Christmas trees painted all over it. I lean forward to look at the label: *To grumpy Carl, Merry Christmas, love Maggie.*

I smile, take a gulp of beer, and switch the Christmas tree lights on. Suddenly the living room is bathed in a magical sparkle. As the lights fade and brighten, it is as if the tree beneath them has come alive with an illuminated heartbeat of its own.

For the first time, the cottage doesn't feel like a house

any more, it feels like a home. A home with a Christmas tree and a present under it, and a home-made cake in the kitchen.

I'm fizzing with excitement at the prospect of Sarah seeing it for the first time, when suddenly something Maggie said a few days ago comes back to haunt me. She was telling me about Roz staying up late to make the cake and said that her German grandmother had taught her that, in Germany, nutcracker dolls are symbols of good luck.

'They're supposed to protect your home from evil spirits,' Maggie said.

At the time, I smiled. But now I feel uneasy, because one thing life has taught me is that the minute you think you're getting on top of your evil spirits, they have a horrible habit of kicking you in the gut.

The cloud of anxiety I've been fighting all day hovers directly over me again, and I wish Sarah was already here.

A Christmas movie and an early night, I tell myself, *and before I know it I'll be on my way to pick her up.*

I flick the TV on and *Scrooged* is just starting.

The noise from the TV wakes Mr Jones from his sleep.

'It's okay,' I tell him, reaching down to pick him up and put him on my lap.

I scratch his belly, which has been so close to the fire that it feels hot to the touch, and notice that my hands are stained orange – I must have disturbed the dusty orange pollen on the lilies when I moved them out of the way of the cake.

I should go and wash them but I don't want to disturb Mr Jones, and besides, I'm so comfortable and warm by the fire, and I don't want to miss the film . . .

I wake with a start.

The fire has almost gone out, and I feel myself shiver. Not from the cold but from the dream I just had of a crater in the road by a mud-brick wall and blown-out shop windows, and a local man with stained orange hands.

He is a regular visitor in my dreams. Sometimes he is leering at me with his tanned, leathery face and knowing eyes. But mostly it's his hands that haunt me. His orange hands that look startling, next to his pristine white clothes.

The apparition is a reminder of that day – the day of the last explosion I saw in Afghanistan, before coming home for good. I thought the orange dye on the bomb-maker's hands was henna, that it was some sort of religious marking. It was only later that I learned it was dye from the explosives he had been touching minutes before.

In my dream I saw Danny being thrown into the air, landing in a twisted heap on the other side of the road, and I saw his bleeding arms and lacerated cheek. Stared into his eyes, brimming with fear.

At the time, I blamed myself for not seeing the signs that there was about to be an attack. They had been so obvious, when I looked back. How could I have not picked up on them?

The work site we had walked past earlier, where all the labourers had downed their tools and disappeared. No one leaves their tools unattended in Afghanistan – they're too valuable. The son of a prominent local tribal leader had been cycling lazily past us in the bazaar. It wasn't me who spotted him, it was Assami. He was spooked, said he thought the youngster had been marking us out for something, but I told him not to worry.

I should have listened to him.

I should have protected Danny.

The final scene of the movie is being played out on the screen now, where Frank is given a chance to re-evaluate the decisions he has made. A chance to right the wrongs of his past.

It feels like a sign. That I am being given a second chance too. A chance to move on from the past and find happiness with Sarah. And this time, I will not get it wrong.

Before heading up to bed I pour myself a glass of water. As I drink, I stare at the cake.

At the nutcracker doll protecting my house from evil spirits.

50. Sarah

My taxi has just pulled into Cardiff train station when I get the phone call telling me that Danny is dead.

I hear the words. Understand what they mean. But my brain just refuses to take them in. They are too unbearable, too overwhelming. I can't, won't listen.

'But he can't be!' I interrupt his uncle who is still talking and clearly doesn't know that Danny's been found. 'He's in hospital.'

As I climb out of the taxi, I patiently explain what has happened.

'I was there when the hospital rang to say he'd been brought in. Annie and Joanna went to visit him there last night.'

'I know, *cariad*,' he says, a sort of muffled cry catching in his throat. 'But he checked himself out this morning. By the time Annie got there to take him home, he'd already discharged himself.'

None of this makes any sense. 'I don't understand,' I say, 'there must have been a mix-up.'

Danny's uncle is sobbing now. Great, guttural heaves of despair. He takes a loud, deep breath.

'I wish there had been, love. But I spoke to the hospital myself. Danny was hit by a car on his way home. They called an ambulance, but there was nothing they could do. It seems the driver who hit him was still over the limit from a party he'd been to last night.'

I think of the packed pubs I visited yesterday. All those people at the bar, jostling for more drinks.

'Poor Annie had to go in to identify the body.' Danny's uncle is talking again. 'She asked me to ring you, said she couldn't bear to do it herself.'

Identify the body? Oh my God. A terrible noise comes out of my throat that I don't even recognize.

Danny is dead.

It is the news I've been afraid of hearing for so long, but still I'm nowhere near prepared. It is simply too awful to think of Danny being gone. Of never seeing him again.

This man who has lived in my heart for all these years. Who I have loved, admired, pitied, even feared. An ordinary, decent man who used to want ordinary, decent things. Who used to want me.

And then he was sent to fight in a terrible war. And he saw and did terrible things. And those things broke his gentle soul.

And now I will never see him again. Never see his ink-black hair, his grey eyes, his scarred cheeks, his chipped front tooth . . .

How can that be?

I feel sick.

'Oh God, no,' I say. 'He can't be, he can't be.'

Danny's uncle can hardly speak through his tears. 'I know, love, I'm so sorry. I'm so sorry to have to tell you like this. Will you be all right?'

I hear Annie's desperate voice in the background, hear Danny's uncle tell her he's coming.

'I have to go, love –' he says, and the line goes dead.

Annie. I never should have left her and Joanna last night. I have to get back to the house, be there for them.

I hear myself call Danny's name. I call it, again and again, louder and louder, until people stop and turn to see whose name I'm calling.

'Have you lost someone?' the man running the taxi rank asks. The bell on his Santa hat jingles. 'Are you okay?' he asks again, as I stand unsteadily in front of him.

'Annie,' I say. 'I have to get to Annie.'

'Right you are, love,' he says, looking puzzled.

A taxi pulls up behind us, beeping its horn. I watch as the man in the Santa hat opens the door and helps an old lady out of the back.

'I hope you find your Annie,' he calls over his shoulder, his hat jingling again.

Annie. I need to get back.

Dazed, I look around me, at the people crowding into the booking hall and concourse, and catch sight of the giant clock that sits on top of the station roof.

The time! The train to Leeds will just be leaving. Oh God, the train to Leeds!

Carl is expecting to meet me off it. An image of him waiting on a deserted platform swims before me. People have let Carl down all his life. I won't be another one of those people.

It's okay, I just need to ring him, tell him what's happened. Carl will understand, I know he'll understand.

309

Without looking, I reach down into my bag for my mobile phone. But my bag isn't there. I scan the floor around me. My suitcase is still sitting on the ground in front of me, but my handbag – which I thought was on top of it – has gone.

Turning in circles, I search for the bag. But there is no sign of it. I don't understand. I don't understand any of this. My mind is spinning. My bag. My phone. Danny. Carl. Danny.

Danny is dead.

'My bag,' I scream.

The man with the Santa hat turns to look at me.

'My bag . . .' and I start to cry. Loud, hysterical sobs.

The parking bays are full. People weave in and out of the cars, pulling suitcases behind them. The same taxi that had beeped its horn earlier is beeping it again now, angrily signalling for me to get out of the way, but I am frozen to the spot.

I don't know where to go or what to do.

Somewhere in the distance I can hear a small band of carol singers, while all around me passers-by jostle with suitcases on wheels and small children and bags full of presents.

A small boy with hair the same Celtic black as Danny's stares up at me.

'Danny is dead,' I offer by way of explanation.

His mother, clearly alarmed by what I've just said, tugs on his arm and pulls him away.

Danny is dead. The handsome dark-haired schoolboy who captured my teenage heart all those years ago, who made moving to Wales bearable. The young soldier brimming with hope, who craved adventure. And the broken man he became.

He's dead.

Not killed in the war he risked his life for, but mown down by a drunk driver on his way home from a Christmas party. On the one morning we all assumed he was safe, because we thought he was tucked up in a hospital bed.

How can that be? How can life be so cruel?

'My bag,' I wail.

The man with the Santa hat is suddenly by my side, pulling my suitcase and shepherding me through the hordes of people in the direction of two policemen standing at the front of the station next to the carol singers.

'You're the fourth person this morning to have their bag snatched,' the man is saying. 'It makes my blood boil. At this time of year as well. You're meant to think of your fellow man at Christmas, not swipe their belongings when they're clearly vulnerable.' He looks at me. 'If you don't mind me saying.'

He pulls me in front of the policemen, and I listen as he explains what's happened.

He nods his head at me when he finishes talking. 'Good luck,' he says, and then he disappears into the crowd.

The policemen look at me sympathetically and I start to cry again.

When, finally, I manage to explain about Danny, they tell me they'll arrange a lift.

'Don't worry,' one of them says. 'We'll get you home.'

'Thank you,' I say, dissolving into tears all over again.

I'm sitting in the back of a police car, with no idea of how I've got here. It's being driven at speed, but even so the journey home seems to take forever.

I stare at my reflection in the rear-view mirror. At the dark smudges of make-up beneath my eyes.

When I woke up this morning, I felt the same spirit of hope and optimism I'd felt yesterday when I was wrapping all the Christmas presents. After the drama of last night, I thought Danny was safe. Mum was packed and ready to go to her sister's. And me . . . finally, I was going to be with Carl.

Even the bruising on my face had gone. Everything was going to be better now, I'd told myself stupidly.

Looking in the mirror, my scars are bright red and angry. My face looks like I feel.

Danny is gone. Forever. I will never see him again. Never talk to him again.

I should have gone with Annie and Joanna last night, told him one last time how much I loved him.

Why didn't I?

Why didn't I tell him how sorry I was for the way things had turned out for him? For how much he had suffered. For how much he had lost. The life he dreamed of, back home, the life he never got to live. The house he never built, the rugby team he never coached, the children he never had.

I have a sudden image of teenage Danny running off

the rugby pitch, cheeks flushed red in the cold. So full of energy, even though the game was over. So full of love for all his teammates out there with him, for me, for his mum and Joanna, waiting for him in the stands.

I never let go of the thought that, one day, he would be that Danny again. If not for me, then for his mum and sister. For himself.

I trace my finger across the scars that will always be with me, and I start to cry.

I'm sorry, Danny. I'm so, so sorry.

51. Carl

Six hours until Sarah's train arrives in Leeds.

Five hours until I leave to pick her up.

The lost hours between then and now feel like the agonizing hours back on Camp Bastion, counting down the minutes to our next patrol. We'd pass the time in the gym, or playing football or volleyball. There'd be a lot of banter and jokes.

But at a certain point I'd see the bravado slip from everyone's face. Glimpse the fear that burrowed away deep inside us all. The fear that we might not make it back. The fear that our lives would never be the same again.

All of us nervous. All of us pretending not to be.

That's exactly how I feel right now. Except suddenly it occurs to me that, this time, it isn't fear that my life will never be the same again. It's hope that my life will never be the same again.

Because this is everything I've dreamed of, and something I never thought I'd have. The chance to be with Sarah, to share my world with her.

Back then, counting down the hours to an operation, I'd sneak away for a walk around the perimeter to get my head together. And that's exactly what I need this morning. A long walk across my beloved moors.

We set off on my favourite route, the one I'm going to bring Sarah on for her first glimpse of this magical place. I can't wait to share it with her. For it to be just me and her out here, and not another soul for miles around, as if we are the only people in the world.

For once, it's just the four of us – me, Elsa, Mungo and Mr Jones. We skirt around the moorland, bracken crunching beneath my feet. It's not too steep a climb this way – just a gentle uphill trail across farmland – and we keep on going, Mr Jones zipped safely inside my coat, until we reach the ancient burial ground where I finally set him down.

The prehistoric tombs rear up behind him, great mounds of heather-covered earth and stone, and I wonder, like I always wonder when I'm here, about the people buried beneath them, and if they have found their peace.

The rock feels cold as I run my fingers across the Palaeolithic art, the carved circles that run out towards a cup, with a second cup close by. The stone is wet today, which makes the image clearer. It almost seems to move beneath my hand – is it trying to tell me something?

Is it a story, like the tattoo art on my back? And if it is, whose story is it? I hope it belongs to the king and queen of my imagination. I hope the cups were a symbol of them toasting each other. A toast to their happy ending.

Here on this spot of moorland, it could still be the Stone Age. Nothing has changed. It makes me feel insignificant – and the things that have happened to me insignificant – and I find that consoling.

Everything about this place I find comforting. The ancient, wild heathland. The huge sky that stretches for miles around, the silent birds that swoop overhead. Being embraced by the only type of wilderness that manages to quieten the hubbub of my mind.

Feeling calm now, the first part of the exercise is complete. Now for the second part of my Camp Bastion pre-patrol routine. To anticipate what might happen and prepare my kit accordingly.

In other words: make sure the cottage is ready.

On our way back, I stop off at the farm to chop some wood. Enjoying the familiar thwack of the axe, I do an extra load, enjoying the rise and fall of the blade, until there is too much wood to carry and I have to take it home in a wheelbarrow, with Mr Jones perched happily on top.

Extra logs, I tell myself, *so Sarah won't be cold.*

After their long walk across the moors, the dogs sleep while I change the bed sheets and clean the shower. I wash the mugs stacked in the kitchen sink and wipe down the surfaces.

I sweep the floor and make sure there is toilet roll and a clean towel in the downstairs loo. I'd plump the cushions if I had any to plump.

And then, it's time. I want to leave early, in case of Christmas traffic. Grabbing my keys, I take one final glance around the kitchen.

Everything is perfect. The flowers with their curly

white petals and shocking orange pollen are in the middle of the table, and the Christmas cake is in pride of place on the counter.

I flick on the lamp, just in case it's dark when we get back – I don't want Sarah coming into a gloomy house – and then I pull the door shut behind me.

The van struggles to get going in the cold, but eventually the engine turns over and, as I indicate to turn on to the main road into Leeds, I relax in the knowledge that I'm fully prepared for 'Operation Sarah'.

At 1.30 p.m. I park the van.

So far so good.

At 1.45 p.m. the arrival board flutters into life. The train from Cardiff will be arriving at 14.05 on Platform One.

At 1.50 p.m. I wait in line to buy two steaming cups of coffee in red paper cups decorated with pictures of snowflakes and gingerbread men.

At 2.00 p.m. I go to stand by the metal barriers that separate Platform One from the station concourse.

At precisely 2.05 p.m. the train slows to a halt, its high-pitched brakes screeching down the tracks. Doors fling open like collapsing dominoes all the way down the train as passengers pour out.

Within seconds the platform is entirely swallowed up by people. They start streaming through the barriers, their tickets being gobbled up and spat out again, releasing gates that swing open like saloon doors in a cowboy film.

Suddenly I catch sight of a woman with blonde hair and a bobble hat, and my heart leaps into my mouth, but a moment later she turns her face towards me.

She isn't Sarah.

Urgently, I scan the remaining passengers making their way towards the barrier.

None of them are her.

At 2.20 p.m. I glance down the platform one last time. There is no movement of passengers now, just a team of cleaners, laughing at one another as they clatter along with their buckets and their mops.

At 2.30 p.m. I accept it. Sarah isn't coming.

52. Sarah

When I get to Annie's house that bleak afternoon, there is no giant swaying Father Christmas to greet me. Just his deflated, lifeless form with a pair of black plastic eyes staring up at me in despair.

A young policewoman opens the door and shows me into the living room where Annie sits rigidly upright in Danny's armchair. She doesn't see me but stares straight ahead, just like he used to.

I kneel in front of her. 'Annie, Annie . . .'

She looks at me but says nothing.

'Annie, I'm so sorry.'

I put a hand on her knee, and she folds hers over it. With her other hand she reaches out and strokes the top of my head.

'I know,' she says. 'I know.'

And then we cling to each other.

Over my shoulder I watch the policewoman gingerly sit down on the sofa. Her microphone crackles in her yellow jacket. I wonder if it makes her feel safe, being zipped inside that big, cushioned parka with its epaulettes and its police badges and its distinctive Battenberg-pattern fluorescent strips.

If it does, it shouldn't. Because nothing keeps us safe in the end, does it?

The policewoman's eyes move nervously across my face, and her expression settles into one of hopefulness, as if I might be the person with the right words to offer to make this unbearable situation better.

But I have nothing.

Danny's Uncle Meyrick pops his head round the kitchen door. 'Can I get you a cup of tea, *cariad*?' he asks.

'That would be lovely,' I say, releasing Annie and getting to my feet.

I think of all the times I've offered bereaved relatives a cup of tea in the hospital. The universal drink we all reach for in a crisis, clinging to the notion that somehow the familiar hot, sweet liquid will make us feel better. I doubt any of them really wanted a cup of tea, any more than I do now.

Meyrick shuffles back into the kitchen. A few seconds later I hear the tap being turned on, but the running water can't drown out the sound of him crying.

'Where's Joanna?' I ask Meyrick when he returns to the living room, his face red and blotchy, his eyes swollen.

He carefully places a tray of teacups down on the coffee table. Only the police officer reaches for hers.

His eyes dart anxiously to Annie. 'In her room,' he says quietly. 'She's sleeping. The doctor had to give her something.'

Poor Joanna. So distressed that she's had to be anaesthetized out of her pain.

She's always worshipped Danny. When I first knew her, she was a tomboy desperately trying to emulate him. She lived in his hand-me-down rugby tops and spent hours outside, in all weathers, happily throwing a rugby ball to him. When he signed up, she got a buzz cut just like his. And then, when he got ill, she chose to study a subject that she hoped might one day help him.

Now she'll never get the chance.

Poor Annie, too, stunned with grief. Her only son, and the man of the house from the age of six when Alwyn, her husband, died. A routine operation, a new hip to replace the one destroyed by playing rugby. He never woke up from the anaesthetic.

She looks so alone. And small, so much smaller than she appeared last night, even. As if her body, which has functioned for so long in battle mode, has finally given up and now, drained of its adrenaline, is shrivelled and slack with grief. Even her fluffy slippers look too big for her.

She says something, but I don't catch it. When I move closer to her she reaches for my hand and clasps it tight.

I hear her say, 'My sweet boy. How can he be gone?' And then she mumbles the words to herself, over and over and over again, lost in an abyss of private pain.

And so, I stay holding Annie's hand, grieving with her for Danny. All the while, the image of Carl standing alone at the train station, thinking I've changed my mind, gnaws at the edge of my imagination, until I feel the bile rising in my throat and I think I'm going to be physically sick.

When Mum arrives, I ask to borrow her phone and

step into the hall, but then I realize that without my phone I don't know Carl's number. I don't even know Jenni's mobile number, so I can't ring her to ask Cherub for it. There's no point messaging him on Facebook either, as he's already told me he never uses it.

I leave a message for Jenni and Cherub on their landline instead, telling them to contact me as soon as possible. But I know they were due to take the boys to see Father Christmas today, so I don't expect them to be home and checking their phone messages any time soon.

Defeated, I lean my forehead against the wall and let myself cry. Huge, juddering sobs that shake my whole body. I'm done being brave. I'm done doing the right thing. I just want to see Carl. Hold him. Let him hold me.

I don't know how long I stay in the hall like this, but it's long enough for me to feel like I'm no longer fully present. As if my body, entirely hollowed out by grief, has floated away.

I hear a rustle behind me and turn to see the police officer staring at me.

She clears her throat. 'I'm so sorry for your loss,' she says kindly. 'Is there anything at all that I can do?'

And it occurs to me suddenly that, yes, there is something she can do. I explain that I urgently need to speak to someone, but as my phone was stolen I don't have their number.

She looks at me thoughtfully for a moment, then she smiles. 'What about a business number?'

Of course! Carl's dog walking business. The police-woman looks him up online, and I watch as she punches his number into her mobile phone.

She hands it over to me triumphantly, relieved that she has managed to do one positive thing on this otherwise unremittingly awful day.

'I'll leave you to it,' she says tactfully, and disappears back into the living room.

My heart flips when I hear his voice, but it's only a recorded message. 'You know what to do,' he says, in that warm northern accent of his.

Suddenly I'm lost for words. I've been so consumed with getting hold of him, I haven't thought about what I'm actually going to say to him when I do. How do I tell him that Danny is dead? A friend of his, another comrade in arms that he has looked out for, for so long. Even when Danny had no idea that Carl had his back.

Another death to lay at Carl's door. Another reason for him to beat himself up with guilt.

'It's me,' I say in a small voice. 'I'm so sorry I wasn't on the train. Something terrible has happened.' I start to cry, I can't help it. 'Danny's dead. Call me when you get this, so I can explain.'

I hang up the phone and go back into the living room. As I do, the ancient mantel clock chimes. Its low off-key chime sounds appropriately solemn on this sad, sad day.

I glance up and my eyes settle on the photo propped next to it of us all standing together in Afghanistan. Danny, who was still feeling well then, looking young and fit and full of life. Me, looking at Carl, who stares straight ahead at the camera.

Then I look at the clock. I never normally look at that clock. I've always found it creepy. Sitting in its antique wooden box, the one old thing in an otherwise modern, lively house.

But I look at it now.

The time is 2.30 p.m.

53. Carl

Sarah isn't coming.

As if rooted to the spot, I carry on standing by the ticket barrier, pathetically clutching my two paper cups, until finally I am moved along by a guard.

Slowly, I walk back to the main concourse, throwing the full cups of steaming coffee into a nearby bin. But I can't bring myself to leave, not yet. So I take a seat on a bench next to the station's giant Christmas tree.

As I sit down I feel my mobile phone in my pocket. My heart leaps pathetically at the possibility that if I look at it there will be a message from Sarah. A simple explanation for her missing the train, a mishap that we'll laugh about later.

There is no message.

A sea of passengers spill out from the platforms into the station concourse. They pass by me, and I stare at their faces splitting into smiles as they see their loved ones waiting for them. Their worlds are lighting up as mine grows dark.

It's bad enough to consider that she's changed her mind. That she doesn't want to be with me. But what if it's not that? What if something bad has happened to her? What if Danny has hurt her again?

I stare at the Christmas tree, at its dancing baubles and bright lights, and think of my own tree at home. The sadness, the loneliness is the same as when I was a little boy watching Mum go out for the evening. Knowing that she wouldn't be back before I fell asleep, even though she said she would.

It's always going to be like this from now on, isn't it?

The world, which just twenty-four hours earlier seemed to finally have a place for me in it, feels heavy and dark again, just like it used to then.

'Everything all right, lad?' It's the same guard who ushered me along from the platform earlier. 'You've been sitting there a while.'

He looks tired, his eyes sunken, defeated by age. Or loneliness perhaps?

There's something about the sympathy in his voice, it's just too much. I fight an overwhelming urge to cry.

'Yes, I'm fine,' I say, springing up from the bench. 'Just leaving. Thank you.'

'You take care of yourself now,' I hear him call after me.

When I get back to the van there is a parking ticket on the windscreen, and I almost want to laugh. Of course there's a bloody ticket on it. What did I expect?

That Sarah and I would live happily ever after? When has anything ever worked out like that for me?

I snatch the ticket from behind the windscreen wipers and scrunch it into a ball. 'Fuck. *Fuck*. *FUCKKKK*,' I scream before tossing it on to the pavement.

A woman walking past with a little girl grabs the girl's hand and scowls at me.

'Sorry,' I call after them.

I climb into the van and my phone buzzes to let me know I've got a message. I look at the time the message was left – 2.28 p.m. I mustn't have had a signal in the train station. Maybe there's a simple explanation, after all. Thank goodness I hadn't already left – she's probably on the next train.

I hit 'play'. I listen to Sarah's message. I hear the sound of her crying, and my body goes rigid as I listen to what she has to say.

Afterwards, I sit staring at the hordes of Christmas shoppers weaving in and out of the crowds on the pavement up ahead of me, eager to get to wherever it is they need to be.

But I have nowhere to be. Nowhere to go. So I stay, I stay sitting, silent and immobile, until it's so cold in the van that my hands are numb and I can see my breath in front of me.

A long while later, I turn on the ignition. I start to drive, automatically retracing the route I took just a few hours ago, when the world looked bright and everything still felt possible. The same roads feel dark now. They are leading me nowhere.

The radio has been burbling away without me listening, but now there is a song I can't ignore. 'Stay Another Day,' blasts through the speakers, taunting me. It's the song Danny had been singing in the tent, the day Fridge died.

I pull over to the side of the road, bang my hands hard into the steering wheel, then I let my head fall forward and start to cry.

I cry for my sixth lost friend. I cry for everything he went through out there, and everything he went through when he came home. I cry for the future he was so desperate to make it back for but never got to see. I cry for the hurt he caused Sarah. And I cry with shame for the feelings I've let myself have for her.

It's dark when I let myself back into the cottage, but I don't turn the Christmas lights on. I don't turn any lights on. And I don't go mad, greeting the dogs enthusiastically, like I normally do. They all stare at me, a row of puzzled eyes.

I sit down at the kitchen table, and Elsa lays her head on my knee and sighs.

My phone pings. I take it out of my pocket and put it on silent. Then I open one of the bottles of red wine I bought to drink with Sarah. I take a tumbler from the draining board and fill it halfway. Then I pick the bottle up again and fill it to the top.

I down it in one. Then I pour myself another, and another, until the bottle is empty.

I stand up to get another bottle, but as I reach across the kitchen counter for it I catch sight of the soldier on the Christmas cake.

His eyes, in my drunken state, blur and then come sharply back into focus again. It's as if he's judging me, and I feel a sudden rush of pure rage, like on those days in Afghanistan when I learned my friends had died.

I judged myself then, for not being there for them, just like I haven't been there for Danny. And now he's gone too. I don't want to listen to any of Sarah's messages, because I know she'll tell me Danny's death had nothing to do with me.

But my heart, my conscience, every fibre of my being, tells me otherwise.

The icing-sugar soldier knows it. He knows how many people I've let down. He's not here to protect my house from evil spirits. How can he, when the evil spirit is me?

I can't stand it. I pick up the cake and hurl it at the wall.

For a moment it settles where it lands, glued to the wall, unmoving. Then I watch, grimly fascinated, as the soldier's face falls apart.

'Can't stare at me now, can you?' I mumble before pouring myself another glass.

I knock it back, then stare as the disfigured chunks of the nutcracker soldier's face break loose and start to slither slowly down the wall, until finally it all comes away in one ugly piece and crashes to the floor.

I know how and where I'm going to do it. And it's okay. I'm ready. Because even though I'm not sure that I want to be dead, I *am* sure that I don't want to be alive.

If I'd never known what it was like to have the door opened, to be given a glimpse of another life, and to step inside, I might have been all right. I might have lived the rest of my life on the outskirts, as a spectator. Gone back to how it always was.

But Sarah opened the door, and I don't know how to close it. I don't know how to live the rest of my life without her. I don't know how to live the rest of my life with all this guilt.

I never did call Sarah back. I can't stand to hear how Danny died. It would be too painful. But he must have killed himself, like all those other poor bastards with PTSD. How can Sarah and I be together, knowing that? Building a future after the pain of his death.

And if she doesn't hate me for that now, it's only a matter of time before she does. Before she realizes what I've done. To Danny, to everyone. To all those people I've let down.

And when she does, those beautiful green eyes of hers will look at me differently. And I won't be able to bear it.

No, this is for the best. The world will be a better place without me in it. Sarah will be better off without me. She may not see that now, but I know she will eventually. Freed from the baggage that we both carry, she'll meet someone new. Someone good. Someone whose mind doesn't take them to the dark places I've been. Someone who deserves her. Who can make her happy.

As for Danny, I failed him like I failed the others. I should have gone down to Wales to see him after Sarah told me how bad things were for him. Maybe if I had, he might still be here. I as good as left him on the battlefield.

My phone rings again. It's Sarah. I don't pick up. I don't want to talk to her. Well, that's not strictly true. I do want to talk to her, I really want to talk to her, to hear the sound of her voice. But I'm scared that if I do, I won't be able to do this.

It rings one more time. My hand hovers over it. I imagine Sarah telling me that everything is okay. Telling me that she still loves me. But she's not going to say that, is she? How can she?

Danny is dead.

I sit for a minute. Listen to the rain. Normally I like listening to the sound of the weather coming in from the moors while I'm cosy inside the cottage, but tonight it's making me feel even more agitated than I already am, so I turn on the radio.

My head feels heavy. It's as if it can't stand the weight of all my thoughts struggling inside it. I want to close my eyes, but I can't, because I know that when I do, I'll see his face.

I hear him instead. I hear him in the lyrics of the song on the radio. Stereophonics, 'Maybe Tomorrow'. A sorrowful male voice is singing about black clouds.

That's what I am. A little black cloud. Stumbling around. Because everyone I love always ends up dying. It's like an endless hall of mirrors, all their faces, great and small, staring back at me accusingly in the warped glass.

331

I can't take that chance with Sarah.

That day with her, that amazing night, it really felt like the start of something. But I should have known that our happiness was borrowed, our romance doomed. That the idea of me and Sarah, front and centre, could never be allowed. I don't deserve it, and I should never have let myself think that I did.

The darkness is here again. It's descending inexorably, like a shutter being closed.

Is this how it felt for Danny?

I don't know. But I soon will.

I must have dozed off, because it's dark when I wake up. I let the dogs out and put the kettle on. Then I go upstairs and splash cold water on my face. I purposely don't look at my reflection in the mirror. I don't want to see myself.

Elsa has followed me upstairs; I can hear her tail thumping on the bathroom floor. I can't bring myself to look at her face either. To see in her eyes the faith she still has in me, when I have none left in myself.

Back downstairs, I make myself a cup of coffee. There are three new messages from Sarah, but I don't listen to them. I need to focus. There are things I need to do.

I take the pad and pen that Maggie left on the side to write down the names of the dogs we're looking after, and their schedules. I sit down at the kitchen table and begin to write.

Dear Maggie,

I need to ask you to do something for me. It's a big ask, I know, but I don't trust anyone else.

Will you take care of the dogs? Elsa and Mungo and Mr Jones? Please don't let anything bad happen to them. They've all been through enough already.

They deserve better than me. You all do.

For a while there I told myself I was a good guy. I thought I could start again. Try to live a good life. A simple life. A life that had good people in it, like you and your mum.

But I'm not a good guy. And I'm scared that if I hang around, then I'll ruin things for all of you too. I don't mean to. But that doesn't matter, because I always stuff it up anyway.

My dad had the right idea. Walk away. Leave me to it.

The one decent thing I ever did was being a soldier. And it turns out I wasn't even good at that. I can't have been, because all the people I charged myself with taking care of are dead now.

I'm sorry, Maggie. You and your mum are two of the best things that have ever happened to me. You gave me a reason to be, and a reason to get better. It should have been enough. This – you, the dogs, the business. But I got greedy. I wanted more, so I told myself that what I wanted was okay.

But it wasn't okay. And now I have to answer for that. And I'm okay with that. Really, I am.

Be good to your mum. She's amazing. And your dad.

The truth is, you're all better off without me.

I don't have much, but what I do have is yours. You can use it for the business, or you can use it for yourself. I trust you and

I want you to be happy. Live your best life, Maggie. Be the amazing person that I know you are going to be. That you already are.

Love,
Carl xxx

I carefully fold the letter in two, then I reach into the drawer of the kitchen table and pull out one of the envelopes Maggie uses to put the bills in. I stuff the letter inside and carefully write Maggie's name on the front.

Then I take another piece of paper. 'Dear Mum,' I write at the top. But then, not knowing what to say, I get up and pour myself another glass of red wine. I knock it back in one.

I want to screw the piece of paper up and not bother, but then I think about something Sarah said after the wedding. She talked about how happy it had made her, giving her dad another chance.

It makes me want to do the same thing with Mum, to put things right between us. I was going to ring her on Christmas Day. Ask her to come and stay. Well, I won't get that chance now, but I can at least tell her goodbye.

She deserves that much. She tried her best to be there for me. I see that now. She tried really hard when I stayed with her after I got back from Afghanistan. That's when she told me that she'd spent time in care herself when she was a kid.

She wouldn't tell me anything more; this is the woman who, after all, has spent a lifetime avoiding emotional issues. Whose mantra has always been, 'Don't go there, Carl, why open that can of worms?'

I understand now that it was just too painful for her. Whatever happened that led to her being in care. The guilt I know she felt at history repeating itself. At feeling like an utter failure when her own children were taken away from her. And I feel nothing but sympathy and love for her.

I wish I'd told her that. I should have done. But fresh back from Camp Bastion, I was in pieces. I was struggling to survive in my own shoes, let alone put myself in someone else's.

And it was just so hard, seeing her drunk all the time with that no-good boyfriend of hers. Maybe if she hadn't been, I would have tried to talk to her. Maybe if he hadn't always been hanging around.

Maybe. Maybe. Maybe. That's the theme of all my regrets, isn't it? Of my life. Anyway, here goes.

Dear Mum,

This is the second letter like this I've had to write to you. You never got to read the first one, because I made it back from Afghanistan.

Maybe I shouldn't have. Maybe it would have been easier for everyone if I'd been killed over there. You would have read that letter, been proud that I'd carried out my duty, and we could all have been done with it.

I wish you were here, instead of up in Scotland with your latest boyfriend. I'm not mad at you for going. I hope you're happy. I hope he's treating you right. I just miss you. I just wish I'd had more time with you. Had a chance to talk – tell you how much I love you, how hard I know things have been for you. But then I know how much you hate to talk!

I'm so tired, Mum. I'm so tired of trying – and what's the point anyway? What's the point, when all the time I'm doomed? When every time I try, I mess things up again.

The sadness and the shame are too much.

I'd sort of learned to live with the sadness. I'd told myself that I had the dogs and the business, and that I could move on. But then I let myself fall in love with someone, when I knew, in my heart, I shouldn't. And now another person I used to care about is dead too.

I've let everyone down, Mum. All of them. Adam and Scott. You.

But mostly I've let myself down. The soldier I thought I was. Because the people I should have stood guard over, have all gone.

And each time I lose someone else, it gets harder to convince myself it wasn't my fault. I don't have it in me to fight any more. To run away from these feelings.

It's time to face them head on. To just jump right in. It feels less scary, that way, because then the sadness is no longer creeping up behind me, waiting to wash over me.

Like the sea, that time in Scarborough. Do you remember the day trip we had there? The day you let me bunk off school, and that new boyfriend of yours drove us there in his Triumph sports car?

The roof was down. I can even remember what song was playing on the radio – 'I'm In The Mood For Dancing' by the Nolan Sisters.

336

You were singing along and waving your arms above your head, and I was shouting at you to stop, pretending to be embarrassed, but actually I just felt happy because you were happy. Don't ask me why, but it feels important for you to know that now.

When we got there, we bought fish and chips, and ate them on the beach, and then you and I walked down to the water's edge. It took forever – the tide was so far out! And when we got there the water was so cold, I screamed. I didn't want it splashing over me so every time a wave came close, you lifted me out of the water.

Well, the thing is, that's how it feels now. The waves are roaring up behind me. They are about to sweep me off my feet, but this time you can't lift me out of the way. Even if you could, I wouldn't want you to. This will be a release. An end to it all.

My mind feels so destroyed, I'm not sure if any of this makes any sense? But I think you know how that feels. I think you drank to escape it.

I know how hard things were for you. I see that now. You tried your best, Mum, you really did.

I'm not afraid. I want you to know that. I'll be with my pals – where I should be. All together on the other side.

But I will miss you. I will miss what we could have been to each other, and I need you to know that I'm sorry for that.

It's too hard to say anything else, so I'll leave it there.

I love you, Mum. Thank you for trying.

Your Carl

xxx

337

I put Mum's letter next to Maggie's and then, in a third envelope, I put the photograph Barry took of my tattoo. This one I address to the journalist who helped me with Assami, and I write.

It was only ever supposed to be for me. The tattoo.
     Each poppy is for one of the friends I lost in Afghanistan. I wanted to tell our story on my skin. Maybe you can tell that story now?
     These are their names:
          Fridge
          Squadron
          Tom
          Caroline
          Assami

I want the world to know who the poppies represent, and what happened to them. But, as always, the words fail me, so I head up to the spare bedroom and pull out the box marked 'Afghanistan' in black capital letters.

It is packed with newspaper cuttings, photographs, letters. Soon, their yellowing pages won't mean anything to anyone. And that's fine, when it comes to me – but not for the comrades I love. They deserve more. I want them to be remembered, if only for a little while.

I find the stories I'm looking for. Pictures of the hearses at Wootton Bassett that carried Fridge and Squadron and Tom's coffins, covered with the Union

Jack, back to base. Flowers strewn on their roofs, flung by crowds who never knew them but who turned out for those sad, final parades.

There's a picture of Squadron's mum, Lorraine, her hand resting on the glass window of the hearse. There's a picture of Tom's wife, her face crumpled with despair. There are pictures, too, of Fridge's coffin and Caroline's, accompanied by a long story of the friendly fire incident that led to her death.

I fold everything carefully and stuff it into the envelope. Then I write.

I am telling you all this, not to give myself any glory – I don't deserve that, and I beg you not to credit me with any – but so that what they all gave, the sacrifices they made, might mean something.

So that their memories might be kept alive.

They were all such extraordinary people, they deserve that.

Best,
Carl

The last letter is the hardest of all to write.

Dear Sarah,

I wish I was better with words. I wish I was cleverer, so I could make you understand, but it's too hard.

I need you to know that the only time in my whole life I ever truly saw myself was when you were looking at me. When you smiled at me. When you said my name.

339

With you everything was good, better than good, it was
electric. The only time I ever felt special was when I was with you.

I'm so sorry, Sarah, for everything that's happened. I never
meant to cause you any pain, and I hate myself, knowing that I
have. I'm doing this for you, so that I will never hurt you
again. Never hurt anyone else again.

We didn't have long, did we? Just a beginning, really. I
wanted more. So much more. I wanted all of it. A home, a
family, all my winters and summers growing old next to you.

But that wasn't in the script for us. I knew that when I
listened to your message — when I heard you cry over Danny. I
never want to have to hear you cry again. I never want to be the
person who makes you cry.

You were never meant for me, and I should never have let
myself believe that you were. If I was a decent man, a decent
soldier, I would have owned that from the beginning. Maybe
then I could have helped Danny, my comrade and my friend,
and he would still be here. And our future wouldn't feel like
one we had stolen from him.

You will meet someone so much better, and I hope more
than anything that you will be happy. You deserve the best.

I had no right to love you. I see that now.

I'm sorry.

Yours, always,
Carl xxx

I put the star earrings in the envelope with her note
and place it next to the others. Then I pick up the pills
and the half-drunk bottle of whiskey, turn off the light,

and go upstairs. I sit on the edge of my bed and empty the pills into my hand.

For a long time I stare at them. So long that they go clammy in my sweating palm.

My head feels heavy, overloaded.

Slowly, deliberately, I put the tablets on my tongue, then I close my lips tight around the cool glass of the bottle and take a large gulp. The pills swim in my mouth for a while, then I tilt my head back and swallow.

The liquid burns the back of my throat as it tries to flush the pills down, but there are too many and I start to choke. I take another glug of whiskey, then another, until I finish the bottle and the tablets are gone.

The back of my throat feels numb.

All of me feels numb.

I stare at the picture Sarge took of us all together. Me, Fridge, Squadron, Sarah, Danny, Jenni, Cherub, Jobbo, Caroline and Assami.

I don't recognize the person squinting through the Afghan dust clouds, surrounded by all his mates. Back then, everything still seemed possible.

I take one last look at Sarah's face.

Then I undo my army dog tags from around my neck and turn them over in my hand, like I used to do in my bunk, back in camp.

I don't deserve to wear them any more.

I lie down. I can't breathe. My mouth is dry, and my tongue feels thick. But my brain, which these last two days has felt as if it's spinning out of control in my skull, whirring and gyrating and tormenting me, is quiet.

Sensing victory, it has started to slow down.

It's time.

I close my eyes. Sarah's face swims before me as if in a dream. I wish I could touch her one more time, hold her hair in my fingers, feel her skin next to mine.

I think of waking up with her beside me, the night after Jenni and Cherub got married. I've never woken up next to another woman in all my life. But with Sarah I always wanted to go all in.

I would have loved her forever, until we were old and grey. I would have done anything for her.

Elsa jumps up on to the bed beside me and lies down. She reaches her chin up to rest on my stomach, and I wrap my arm around her and close my eyes again. There's a strange sensation at the back of my head. I feel myself falling. The lamp by my bed is on but I'm already in darkness. A black lid is closing over me.

I feel curiously peaceful. The guilt that has had its hands around my neck my whole life is loosening.

Guilt for not being enough to make Dad want to stick around.

For not being able to take care of my brothers.

For not being able to stop Mum's drinking.

For Fridge and Squadron and Tom and Caroline.

For Sarah being injured.

And now for Danny.

It's as if I've swum against the tide always, but now? Now I can just let myself sink into the warm waters. I let the sensation rush over me. I won't fight it any more.

I'm so tired.

I feel the dog tags in my hand and rub my thumb backwards and forwards over the inscriptions on the discs.

Blood type: O negative
Service number: 662582
Religion: Roman Catholic
Name: Wilson, C.
In the end, that's it.
That's all there is.

54. Maggie

'Hey, there's a Fortnum and Mason hamper on the doorstep and a box of champagne!' I call out. 'Someone's planning a fancy Christmas!'

He doesn't respond.

'I'll fetch them in, then, shall I?' I say, heaving in first the hamper and then the champagne, and leaving them by the back door. 'I mean why bother getting the strong ex-soldier to do the manual labour when you've got me around, eh?'

I address my comments to the dogs. Mungo and Mr Jones eye me sleepily from their beds.

It's a flipping big box. 'So who's your fancy admirer, then?'

It's so like Carl not to respond. Not to acknowledge something as exciting as finding a hamper from Fortnum & Mason on the doorstep. As if it's something that happens every day of the week, as mundane as a delivery of dog food.

Only Mr Jones looks excited. He staggers towards me, wagging his tail.

I bend down to pick him up, and kiss him on the nose. 'Hello there, little one,' I say, scuffing him behind the ears, then gently laying him back down on the floor while I take my coat off. I hang it on the back of the door, on top of Carl's leather jacket.

I smile when I see it, because it means he must be in. 'So you *are* here,' I call out.

I thought this new girlfriend of his was coming to stay, but maybe I got that wrong, because there's no sign of an extra coat or pair of shoes. I won't pretend I'm not secretly relieved. I hate the idea of someone taking Carl away from us – away from me.

I call out his name. 'Carl?'

No answer.

'I've just come to drop off Mungo's eye drops. I took them home with me by mistake last night.' I did take the drops home with me, but accidentally on purpose. I want to check out this girl, whoever she is. See if she's good enough for Carl.

Still no answer.

He must be next door in his chair, probably dozing in front of the fire. I pop the eye drops on the kitchen counter, then I fill the kettle, jam the lid down, and put it on the hob to boil. A couple of minutes later, it begins to emit a threatening hiss.

'That's it,' I say decisively. 'I'm buying you an electric kettle for Christmas. I swear this one has it in for me. D'you want tea?' I ask, already reaching into the cupboard for our favourite mugs. Carl's is the ancient, chipped Leeds United one, and mine is a white mug Carl bought me for my birthday, with *Smash the Patriarchy* in big, angry black capital letters.

I pick Mr Jones up again. I feel his warm little body wriggle against mine until he eventually settles his head on my shoulder. I stare down at him. Sweet little Jonesy. I love him to bits. I love all the dogs to bits. I even love grumpy old Carl.

I'm so lucky to have this job. Not that I'd ever admit that to him. I listen to my mates complain about how much they hate their office, their boss, their lecturers, or whatever degree it is they've decided to study, and I feel so lucky that I get to spend my days here, with the dogs, on the moors, joking around with Carl.

And while he does his best to pretend to be crotchety, I know it's all a front. I see how gentle he is with the dogs. How lovely he is to my mum. For such a giant of a bloke he's actually the biggest softie I know.

'You'll never guess what happened at the pantomime,' I call out to him, warming myself up in front of the Rayburn.

Just thinking about it again makes me laugh out loud. Mr Jones lifts his head, eyeing me momentarily, then he puts it back on my shoulder and exhales, as if I'm boring him.

'They only went and had a fight onstage!' I laugh. 'And to think I only went because Mum made me. Turned out to be the best show I've ever seen! I mean, not really, obviously it was every bit as awful as I thought it was going to be. Until the fight. Captain Hook and Tick-Tock the Crocodile tearing chunks out of each other. I told you! I told you Peter Pan was up to no good with Captain Hook!' I wait. 'Carl? Come on, that's funny!'

Still no response.

But then I'm used to our one-sided conversations. Carl isn't exactly what you'd call chatty. Unless you count having a conversation with his eyebrows as being chatty. He does this thing where he arches them so high you could park a bus under them. You can have entire conversations with his eyebrows, with him not saying a thing, and still know what he means. I imagine him listening to this story now, and raising those eyebrows at me.

The kettle starts to whistle.

'Why is it so dark in here?' I ask, suddenly realizing it's so gloomy I can't see the oven gloves I need to pick up the kettle.

The only illumination is coming from the little night light Carl bought for Mr Jones, because he cries if you leave him alone in the dark.

'Carl?' I call again, suddenly feeling anxious. I walk back to the door to flick on the light switch. I turn back to face the kitchen, and that's when I see it. 'What the – ?'

Mum's Christmas cake is splattered all over the wall. It looks like something from a crime scene.

Carl's phone buzzes, for the second time since I've got here. I follow the sound to the kitchen table, where I spot it lying next to three empty wine bottles, one of which has a stack of envelopes leaning up against it.

The phone lights up as someone leaves a message and as it does, I catch a glimpse of my name scrawled in Carl's handwriting across the first envelope.

My stomach turns to water. Panic rushing through me, I sprint to the living room, but his chair is empty, and I know. I just know. I know what he's done.

'*CARL!*' I scream.

I put Mr Jones down and rush to the door to get my phone out of my coat pocket. Then, my fingers jerking convulsively, I dial 999.

A female voice asks me what the nature of the problem is, and I don't know how to respond. I feel so inadequate. Poleaxed by the horror that looms in front of me. I don't know what to say.

I start up the stairs, two at a time, screaming Carl's name, but when I get to his bedroom door I stop. I don't want to open it, because I'm absolutely terrified of what I'll find on the other side.

'Help me, please help me,' I beg the operator. 'I don't want to go in. I'm scared.'

She is calm and kind and efficient. She asks me what my name is but I can't remember. In my panic, I can't even remember what my name is.

'Maggie,' I eventually stammer.

She asks my address and I hear her tapping away into a keyboard as I tell her the address of Carl's cottage. And then we're back to her asking me what the nature of the problem is.

'I need to know the nature of the problem so I can send the right help,' she says. She is infuriatingly calm but insistent.

I push open the bedroom door. I see Elsa first. It's the one and only time she hasn't come running downstairs

348

to greet me, and I realize now it's because she doesn't want to leave his side.

Downstairs the kettle is still whistling. It sounds angrier than ever.

'Is he breathing?' the operator asks.

I can't speak. Giant waves of panic are crashing over me, and I daren't step into the room. What if he's dead?

'I need you to find out if he's breathing,' she repeats firmly.

I force myself to walk towards the bed. I bend down so that my ear is over Carl's mouth. 'I don't know,' I say. 'I don't think so.' I start to cry.

'It's okay,' she says. 'The ambulance is on its way. It's going to be with you soon, but right now I want you to check his airways. Can you do that for me?'

'I don't know how to do that,' I say, panic rising in me again.

'It's okay,' she says kindly. 'I'm going to tell you exactly what to do, and I'm going to be right here with you.'

She asks me if Carl is on his back, and I answer that he is.

'That's good,' she says. 'Now I want you to take away any pillows so that he's lying flat on the bed. Okay?'

'Okay,' I say.

I pull the pillow from under Carl's head, and something falls to the floor with a crash, but I don't look to see what it is because the light from the bedside lamp flickers over his face, and I see that his lips are blue.

'Oh God, his lips, they're blue!' I tell her.

349

'It's okay,' she repeats reassuringly. 'I know this is really hard for you, but the ambulance is nearly there.'

'But his lips!' I'm screaming at her now.

'I understand,' she says, super calmly. 'That's why I'm going to ask you to work on his breathing for me. I want you to put the heel of your hand on his breastbone. Can you do that for me?'

I do exactly as she tells me. I put one hand on his breastbone, then I put my other hand on top of it and I push down, with only the heel of my lower hand touching Carl's chest. I pump his chest, two times a second, precisely as she says to.

'Keep doing it,' she says. And again, 'Keep doing it. Don't stop.'

And I don't. I keep pumping at Carl's chest until my arms ache and the horror of what I'm actually doing no longer feels real. It's as if I'm watching myself from above.

'I know it's really tiring, but you're doing really well,' she says. 'Not much longer now.'

That's the last thing I hear her say, because then the ambulance pulls up in the lane outside. I see the flashing lights first and then I hear the sound of heavy footsteps on the stairs and two men in green trousers and rustling, bright yellow jackets burst into Carl's bedroom.

'It's all right, love, we've got this now,' says the older-looking of the two men.

He gently pushes me out of the way and takes over the compressions while the other, younger-looking one, rummages in a bag, then pulls out a plastic mask that he puts over Carl's face.

'You've done a brilliant job, lass,' the first paramedic adds before nodding at his partner.

I slide to the ground and pull my knees up to my chest. Next to me, Elsa has curled herself into a shivering, scared ball. 'It's okay, girl,' I say, stroking her back and pulling her towards me. 'It's okay.'

The words sound like my mouth feels. Sour.

I put my arm around her neck, and as I sit with her I notice the framed picture that Carl keeps on his bedside table, lying now in a jumble of broken glass on the floor by my legs. That must have been what fell to the ground when I pulled the pillow away.

Outside, the lights from the ambulance blink in the evening sky, throwing an eerie blue shadow over Carl's unlit bedroom. I've never felt fear like this. It's a choking, black fear. My body shivers like Elsa's, as if an unseen frost is closing around my heart.

I reach for the photograph, shake off the broken pieces of glass, and rest it on my knees. Then I stare and stare at the picture. I stare so that I don't have to look at what the paramedics are doing to Carl.

It's a photograph of him and a group of others, all in running gear. They look suntanned and hot and happy.

There are three women. The one in the middle looks like one of those old-fashioned women in the war, who used to work on the farms. Her hair is dyed an orangey-red and it's been set in rollers, giving her big, sausage-shaped curls — like my nan's hair in the pictures of her when she was young. She's wearing red lipstick, which doesn't look very army-like, and terrible foundation, and she's a bit plump. But she looks really smiley and kind, not at all like a soldier – I bet she'd be rubbish at fighting.

The other two girls are much slimmer, and neither of them are wearing any make-up. One has long, dark brown, shiny hair braided neatly and pinned on top of her head. She's leaning back into a man who has his arms around her, pulling her protectively towards him. They look like they've just started dating and want everyone to know they're a couple.

There's a massively tall guy with a big goofy grin and very small T-shirt, and in front of him a man in robes with a beard. And Kath and Michael's son, who Carl calls 'Fridge' and always refuses to tell me why.

Then there's some other soldier dude who has his arm around the third woman, a blonde beauty, with long, thick, straight hair and teeth so perfect she looks like an American.

Everyone is staring at the camera, apart from her. She has her head tilted to the side, and when I follow her gaze I realize she is staring at Carl. And there's something in her gaze that I can't figure out. But then I get it.

Whenever we watch a film with Cary Grant, or Steve McQueen, or Paul Newman and, lately, Brad Pitt, my mum sighs and says, 'Oooh, he has *such* presence.' And we all laugh. She says it means that some people just shine more brightly than others.

I never understood what she meant, but now I get it,

because that's exactly what Carl has. A powerful presence. It's not something you can put your finger on or articulate. It's not even about his looks. He's just one of those magnetic people who draw you in. He's like a sugar fix.

She gets it. The woman staring at him in the picture. I can tell by the way she's looking at him. I wonder if he felt the same about her?

Next to Fridge is another tall and hefty bloke. He's smiling, too, but he looks a bit more menacing, like he's left unfinished business on the battlefield and is going back any minute. As my nan used to say, he looks like he wouldn't take any prisoners. He's standing behind the friendly-looking woman with the red lipstick, and they look like they might be a couple too.

I stare at Carl, who is standing on the edge, his hair buzzed short, the same length as his stubble. Suddenly I feel angry. Why? Why would he do this? The dogs need him! I need him!

Is it because of something that happened when he was out there?

Or maybe it's to do with these mysterious appointments he's been disappearing off to, over the last couple of months. When he gets back, hours later, he seems dazed, as if he's in pain.

And the cake? What could have made him so angry that he would hurl it against the wall? Mum spent hours making that cake. She dug out my old copy of *The Nutcracker* that Granny gave me, so she could do an exact iced copy of the soldier. I used to love that story – Mum used to read it to me over and over again.

Mum. How I wish she was here with me now.

I think of her staying up late, lovingly icing this cake, painstakingly piping on the eyes and the buttons and the hair, because she thought it would make Carl happy.

It did make him happy though. The cake. Mum said he was over the moon when she gave it to him. She told me he actually swept her off her feet and kissed her on the cheek.

So what happened? None of it makes any sense.

He's been so happy since he got back from the wedding. All skippy and perky – so different to how he used to be when I first met him. Back then, he had a permanent faraway expression on his face, as if what he was seeing was totally different to what everyone else was seeing. His body stayed in the room, but his mind was far away. And wherever it went, well, I don't think it was a very happy place.

Mum told me not to push him. She says he's seen things that no amount of positive thinking can rescue him from. Stuff from when he was a soldier that he's not ready to talk about. That he might never be ready to talk about.

Grandad was a soldier, too, and I can imagine him being a soldier, because he was always dead stern and strict, and a bit mean sometimes. But Carl? I still find it hard to imagine Carl fighting in a war.

I mean he looks like a soldier, all right – he's built like an armoured tank – dead broad and fit, with these super-muscly arms. But I just can't see him deliberately hurting someone. The Carl I know won't even kill spiders. He carefully catches them in a glass and then takes them outside to stop the dogs tormenting them.

Sometimes, when he doesn't know I'm looking, I watch him playing with the dogs in the garden, lying on the ground and letting them roll all over him and lick his face, or chasing after them like a little kid.

He's so nice to Hatty, and all the other dogs, and to Mum, and to the old farmer's wife. I know he does chores for her around the farm, chopping wood for her and that. He spent ages fixing her fence in the pouring rain last week.

He never, ever tells me what to do, and he draws silly, smiley stick pictures of me and the dogs on the envelopes he gives me my wages in every week. And he always puts too much money in and when I tell him, he pretends he can't count very well. But I know he can, because sometimes we watch *Countdown* together and he is totally amazing with numbers.

But I don't care. I don't care how good or nice he is, because how could he do this? I don't understand.

'On my count,' I hear one of the paramedics say.

'One, two, three.'

I wipe away the tears from the corners of my eyes and look up as, with a huge effort, they hoist him on to the stretcher.

They must have cut his T-shirt off to treat him, because his back is bare.

Totally bare but for the most shocking, stunning, beautiful tattoo.

Nine months later

55. Sarah

I wake from a fitful sleep, dreaming about him. I dream of lying next to him . . . him with his back to me. I am staring at red poppies – and then I reach forward to kiss the tip of one of the flowers . . .

And suddenly he is awake.

He turns and reaches out, and our bodies twist together in a tangle of crisp, scented, white hotel sheets.

His eyes are bright and he is dotting my face with kisses. We are rolling in the sheets and laughing, and then finally Carl wrestles the sheets away and there is nothing between us any more.

I feel his warm skin next to mine.

He gazes at me and then he smiles. 'Sarah,' he says.

As he says my name I can feel his breath on my face. 'Sarah,' he says again.

He is in my head and in my heart.

I can hear his voice. I can smell him. I am back here with him. His weight on top of me.

He is saying my name. 'Sarah, Sarah, Sarah.'

Poppy #6

I push open the heavy glass door to the tattoo parlour, and the old-fashioned bell rings above my head. It feels like a lifetime ago now that I first heard that noise.

Hearing it again, the chiming sound is comforting. It lets me know I'm on familiar territory. It makes me feel safe. Even the smell – a mix of ink and antiseptic – feels reassuring.

Everything is exactly as it was. Shiny concrete floor. Big, squishy velvet sofa. Electric-blue neon sign that says 'Tattoo'.

A door opens in the back and Barry emerges.

'Carl!' he says, beaming.

He comes towards me and I hold out my hand in greeting, but he brushes it away and pulls me towards him in an affectionate bear hug instead.

'Carl,' he repeats. 'It's so good to see you again.'

He pushes me away from him, holds my shoulders with his

hands so he can study my face. Then he pulls me towards him and hugs me again.

'It's good to see you too,' I say.

And it is. His warm, dark eyes that remind me of Assami. His mass of dark hair, tied up in a knot on top of his head. The crazily big holes in his ear lobes with the copper rings in them.

I never thought I'd see him again.

'So, one more poppy, eh?' he says, grinning.

I nod.

'It's a good job you've got a wide back.' Chuckling, he leads me to his room at the back of the shop.

He opens the door and beckons me inside.

I stare at the red walls, the small electric fan heater in the corner, the metal medical trolley with its surgical spirit, swabs and cotton wool. The single stool. The bed covered in a layer of cling film.

A shiver runs down my back, just like it did the night we were heading out on the Christmas Eve patrol, the night Fridge was killed. It happened again the very first time I was here, and suddenly I feel overwhelmed. So much has happened between then and now. And it hits me all over again. How lucky I am to be here.

Barry looks at me. 'Are you okay?' he asks.

Gently, he puts his hand on my shoulder, guides me down on to the stool. He pours me a glass of water.

'It's okay,' he says, passing it to me. 'Take your time.'

I sip the water. I breathe in. I breathe out.

'I'm okay now,' I tell Barry after a while.

He looks at me with concern. 'Are you sure? Because we don't have to do this now.'

'I'm sure,' I say, pulling my jumper up over my head.

'Okay, then,' he says, and I hear him gather together his equipment. 'Music?' he asks.

I shake my head. 'Not today.'

I can't do music any more. Not since that night. It makes me feel too much. Brings back too many difficult emotions, things I haven't yet processed. Memories I still can't face.

He nods. 'No problem.'

I'd forgotten how kind Barry is, how he always manages to put me at ease.

'Let's get started, then.' He smiles.

I lie down on the couch and turn over on to my stomach. I listen to the unsettling sound of Barry snapping on his gloves, then grimace as he brings the needle down on to my back. I practise my deep breathing; I take myself to the safe place in my head, just like my therapist has taught me.

After a while I no longer register the pain. Feeling the outline of the poppy being drawn on my back calms me. And I feel grateful, because this, like all of my sessions with Barry, feels like another chance. A chance to get things right. To put things right.

'Back by five, then?' Maggie asked anxiously as I left this morning.

'Back by five,' I promised, kissing her on the cheek.

Our friendship, our work life, has slipped back into its old rhythms, but I will never forgive myself for what I put her through.

I don't know how to begin to say sorry. How to say in words the gratitude that I feel towards her for saving me. For all the new tomorrows, the happiness, the hope. For all those things she has given me; there aren't sufficient words to express it. I don't have the language.

So I will show her instead. In every way I can. In every

appointment booked, every dog walked, every mug of tea made, every lift home, every detail I can, I will show her. Roz too. I will show them all that their faith in me hasn't been wasted.

Roz's was the first face I saw when I woke up.

'Carl,' was all she managed to say. 'Carl.' She blew her nose, took a few moments to compose herself. Finally, she said, 'Maggie wanted to be here when you woke up, but she's been so upset about it all. She's the one who found you.'

I looked around the bed.

At Roz and Michael.

And Sarah. Those beautiful green eyes of hers, red raw at the edges from crying. She was still crying. I wanted to reach out and wipe her tears away, but when I tried to lift my arm I was too weak.

It hit me then. What had I done to myself? What had I done to them? To Maggie? How could I have inflicted this on her?

Michael came to stand on the other side of my bed. 'You gave us a scare there, lad,' he said. He reached down, laid his hand gently on my arm. 'We've lost one son, Carl. We don't want to lose another.'

He didn't cry but, just as at Fridge's funeral, watching him wrestle with the effort of not breaking down was worse than if he had.

'Son,' he had called me. 'Son.'

My body already ached everywhere, but this new pain was worse. The pain of realizing how much I had made them all suffer.

I looked back at Sarah, at the scars on her forehead. Saw the same vulnerability in her eyes that I had seen when she was the one lying in a hospital bed. The hurt I had inflicted on her may have been invisible, but what I had done was every bit as cruel.

She bent down, pressed her cheek against mine. 'I thought I'd lost you too,' she sobbed.

My heart crumpled, and in that moment I learned that love isn't conditional. I felt what it is to be loved and to love someone, completely and utterly, in return. No matter what they've done. No matter what they think they've done.

I felt such a fierce surge of gratitude to her, to all of them, for not giving up on me. And I vowed, there and then, that I would never cause Sarah or Maggie or any of them another day's pain. I promised that I would get better, that whatever life I am lucky enough to have left, I will live to its fullest.

So I listened to the therapist, and I talked while he listened to me. I realized how wrong I had been about Danny's death. That, like the others, it wasn't my fault. In his case, it was just a terrible accident.

I worked through the deaths of them all, and I realized that I had forgotten, or had not let myself see, that for all the loss I had endured, there had also been so much love.

The sort of love I'd never understood. Not conditional love, or one-night-stand love, or the love of a soldier trying to protect a comrade. Or the love of a struggling mother trying to do her best by her kid.

Instead, the sort of love that makes you feel safe. The sort of love that makes you feel like you're not alone, even when you are. That's what true love feels like to me now. Safety. Security.

I have given myself permission to be loved, and I'm learning how to love in return. I won't say it's been easy. I still have my moments. Times when my 'self-destructive thoughts', as the therapist calls them, threaten to floor me. I know I will always have to work to keep them at bay.

But every day, I try. Every day, I push myself to be better, to make it up to the people I love.

Today it's about making it up, in some small way, to Danny.

'So,' Barry asks, 'ready to tell me who this sixth poppy is for?'

56. Sarah

He starts to take off the blue cashmere jumper I bought him, and as he reaches up to pull it over his shoulders I glimpse the dressing over the fresh red poppy before his T-shirt falls back and covers it again.

It meant so much to him to get it done. A way to let Danny still be a part of our world. I know it is Carl's way of saying sorry too. For not being able to save him. Just as the other poppies are his request for forgiveness from the other five souls they're dedicated to.

The friends and comrades he still misses.

My sweet Carl. He still doesn't believe he deserves to be this happy. He tries to prove himself worthy. Not just with me and Maggie but with all the others whose lives are being touched by the charity we've set up.

Watching him work with his reporter friend to track down Assami's family, and with my dad to persuade the Home Office that Habiba and the children should be allowed to come to this country, has been like watching him come alive again.

With each new piece of good news, every new phone call from Dad or the reporter, his optimism would grow. Slowly at first. But then, the night after they finally arrived, just before he fell asleep, I realized that something had changed in his eyes.

There had been a darkness to them since Danny's death, but that night the life came back into them. I saw the same clear blue that had dazzled me all that time ago, in the camp canteen. It was as if helping Habiba and her children had given him back a spark of hope and begun to restore his faith in the world. And every day, with each new person he helps, I see that faith grow.

Carl turns to look at me now. He arches his eyebrows, and I smile, reaching up to ruffle my hands through his hair – which is longer now, the curls finally getting their way.

He is just the same, and yet not the same at all. But he is here, and nothing will ever separate us again.

'Are you playing the football?' calls Mustafa from the field beyond the drystone wall that marks the end of the cottage garden.

Carl looks back at Mustafa, and beams. 'I'm playing the football,' he shouts back. 'Do you need anything?' he asks as he gets up from the picnic blanket.

I shake my head.

'You sure?'

'I'm sure.'

He turns and calls out to Rangina. 'Come on, lass,' he says, 'you can come and play the football too.'

She appears at the kitchen door and rewards him with one of her lopsided grins. Then she skips towards him and holds out her hand.

'We can do better than that,' he says, swinging her into the air and hoisting her on to his shoulders. He clasps her ankles, easily enfolded in his enormous hands. 'Are you ready?'

She giggles, then starts to scream as he turns and runs in zigzags across the garden to the far wall.

'Everything okay?' calls Roz from the kitchen where she and Habiba are busy preparing tonight's dinner – a Ramadan feast of slow-cooked meats and sweetbreads. And, at Roz's insistence, scones with home-made strawberry jam and cream.

I smile and nod at Roz. She is peering out of the kitchen window, a wooden spoon in one hand and a mixing bowl in the other. Next to her, Habiba, with her lilac silk scarf draped elegantly across her head and shoulders, smiles shyly and gives me a small wave.

Then Roz says something and they both laugh. Firm friends, they have bonded over the universal language of the kitchen. A language that is never better understood than when one of them is complaining about Carl's unpredictable Rayburn.

Suddenly I see Carl sprinting back up the field towards me. For a second I panic, thinking something is wrong, but then I see that he's grinning.

'What's up?' I shout.

'I forgot to say goodbye to the nipper,' he pants, kneeling down beside me. He bends down to kiss my stomach, then he rocks back on to his ankles and stares at me. 'You look cold,' he says, reaching for his cashmere jumper.

He holds it above me and then gently pulls it down over my head. He brushes the hair that has fallen over my face out of my eyes, and stoops forward to kiss me.

'I love you,' he says.

'I love you too.'

'Are you sure you've got everything you need?'

'I'm sure,' I tell him.

Then he leaps up and is gone again.

I lie back down and close my eyes.

I can hear birdsong. I can hear Carl's laughing voice telling me it's the sound of a wood pigeon not an owl.

I see him standing over the Rayburn making scrambled eggs for me and Maggie. I see him stroking Elsa's ears. I see his eyes light up at the news that I am pregnant. I see six poppies.

Somewhere in the distance I hear him calling for the ball, then the sound of the boys laughing.

I can smell lavender mixed with the occasional waft of freshly baked scones.

I rub my hand over the soft fabric of Carl's jumper, stroke the smallest hint of a bump beneath it that will one day be our baby.

Yes, I think, *I've got everything I need, and more besides.*

Author's Note

This book came about because of one extraordinary man, Rob French. Rob, a former Royal Marine, first came to my attention in a newspaper article in November 2017.

In the story Rob was quoted as saying, 'Around this time of year the public start wearing poppies to show that they remember the fallen, but for me and all the other servicemen and women who have been to war, every single day is Remembrance Day.'

But it was not Rob's words that gripped me, so much as his photograph. Taken from behind, with Rob wearing nothing but his ceremonial green beret, it showed the enormous and very beautiful tattoo he'd had inked across the whole of his upper back.

A tattoo of seven large poppies.

Above the poppies sat the silhouettes of seven Royal Marines, drawn to represent Rob's seven colleagues who all died within weeks of each other in Afghanistan, in December 2008.

Rob's quote continued. 'I decided to get the tattoo on my back so that they are with and behind me, pushing me on, rather than in front and holding me back.'

A few weeks later, unable to get Rob's story out of my head, I tracked him down. He warily agreed to meet me on condition that the story wouldn't focus on him or portray him as a hero. On this he was adamant.

He had only agreed to have the original story published, he said, to raise awareness for the Royal British Legion's Poppy Appeal.

'This is not for me,' he insisted. 'It is for them. I am always remembering them. I carry on with my life, but with them on my back they are always with me.'

Three of the seven were particularly close to Rob – Lance Corporal Steven 'Jamie' Fellows, Lance Corporal Benjamin 'Ben' Whatley and Lance Corporal Jason Mackie.

'They were very, very good friends of mine. The other five were people I met and fought with out there.'

He told me how they had all died. Marine Damian Davies, Sergeant John Manuel and Corporal Marc Birch died when a thirteen-year-old suicide bomber approached them with a wheelbarrow packed with explosives.

Lance Corporal Steven 'Jamie' Fellows was blown up in a separate incident the same day.

Marine Georgie Sparks and Marine Tony Evans were killed by insurgents armed with rocket-propelled grenades during a foot patrol in Helmand province.

Lance Corporal Benjamin 'Ben' Whatley, aged twenty, was killed by enemy fire during a fierce battle on Christmas Eve.

Rob, who served for nine years in the Marines, had been diagnosed with post-traumatic stress disorder, and was clearly haunted by their loss, especially Ben's.

'I have always carried the weight of Ben's death on my shoulders, as he was killed on Christmas Eve, two weeks after I was sent home. I have always felt that if I was still there, I might have been selected to take that position on the same rooftop, and therefore taken the round that hit Ben. I still live with that guilt now.'

Beyond this, he sought no credit for his time as a soldier – or for having his tattoo done to remember his comrades – and the last thing he wanted was to be seen as a hero.

But Rob's story got me to thinking. I began to research the war in Afghanistan. I was shocked by the statistics of how many soldiers had, like Rob, been diagnosed with PTSD.

I read countless newspaper articles and testimonies of British soldiers who had served in Afghanistan. I read about the horrific things they had been through, the shocking things they had seen.

I learned that, as of 23 July 2015, a total of 454 British forces personnel or MOD civilians had died while serving in Afghanistan since 2001. Of these 405 were killed as a result of hostile action.

I also discovered that more than 2,000 British soldiers and veterans are feared to have killed themselves since the Afghan invasion. Veterans United Against Suicide believes this figure may be an underestimate.

In 2012, more soldiers and veterans took their own lives than were killed in combat in Afghanistan.

More British service personnel have killed themselves since 1984 than have died in combat.

All good people, like Rob, who had fought for their country and paid the ultimate price.

And so I decided to create a 'fictional' hero. A decent

man struggling to get his life back together after serving in Afghanistan. A good man, like Rob and so many others, still haunted by the deaths of the friends they lost out there.

When, many years later, I rang Rob to tell him I had a book deal, he was thrilled. Not for him – again, he begged me to tell him that the story was not about him – but that it might raise awareness of the issues surrounding PTSD.

Rob, this book is for you, and for all of your comrades who bravely stood beside you in Afghanistan. Who gave so much and asked for nothing in return.

I salute you.

Acknowledgements

Firstly, thank you to the straight-talking force to be reckoned with that is my agent, Eugenie Furniss. Thank you for believing in *Six Poppies* before I even started to write it, for the sixth-sense phone calls when I needed a boost, for knowing that Michael Joseph was absolutely the right team to submit it to. For making *Six Poppies* happen.

Also, to Emily MacDonald at 42 Management, another early cheerleader. Thank you for all your thoughtful feedback and kind encouragement.

To my publisher, the extraordinarily talented Clio Cornish, whose vision, hard work and dogged determination to make this book the best version it could possibly be I am forever indebted to. Thank you for your guidance, for pushing me to do better and for believing that I could.

To the gorgeous Hannah Smith, for so expertly and cheerfully directing me through the publishing process, and the rest of the amazing team at Michael Joseph – Phillipa Walker, Frankie Banks, Yasmin Anshoor and Beatrix McIntyre – who have all worked so diligently and enthusiastically on the book.

Thank you also to Shan Morley Jones for her magical edit and Lauren Wakefield for the stunning artwork on the cover. I am so honoured to be surrounded by such a talented cast of people.

To all my friends.

To Anna Pasternak, for being generous enough to introduce me to Eugenie in the first place. You truly turned everything around for me.

To Paul Jefferson, a former army bomb disposal expert, who was totally blinded and lost a leg in Kuwait. Thank you for sharing your story with me. And for patiently explaining the order of ranks in the army over and over again!

To Ian Falconer and Wendy and Jules Walker for being eager early readers, and for all my other marvellous rosé-drinking, dog-walking, cake-eating, night-out-accompanying friends for all your love, generosity and support over the years with particular mention, of course, to the Monday Night Supper Club.

To every single member of my enormous family. They say that writing a book is a lonely journey, but I never once felt lonely because of all of you.

To my brothers Nick, Simon and David and my sister Jane. Mum and Dad may not be around anymore, but I have all of you. Thank you for a lifetime of love and adventures and laughs. Thank you for always, always being there for me.

To my three gorgeous sons – Jack, Alfie, and Ted.

To Jack, for picking me up on the bad days and for being so thrilled for me on the good ones.

To Alfie, the first person to read the manuscript. Thank you for making me think there might be something there.

And Ted, for never ever minding when I'm on a deadline. For always knowing when to give me space and when to interrupt me with a cup of tea and a Twirl.

Thank you all for being so supportive. I am so proud of the wonderful men you have grown into.

And finally, of course, to Andrew. For believing in me, making me laugh and for taking care of everything else so that I don't have to. You are the person that makes everything okay. I love you every day.